The Last Watchman of Old Cairo

בראשית ברא   בין האור ובין   ויבדל ב

אלהים את ה   החשך ויקרא   אשר מ

השמים ואת   אלהים לאור   לרקיע

הארץ והארץ   יום ולחשך ק   המים א

היתה תהו ובהו   קרא אלה רי   מעל

וחשך על פני   ויהי ערב ויהי   ויהי כן ויק

תהום ורוח א   בקר יום אחד   אלהים לר

אלהים מרחפת   שמים ויה

על פני המים   ויאמר אלהים   ערב ויהי בקר

וי ..ב אלהים   יהי רקיע בתוך   יום שני

יהי אור ויהי א   המים ויהי מ   ויאמר אלהים

ור וירא אל   מבדיל בין   יקוו המים מר

אלהים את׳   מים למים וי   מתחת השמית

ה .י כי טוב   ויעש אלהים   אל מקום אחד

ו .. אלהים   את הרקיע וי   ותר .א

The Last Watchman of Old Cairo

A NOVEL

Michael David Lukas

SPIEGEL & GRAU
NEW YORK

Published in the United States by Spiegel & Grau, an imprint of Random House, a division of Penguin Random House LLC, New York.

SPIEGEL & GRAU and Design is a registered trademark of Penguin Random House LLC.

Frontispiece photo reproduced by kind permission of the Syndics of Cambridge University Library.

LIBRARY OF CONGRESS CATALOGING-IN-PUBLICATION DATA

Names: Lukas, Michael David, author.
Title: The last watchman of old Cairo: a novel / Michael David Lukas.
Description: First edition. | New York: Spiegel & Grau, [2018]
Identifiers: LCCN 2017007153 | ISBN 9780399181160 | ISBN 9780399181177 (ebook)
Classification: LCC PS3612.U258 F67 2018 | DDC 813/.6—dc23
LC record available at https://lccn.loc.gov/2017007153

Printed in the United States of America on acid-free paper

randomhousebooks.com
spiegelandgrau.com

987654321

FIRST EDITION

Book design by Simon M. Sullivan

For Mona,
her mother,
her grandparents,
and on back through the generations

In times gone by, when storms threatened us,
we wandered from place to place; but by
the mercy of God we have now been enabled
to find a resting-place in this city.

—MOSES MAIMONIDES

The Last Watchman of Old Cairo

Along, long time ago, before Mubarak and the revolution, before Sadat and Begin, before Nasser, the Free Officers, and the Suez Crisis, before the Suez Canal, before Herzl, before Dreyfus, before Solomon Schechter and the Cambridge University Library, before Ismail Pasha and Muhammad Ali Pasha, before the British, the French, the Ottomans, the Mamluks, and the Ayyubids, before the Great Plague and Saladin, before Maimonides the great sage—may his memory be a blessing—our story begins before all this, in the reign of al-Mustansir, when Cairo was still two cities and the Jews but a tribe among them.

It was late summer in the forty-eight-hundredth year of creation, four centuries after Muhammad's migration to Medina and more than a thousand years after the birth of Jesus. The Nile had crested a few days earlier, and its entire shallow valley shone with damp brilliance. Beneath the purple silhouetted swoop of storks, the clang of an eager blacksmith mingled with the call to prayer and the smell of baking bread. That particular morning there was another smell too, something sharp and unfamiliar at first. No one could put a name to it until, bleary-eyed and still warm from bed, they stepped out into the day and saw that neat black thread of smoke rising from the Ibn Ezra Synagogue.

Before long a crowd gathered in the courtyard of the synagogue: women and children, dyers and glassblowers, pharmacists, money changers, and fishermen. For most, this was their first glimpse of the newly reconstructed synagogue. Still unfinished, still unconsecrated by prayer, and already this beautiful new building was blackened by fire. It was a terrible thing, and yet it could have been worse. Apart from the smell of smoke in the prayer hall, the damage was limited to a shadow of soot beneath the scaffolding where the fire had started.

Who would do such a thing? Some more hopeful members of the crowd thought they saw signs of an accident, a stray coal or a clumsy housewife. Others insisted that the fire would turn out to be the work of petty vandals. And then there were those who regarded it as something more sinister, a reminder and portent of things to come, not that anyone needed reminding. Who could forget the reign of al-Hakim the Horrible? Who did not shiver to think of that sister-loving false prophet who had destroyed nearly a dozen synagogues and churches, including the original Ibn Ezra? Who could forget that hateful despot who had gone so far as to outlaw molokhia, the leafy green vegetable also known as Jew's mallow? He was gone now, al-Hakim, dead for nearly twenty years, and the current caliph, al-Mustansir, had proven himself to be a friend of the Jews. Still, one never knew.

This discussion about the cause of the fire went on for some time. And all the while, Ali ibn al-Marwani was standing at the edge of the courtyard, waiting for the right moment to step forward. Fingering the sleeve of his robe, he tried to recall what he had been told to say, whom he was supposed to seek out. But in the effort to remember the directions to the synagogue—a right at the old palace, a left at the Abu Serga Church—he had forgotten what he was supposed to do when he got there.

Eventually, as the crowd was beginning to disperse, someone noticed him. All at once, he felt the balance of attention shift. They were talking about him—an unfamiliar boy, thin cotton robe and cheap sandals, no older than thirteen—and as the murmur of insinuation collected to a boil, a circle formed around him. For a moment, Ali was alone in the middle of the courtyard. Then a young man stepped forward and grabbed him by the scruff of his robe.

"Did you do this?" the young man demanded, forcing Ali's gaze toward the remnants of the fire. Ali opened his mouth, but he was not able to speak.

"It is said that a thief returns to the scene of his crime," the young man continued. "Could not the same be said for our arsonist?"

There was a buzz of agreement followed by a few muttered calls for revenge.

"Why does he not respond? Why did he not announce himself? What is his business with us?"

The young man paused and looked out over the crowd as if expecting an answer. Instead, the silence was punctured by the sound of an older man clearing his throat.

"Shemarya the Pious," someone said and everyone stepped aside, making way for a hunched man with a mane of white hair tangled in his beard. When he got to the center of the circle, he addressed himself to the young man, who was still holding Ali by the scruff of his robe.

"Amram," he said. "Is it not written that we should judge everyone from his most favorable side?"

"Yes, Father, but would you not—"

"Release him," Shemarya the Pious said, then turned to Ali.

He did not smile, but his eyes crinkled with compassion.

"Tell us your business here, my child."

There was a long silence before Ali could bring himself to speak.

"I have a message from Abu Saad," he said finally.

The crowd grew ever more silent as Ali produced a note from the sleeve of his galabiya. Abu Saad was chief adviser to the caliph and the Jews' most important ally inside the palace. Correspondence from Abu Saad was always important, but on this day of uncertainty the Jews of Fustat were particularly eager for his reassurance.

"You are not Abu Saad's usual messenger," Shemarya the Pious observed. "What is your name, my child?"

"Ali ibn al-Marwani."

"You are Muslim."

Ali nodded.

"And your father's profession?"

"He was a water carrier, but he died before I was born. I live with my mother's brother near Bab Zuwayla."

"May God protect the orphans," Shemarya the Pious said, and a murmur of assent rippled through the crowd.

Once Ali's business, name, faith, and patrimony were established, Shemarya the Pious unfolded Abu Saad's note and read through it twice. He closed his eyes for a moment to think; then he pulled a reed pen from his pocket, requested a bit of ink, and composed a reply on the reverse.

"This is for Abu Saad," he said, handing the note back to Ali. "You must not give it to anyone else. Do you understand?"

"Yes," Ali said, and he returned the note to the folds of his sleeve.

Shemarya the Pious concluded the exchange by addressing himself to the assembled crowd, though his words were clearly intended for his son Amram.

"We should not stoop to unfounded accusations, especially not today. There is too much work to be done."

While the Jews of Fustat scrubbed soot off the light-gray stones of their synagogue, Ali ran back to Qahira with the message for Abu Saad. Through the jumbled crowd of pack animals outside Bab Zuwayla, past his uncle's house, past the market of the coppersmiths and the students congregated around al-Azhar, darting between food vendors, camels, magicians, and slaves, he cut across the market of the money changers and made his way around to the back entrance of Abu Saad's palace.

Larger than all but the most magnificent of mosques, the residence of Abu Saad was one of the grandest buildings in all of Qahira, its outer walls decorated with turquoise banners and a thick band of calligraphy carved so intricately that the letters looked like a nest of snakes. Earlier that morning Abu Saad's usual messenger—Ali's neighbor—had lifted his head from his sickbed to describe the palace's back entrance, a tall cedar door at the end of an unremarkable side street, home to a butcher, a knife sharpener, and a few unscrupulous-looking money changers. Approaching the entrance for the second time that morning, Ali caught his breath, stepped up to the door, and knocked. He waited for some time before knocking again, louder this time. As he did, the door swung open to reveal an enormous guard wearing a white linen robe trimmed with turquoise of the same shade as the banners hanging outside. This guard was much more imposing than the one Ali had spoken with earlier that morning, and much uglier.

"What do you want?"

"I have a message for Abu Saad, from Shemarya the Pious."

The guard stuck out his hand and Ali took a small step backward.

"Shemarya said I must not give the message to anyone but Abu Saad himself."

"To you, I am the same as Abu Saad."

Ali stared at the guard's meaty palm and felt the sun on the base of his neck. As he tightened his grip on the note, a drop of sweat slid down the valley of his spine.

"Shemarya said I must not give the message to anyone but Abu Saad himself," Ali said again. It was a bold request, but he had his instructions and he intended to follow them.

"Abu Saad himself," the guard growled.

A few moments later, Ali found himself standing less than an arm's length from Abu Saad, the chief adviser to the caliph. He was a short man with an enormous stomach, and he wore a fine purple silk caftan embroidered on the collar with white and turquoise flowers. He introduced himself, took the note from Ali's outstretched hand, and returned several minutes later with a tightly folded piece of vellum.

"The note is for Shemarya the Pious," he said. "And this is for you."

A servant stepped forward and presented Ali with a silver cup, filled to the brim with a deep-red liquid.

"Pomegranate juice," Abu Saad explained, noticing Ali's hesitation. "In appreciation of your discretion. May it give you strength."

Over the course of the day, Ali ran seven times back and forth between Fustat and Qahira. Dodging donkey carts, refuse, and stray dogs, he delivered dozens of messages from the Jews of Fustat to their coreligionists, business partners, and other supporters throughout the city. Ali carried notes to tradesmen, qadis, merchants, and priests. Cutting through rank back alleys slick with sewage, squirming under locked gates, and sneaking across the shaded courtyards of great mansions, he delivered messages to the Hanging Church, the market of the glassblowers, the Garden of Kafur, and the secret inner sanctums of al-Azhar. In one day, Ali saw more of his native city than he had seen in his entire life.

All day, Ali performed his duties with the utmost discretion and care. He always announced himself forthwith, never lingered or made inappropriate eye contact, and never once considered opening any of the notes he was carrying. Then, at the end of the day, as he ran back to Fustat with a final note from Abu Saad, Ali tripped over an exposed root and cut his hand on a pebble. He didn't notice the wound at first, but when he pulled Abu Saad's note from his sleeve, he saw that the top edge of it was smeared with red.

"I'm sorry," he mumbled to Shemarya the Pious, mortified by the sight of this elegant paper stained with his own sticky blood.

Sinking into a dim corner of the courtyard, Ali watched the note pass among the council that governed the affairs of the Jewish community, from Shemarya to his sons, Amram and Ephraim, to a Tunisian spice merchant known as Ibn Kammuna, then on to Doctor Mevorakh, the scribe, the head cantor, and finally to al-Zikri, a barber who also served as guardian of the synagogue. Ali held his breath, bracing himself for their censure, but none of the men seemed to notice the bloodstain. They were more interested in the message itself.

While the council deliberated, speaking in hushed but urgent voices, Ali relaxed and let his gaze wander along the façade of the newly reconstructed synagogue. Aside from the subtle stonework just below the roof, the building's only exterior decoration was the main entrance, two heavy wooden slabs adorned with the image of a grapevine twisting around four large Hebrew letters arranged in a square. Lost in his inspection of the mysterious script, Ali did not notice that a silence had fallen over the council. When he glanced up, he saw that the men were all looking at him.

"We have a proposal," said Shemarya the Pious.

"We have decided," Ephraim ibn Shemarya continued, "that it would be beneficial to employ a night watchman for the synagogue. We have al-Zikri, of course, but he cannot be responsible for watching the building day and night."

"Since you have proven yourself to be trustworthy and discreet," Ibn Kammuna said, "we would like to offer you the position. In addition to three dinars a month, you would be free to live in the old schoolroom at the other end of the courtyard."

"I imagine it should suffice for your purposes," al-Zikri added as he motioned toward the small structure, "and with a fresh coat of paint it will be very hospitable."

"Thank you," Ali said, unsure how else to respond.

Three dinars was more than he made in six months as a water carrier, and the schoolroom was larger than the house he currently shared with his uncle's family. It was an unexpected and generous offer, a stroke of good fortune, but Ali had learned to be distrustful of fate and, although the Jews had treated him well, he knew nothing of them or their practices. While he could not see anything wrong with the offer, he was not ready to accept the position outright. Naturally, the Jews of Fustat understood such caution. It was to be expected, valued even, and only confirmed the good sense of Abu Saad's suggestion.

"There is no need to make your decision now," said Doctor Mevorakh. "Sleep will be your best counsel."

There was a murmur of agreement, and it was decided that Ali should send word the next morning with his answer.

Ali stayed up late that night, staring at the mud walls of the storage room where he slept. He wanted very much to leave his uncle Rashid and aunt Fatimah's house. Although he was fond of his cousin Fawziyah and would always be indebted to the family that had raised him, life in his uncle's house had been quite difficult for some time now. A few years earlier, an errant donkey kick had crippled his uncle's right hand, leaving him unable to practice his trade as a blacksmith. The family became dependent on charity, and Ali was forced to work as a water carrier. Meanwhile, Uncle Rashid had grown increasingly bitter. He spent most of his days at the neighborhood café, chewing seeds, drinking palm wine, and gambling away any money he was able to obtain.

The Jews' offer seemed like the perfect solution to Ali's problems. Even so, he was wary. He didn't know if he could trust them—he didn't know anything about them, really—and either way, he wasn't certain how his uncle would react. Following the night shadows across the ceiling of the storage room, Ali prepared a long list of answers to the questions his uncle might ask. In the end, however, all that was unnecessary. Once he learned how much Ali would be paid, Uncle Rashid had only one question; whether he would continue to contribute to the welfare of the poor relations who had so kindly taken him in.

"A small price," he said as he chewed over a mouthful of taamiya and pickled turnip, "to repay all we've done for you."

Eventually, Ali agreed to provide his uncle's family with one dinar a month, a portion of which was to be reserved for the dowry of his cousin Fawziyah. It was nearly twice as much as he currently contributed to the household and he knew most of the money would disappear into his uncle's vices. Still, his uncle was right. It was a small price to repay all they had done for him.

"I will be forever indebted to your kindness," Ali said, and so it was settled. He sent word to Fustat, and the following afternoon he departed.

Waving farewell from atop his donkey cart, Ali felt as if he were a prince leaving home for distant battle. It was a luxury for him, traveling by cart. His possessions—a few changes of clothes, some bedding, a basket of food, and an old teapot Aunt Fatimah had given him as a parting gift—could easily have fit on the back of a donkey, but at the last minute he chose the cart, and he was glad he had.

Following the east bank of the Nile past the Siba bridge, Ali leaned back against his bedroll and watched the midday sunlight reflect white off the sails of ships lining up to unload their cargo. It was a beautiful day, and he felt that all was right with the world. His only regret was leaving his cousin Fawziyah behind. He knew how much she hated being alone with her parents and, homely as she was, she could not count on marriage to deliver her a better situation. She was only fourteen, and already the matchmaker was trotting out widowers and cripples. If anything, Fawziyah's married life would be worse than her current circumstances. Ali wanted to help his cousin, to give her some piece of the good fortune he had stumbled upon, but aside from contributing to her dowry, there was nothing he could do. He was starting a new life in Fustat, and there was no room in it for Fawziyah.

2

T HE PACKAGE ARRIVED on a Tuesday in early August, a bit less than three months after my father died. I must have slept late that morning, because I woke to the squeaky clank of the mailbox lid followed by the sound of the doorbell. The mail lady was gone by the time I got downstairs. But there, in the middle of my green plastic welcome mat, was a package the size of a shoebox, wrapped generously in tape and stamped all over with the logo of the Egyptian postal service. My name and address were printed across the top in a careful schoolboy hand that I recognized immediately as my father's. Someone else had written the return address, along with instructions, in both English and Arabic, to handle carefully.

It was one of those annoyingly perfect Berkeley summer days. A soft-peaked range of clouds hid the progress of a distant plane, and a pair of squirrels chased each other from roof to roof before disappearing into the foliage of a backyard oak. I don't know how long I stood there on the porch—staring down at his handwriting, picturing him hunched over his desk, copying out my address, crumpling up the balls of newspaper he always used as packing material—but at some point the whine of an ambulance broke through. I blinked back to myself. Then I took the package inside and cleared a space for it on the kitchen table.

He had been sick for a long time—seven or eight years, depending on how you counted; still, it took me by surprise when my cousin Aisha called, a few weeks before the end of that spring semester, to tell me that he was in the hospital, that he was going off chemotherapy.

Two weeks later, she called again.

"He died in his sleep," she said.

According to Muslim tradition, a person was supposed to be buried as soon as possible. So there was no way I could make it back to Cairo in time for the funeral, not without getting on a plane that afternoon.

"It's going to be small," Aisha said, to make me feel better about not being there.

Besides family, they expected a couple of employees from Uncle Hassan's produce distribution company, maybe some people from Ibn Ezra. As far as I knew, that was the extent of my father's life: his family, his work, and the synagogue he had watched over when he was a young man.

"Let me know if there's anything I can do."

"I will," she said.

But what could I do? What was there to be done? What was done was done, wasn't it? After I got off the phone, I stretched out on the couch and pulled a throw pillow over my head. I remember noticing its musty thrift-store smell and the flicker of a television across the street. I knew I needed to call my mother, to tell her what had happened. But before I did, I wanted a moment to hold the news myself. We had never been especially close, my father and I. Aside from a few summers in Egypt when I was younger, our relationship consisted almost entirely of phone calls and birthday cards. Still, he was always there, on the other side of the world, occupying the position of father. Until now.

I didn't have much in the way of responsibility that summer—a seminar paper that needed some light revision before I could submit it for publication, the stack of books I was supposed to be reading for my preliminary exams—nothing I couldn't put off for a few months. Plus, people understood. They were understanding. Among my friends in Berkeley, the consensus was that I should try to embrace the grief, indulge its various whims.

"You do what you need to do," my adviser, Steve, had said.

And so, that was exactly what I did.

I spent most of June at home in New Mexico with my mother and Bill, slept in my old room above the garage, took long runs in the hills behind our house, and tore through a couple of the Navajo mystery novels Bill liked to read before bed. We didn't talk much about my father. It was all still too raw. But one night, toward the end of the visit, my mother sat with me out on the back deck and retold the story of how they first met, so many years ago in the courtyard of the Ibn Ezra Synagogue.

"I still remember," she said. "I can see him like he's right here."

It was late. We were at the far edge of the deck, drinking tea and watching the bright white veins of heat lightning flash across the desert night.

"He was always so thoughtful," she said, and then she began a story I had never heard, about a scrawny little cat my father used to look after, how he fed it and protected it from the other kids.

"Such a kind heart," she said, "such a good man."

When I looked over I saw she was crying, her face streaked with the silver reflections of porch light. I put my hand over hers and we sat like that for a long while.

It was always a little strange for me to hear her talk about him like that, to think that they had been together once. When I was younger, I used to picture the two of them as distant planets, at opposite ends of the universe, my Muslim father and my Jewish mother, the bushy-mustached produce salesman and the silver-haired French professor with rectangular red glasses. Most of the time, I told people they were divorced, though the truth was they never married. As far as I understood it, the arc of their relationship was relatively brief. They had met as children and wrote letters back and forth after my mother's family left Cairo in the late 1950s. My father visited her in Paris in the fall of 1973, just after the Yom Kippur War. I was conceived. Then my mother dropped out of graduate school, moved to California, and met Bill. This was the story I had always known. But something in my mother's voice that night—a faint wobble of emotion—made me think that perhaps there was something else lurking in the background. Either way, the question of my parents' relationship wasn't at the front of my mind.

At the end of June, I flew back to Berkeley and let the rest of the summer evaporate into pub trivia and backyard barbecues. I grew my beard out and watched old foreign movies at the art house around the corner from my apartment. I drank too much, made bad decisions, read trashy magazines, and let the take-out containers pile up on the kitchen counter. Some days, I thought about my father all the time. Other days, I hardly thought about him at all. Then, cracking an egg on the edge of a pan, I would remember the sound of his voice or the way his mustache curled down over his upper lip.

There were no stages to my grief, at least not as far as I could tell, no orderly progression from denial to anger, bargaining, depression, and acceptance. Instead, my feelings stalked me in a pack, like wild animals. One moment they were lazing on a distant hillside and then, all at once, they were upon me.

Meanwhile, gurgling up beneath these other feelings was a strangely persistent sense of expectation. Or maybe it was hope. There must be something more, I told myself. How could there not be? All summer, I had been hoping for a message from my father, some last words of advice or reconciliation, a belated birthday card or an errant voicemail lost in the wires between Cairo and California. All summer I had been waiting—and then, just like that, there it was, this package in the middle of my kitchen table.

I ripped through the tape with a key and pulled back the flaps. Inside, peeking out from beneath a layer of balled-up Egyptian newspapers, were a note from my father and an old red leather presentation case that looked as if it might contain a mayoral declaration or a service award from the Rotary Club. The note was in English, written on the back of an index card in dark blue ink.

> *Dear Joseph,*
> *I think you should want this.*
>
> > *Your Father,*
> > *Ahmed al-Raqb*

THE LAST WATCHMAN OF OLD CAIRO • 19

Nestled in the black velvet lining of the case was an ancient-looking piece of paper pressed between two panes of glass. It was no larger than a page torn out of an airport novel, ragged at the edges and speckled with holes that seemed to bloom from the letters themselves. One side was covered almost entirely with an elegant downward-slanting Arabic script, the last few words of which curled up into the margin. The reverse contained five lines of Hebrew and a signature. It appeared to be a letter, or maybe a pair of letters, but I couldn't read Arabic well enough to make out more than a few words, and the Hebrew might as well have been Greek.

Turning it over in my hands, trying to understand the significance of this thing my father had sent me, I couldn't help but feel a little disappointed. There was a general tightening in my chest, and that familiar chorus of self-pity began warming up. I knew I should be glad to have anything from my father. I knew there was no reason to feel sorry for myself. But there was something uniquely frustrating about the package, the scrap of paper, the shortness of my father's note. I had gotten exactly what I wanted, and I had no idea what it was.

According to a small brass plaque affixed to the inside of the presentation case, this ancient scrap of paper had been *Presented to Mr. Muhammad al-Raqb, friend of knowledge and guardian of Ibn Ezra Synagogue, by Mrs. Margaret Gibson and Mrs. Agnes Lewis, February 1897*. The only other information I could find was a business card stuck to the bottom of the case with a piece of packing tape. Printed on thick, cream-colored stock, the card gave no title or company, just a name—Mr. Claude Mosseri—a telephone number, and an address. On the back, Mr. Mosseri had written a short note. *Your father asked me to send you this. He was a great friend. Please call if you ever find yourself in Cairo.*

Muhammad al-Raqb, I assumed, was a distant relative of some sort. But I had no idea who Margaret Gibson and Agnes Lewis were. As for Mr. Mosseri, he was probably someone my father knew from the synagogue. I had never heard of him before, but that wasn't particularly surprising. My father's past, especially those years before I was born, had always been something of a mystery.

Trailing my fingers along the mottled velvet lining of the presentation case, I went through the package again, hoping I might uncover some hidden indication of what it meant or where it came from or how it had found its way to my kitchen table. I removed all the balled-up pieces of newspaper and flattened them out one by one. I looked under the cardboard flaps at the bottom of the package, searched the exterior for identifying marks. It was postmarked June 14, 2000—about a month after my father's death—but that was the only piece of information I could discern. There was nothing else, no explanation or instruction, no last will or testament, only this ancient scrap of paper, its case, and a one-sentence-long note.

It was fitting, in a way. After twenty-six years of long-distance part-time fatherhood, those were his final words to me. I think you should want this. Hadn't that always been how it was? He would send me something—a postcard, a birthday present, an ancient scrap of paper—and I was left to puzzle out its significance. I knew that he had tried, that he wasn't always able to fully express himself in written English. But would it really have been so difficult to write a few more sentences? Would it really have been so hard to explain why, of all the things he might have sent me—a tie clip or an old sweater, a photo album or a strand of wooden prayer beads—he had chosen to leave me with this?

"Would it?" I said later that afternoon, on the phone with my mother. "Would it really have been so difficult?"

"Maybe it was," she said, taking the question at face value. "Maybe he didn't understand it himself."

"Then when did he send it to me? Why did he say he thought I should want it?"

I could have called Mr. Mosseri or Aisha or Uncle Hassan or one of my friends who studied Hebrew and Arabic literature. But my mother was the first person I called. Not because I thought she would be able to shed any light on the meaning of the package. She wasn't. I called her because I knew she would understand.

"He could be difficult," she said, after a pause. "But he had his reasons, usually. And he loved you, so much. You know that, Joseph, don't you?"

"I do," I said, and in spite of my frustrations, I did.

After I hung up, I looked at Mr. Mosseri's business card, calculated the time in Cairo, and thought about whom from the department I might call to help me with the translation. But even then, I think, at the back of my mind, I knew exactly what I was going to do.

For most of my childhood, my father occupied that sector of my imagination otherwise reserved for myths and legends.

Somewhere between King Arthur and Zeus, he was that distant and usually benevolent demigod who oversaw the realm of air mail and phone calls, provider of pharaoh statues, pyramid paperweights, and, for my ninth birthday, a real Egyptian scarab. Playing catch, driving me to school, telling me to buck up when I struck out or skinned my knee—all those more prosaic paternal duties were covered by my mother or Bill. All things considered, they did a pretty good job of it. There was nothing tangible missing from my childhood. Still, I was always aware of a disjuncture, that fatherly lacuna.

I have no doubt that he tried his best, in spite of the distance. There were postcards and visits. His birthday presents always came on time and, for as long as I can remember, he called me every Sunday night just before bedtime. Our conversations usually followed along the same path. He would ask me about school or soccer practice. Sometimes he told a humorous anecdote he had heard from Uncle Hassan or the man who sold newspapers on the corner outside his apartment. And every week, as I settled into bed with the hard plastic earpiece of the phone pressed between my head and the pillow, he would ask if I wanted to hear a story.

My father told stories about dragons and djinns, buried treasure, fishermen, and wayward princes. But his best stories were those drawn from our family history, stories about the long line of al-Raqb men who had, for nearly a thousand years, served as watchmen of the Ibn Ezra Synagogue. There was the story of Ahmed al-Raqb, my father's namesake, who had faced down an angry crowd that believed the Jews were immune to the Great Plague. There was the one about Ibrahim al-Raqb, who convinced the ruthless Mamluk ruler Baybars to accept a fine in lieu of destroying the synagogue. And then, of course, there was the story of Ali al-Raqb, that first and most noble watchman, whose bravery helped to establish our family name.

I often fell asleep before the story was finished and would wake up again when my mother came in to kiss me good night. She would take the phone out of my hand and, as I drifted back to sleep, I would hear her talking to my father in the living room. These were the only times I ever heard her speak Arabic, and I remember how different she sounded then, in her native language, almost nothing like the woman who packed my lunch every morning, kissed me on the top of my head, then went off to teach French at the local community college.

For many years, this is how it was. There were birthdays and sleepovers, ski weeks and a shelf full of plastic trophies. Then, one Sunday toward the end of fifth grade, my father asked me whether I wanted to spend the summer with him in Egypt. He and my mother had already worked out all the details. I would stay with him in Cairo for two months, then come back to Santa Fe a few weeks before school began.

"It's up to you," my mother said the next morning at breakfast. She liked the idea. It was a great opportunity, a chance for me to spend time with my father. "I just want to be sure that you're sure."

"It's a big trip," Bill added.

I didn't understand why there was even a question. Why wouldn't I want to spend the summer with my father in Egypt?

"I'm sure," I said, looking up from my Raisin Bran. "I'm sure I'm sure."

And so it was settled.

There must have been more conversations, discussions of what to pack and whether it was a good idea to drink the water in Cairo, a trip to the travel doctor. But I don't remember any of that. I don't recall how I got to the Los Angeles airport or whether anyone helped me change planes in Amsterdam.

What I do remember, distinctly, is stepping onto the tarmac in Cairo, my little red-and-black-plaid suitcase in one hand and a blank customs form in the other. My father was waiting for me just past border control, leaning against a white pole and smoking a cigarette. He wore an old gray suit jacket, and I remember thinking that his mustache looked like a small aquatic mammal, a river otter maybe, or a ferret. I saw him before he saw me, and for a moment I just stood there, watching him smoke. My father. I repeated the phrase a few times under my breath, trying it on for size. Then I took a step forward and he spotted me.

"You are here," he said, and when he leaned over to embrace me, my head spun with that potent Levantine potpourri of cigarette smoke, cologne, and stale sweat. "Welcome, my son."

On the taxi ride back from the airport he was excited, rustling my hair and talking in his broken shuffle of English about our plans for the summer. I tried to pay attention to what he was saying, but I was tired from the flight and spent most of the ride staring out at the city, at the piles of trash and the crumbling unfinished apartment buildings, the freeway overpasses crammed with honking little taxis and the bright Arabic billboards advertising strange brands of laundry detergent and fruit juice.

"Here we are," my father said proudly as the taxi pulled up in front of a huge cement apartment block. "What do you think?"

It wasn't how I imagined. None of it was. But the last thing I wanted was for him to see the disappointment on my face.

"It's nice," I said, doing my best to smile. "Really great."

That first week in Cairo wasn't easy. Stuck in a strange hot polluted city with a father and a family I hardly knew, I had a bad heat rash and persistent low-grade diarrhea, both of which were exacerbated by my aunt Basimah's home remedies. My father lived with his brother—Uncle Hassan—and his family, which meant I was forced to share a bedroom with Aisha. Or maybe it would be more accurate to say that she was forced to share a bedroom with me. In any case, she made no secret of the inconvenience I caused by being in her space.

"Do you have to breathe so loud?" she asked that first night as we lay across the room from each other. Her slight British accent gave the question an extra sharpness.

"What do you mean?"

"Never mind," she said, then muttered something to herself in Arabic and pulled a pillow over her head.

I told my mother I wanted to come home early and she said to give it a few more days. As usual, she was right. Eventually I got used to the microbes and everyone calling me Yusuf. The heat and pollution began to feel normal and, by the end of that first week, Aisha and I were inseparable.

Most mornings, we spent lounging around the apartment,

watching old black-and-white Egyptian movies on TV, reading *The Cartoon History of the Universe,* or helping Aunt Basimah in the kitchen. We played board games, wrote adventure novels set in Siberia and the Sahara; and Aisha taught me an Egyptian version of Truth or Dare that we played late at night while the rest of the family was asleep.

But as much as I enjoyed spending time with my cousin, the best days were those when my father agreed to take me along with him on his rounds. After lunch, we would catch a taxi to Nasr City, Dokki, or some other unfamiliar neighborhood, and walk together up the main street, drumming up business for Uncle Hassan's burgeoning produce distribution concern. My father was a born salesman and it was a pleasure just watching him work. As he wheedled and joked, smoked cigarettes and drank glass after glass of sweet black tea, I sat quietly in the corner of the restaurant or produce stand, reading my comics and thinking about the rice pudding the two of us always shared at the end of the day. Occasionally, a friendly waiter or shopkeeper would direct the flow of conversation my way and I would respond with the string of stock Arabic phrases Aisha had taught me.

"I don't speak Arabic well. I am American of Egyptian heritage. I like Cairo very much."

This was usually sufficient to slake their curiosity. And it was true. Aside from those first few weeks, it ended up being a great summer. My father and I rode camels behind the pyramids, we saw the mummies at the Egyptian Museum, and we climbed the stairs all the way to the top of the Cairo Tower, from which we could see the entire city spread out below us like a map. But of all the days that summer, the one that stuck with me most was the afternoon my father took me, Uncle Hassan, and a couple of distant male cousins on a felucca ride down the Nile.

It was a bright blue-and-white day. There was a soft breeze blowing upriver and the windows of the skyscrapers along the water glinted with reflected sunlight. I was sitting with my father at the back of the boat while Uncle Hassan and my cousins manned the front. We sailed up the Nile for an hour or so; then the captain dropped anchor near the bottom tip of Zamalek and everyone stripped down to their underwear and jumped in. They beckoned for me to join, but in spite of my father's assurances, I didn't trust the water. It looked like the kind of river—thick with silt the color of coffee ice cream—where you might find leeches and piranhas or, at the very least, those slimy little fish that ate the dead skin off your feet.

"No, thank you," I said in Arabic and leaned back against the side of the boat in an effort to convey my comfort.

After a few minutes of splashing around, Uncle Hassan pulled himself back into the boat. I remember he smiled and made as if to light a cigarette. Then, with a violent lurch, he wrapped his arms around my chest and threw me into the Nile. The abruptness of it knocked the wind out of me and when I came up, sputtering and coughing, trying to tread water in wet shoes and jeans, everyone was laughing. My cousins sang a humorous song in my honor and I tried to laugh along with them, even though I knew I was the butt of the joke.

Back in the boat, I took off my wet clothes and set them out to dry. There were angry tears welling up at the corners of my eyes, but I held them back, knowing from experience that crying only made things worse. I was mad at Uncle Hassan. But most of all, I blamed my father, for allowing it to happen, for not protecting me, and for chuckling to himself as he draped the towel over my shoulders. To his credit, he didn't say anything once he saw that I was upset. He didn't try to explain himself or apologize. He just sat there with me at the back of the boat, watching the murky brown water pass a few feet below us.

"There is a proverb," he said eventually. "'Drink from the Nile and you will always return. Swim in it and you will never leave.'"

Then he leaned over the edge of the boat and cupped out a handful of water.

"This is our blood," he went on, trickling the water onto my knee. "Nearly a thousand years our family has lived on the Nile. This river is in our veins."

He lit a cigarette and we were both quiet for a long while.

"We are watchers," he said, throwing the half-smoked butt into the Nile. When I didn't respond, he explained. "Our name, al-Raqb, it means 'the watcher,' 'he who watches.'"

"'He who watches,'" I repeated, and he smiled.

"It is the forty-third name of God."

He thought for a moment, shading his eyes against the sun; then he asked me the same question he asked every Sunday night.

"Would you like to hear a story?"

"Yes," I said, and he began.

"Once there was a boy named Ali—"

I must have heard that story a dozen times before. But that

particular afternoon—watching the city unfold from its haze—it felt more immediate, more real. This river a few feet below us was the same river that had flowed through the city a thousand years earlier, when Ali al-Raqb first took up the position of watchman, the same river that had flooded the valley every spring for hundreds of years.

"We protect the synagogue," my father said when the story finished, "and we guard its secrets."

"Secrets?" I asked.

He shifted in his seat and, glancing back over his shoulder, dropped his voice slightly, so no one else on the boat could hear what he was saying.

In one corner of the courtyard, he told me, there was a well that marked the place where the baby Moses was taken from the Nile. Beneath the paving stones of the main entrance was a storeroom filled with relics, including a plank from Noah's Ark. And hidden in the attic, behind a secret panel, was the greatest secret of all, the Ezra Scroll.

He leaned in, so close that I could feel his breath on my face.

More than two thousand years ago, he said, during the time of the prophets, there lived a fiery scribe named Ezra who took it upon himself to produce a perfect Torah scroll, without flaw or innovation. He worked on the scroll for many years and when he was finished, he presented it to the entire community. The people assembled outside the walls of Jerusalem. And when Ezra opened the scroll, they all stood, for they knew that this was the one true version of God's word. It was the perfect book, the perfect incarnation of God's name, and it glowed with a magic that could heal the sick, enlighten the perplexed, or bring back the spirits of the dead.

"Have you seen it?" I asked. "Is it real?"

My father lit a new cigarette and stared into the water, as if he might find his story there.

"That's enough for today," he said, eventually, and I knew not to press any further.

For the rest of the ride, as we sailed back toward the 26th of July Bridge, I sat with my father at the back of the boat, looking out on the water and thinking about the heroic history of our family, about the Ezra Scroll and the generations of watchmen who protected it.

For much of my childhood, my last name—al-Raqb—had felt like a burden. I hated the questions it inspired, the taunts, and the well-meaning adults wondering where a name like that came from. I dreaded the moment when, without fail, substitute teachers would pause and glance up from the attendance sheet, apologizing in advance for their mispronunciation. It even looked strange—al-Raqb—the hyphen in the middle, the lowercase "a," and that unpronounceable double consonant at the end. In third grade, prompted by a particularly embarrassing incident with a new teacher, I had waged a semi-protracted and nearly successful campaign to change my last name to Shemarya, like my mom, or Levy, like Bill. But that afternoon on the Nile, I wouldn't have traded al-Raqb for anything.

I was a watcher, I told myself. He who watches.

◆　◆　◆

My father and I often discussed plans for me to visit again. But for whatever reason—money, summer camp, conflicting schedules—it never worked out. And as the years passed, Cairo began to recede from my imagination. Middle school gave way to high school. Video games, pubic hair, and growth spurts were replaced with cross-country practice, AP tests, and bad poetry. I started college, came out, fell in with a group of art students in my dorm and, without much thought to the future, decided to major in English. I took to wearing long knit scarves, thick sweaters, and a tan peacoat I bought at a thrift store in Somerville. Instead of holing up in the library with the rest of my friends, I did my reading—*Mrs. Dalloway*, John Donne, *Invisible Man*—in a humid café off Commonwealth, trying not to be too obvious as I glanced up over the top of my book and noticed the barista or that guy across the room.

Everything was going smoothly. Then one Sunday night, toward the end of my freshman year, I got a call from Aisha. She said my father was sick and that I might think about coming to visit.

"Can I talk to him?" I asked, holding up a finger to let my friends know I might be a minute.

"He doesn't want us to tell you," she said. "But you should come. It will be good for him to see you."

My mother and Bill said they would pay for my plane ticket, and the literary magazine where I was interning that summer agreed to let me start a few weeks late. So I went. Eight years later and twelve inches taller, I returned to Cairo, that gangly oversensitive eleven-year-old transformed into a reasonably self-assured college student, shaggy about the edges, smug, and bristling with the possibility of it all.

Meanwhile, my father was wasting away. Aunt Basimah told me what the doctors had said, but I didn't need red blood cell counts to see that he wasn't doing well. His face was slack and his skin had the sallow appearance of soft cheese. Most days, he didn't have the energy to go out. So I spent the majority of the visit sitting next to him on the couch, watching old black-and-white Egyptian movies while he sipped his tea and counted the pills on his tray.

"You don't need to sit here all day," he said more than once. "Go out. Enjoy yourself."

But I knew he was glad to have me there. And I knew that one day I would be glad to have sat with him. We talked about my classes and my plans for the future. I told him about Boston and my internship. We discussed Egyptian politics, such as it was, and I explained the meaning of the term "postcolonial." But he didn't want to talk about his health. When I asked how he was feeling or whether the chemotherapy was affecting his appetite, he closed his eyes, as if the very question pained him, and changed the subject.

"It is always the same movie," he said one afternoon when I was especially insistent. He looked at me, then turned back to the television, where a handsome older man in a tuxedo was speaking to a desperate young woman. "Always the same movie, even when it is different."

In a way, I was glad my father didn't want to talk about his cancer. I was still trying to understand what it meant, still trying to reconcile that man on the couch with the father of my imagination. And besides, I understood. When you said something, it became real. When you said something, you had to start dealing with it.

"He's so much happier with you here," Aisha said a few nights later. We were at a bar on the roof of the Four Seasons, a birthday party for one of her friends from university. "You can see the difference in his face."

At the other end of the table, the conversation skipped from scuba diving in Sharm el-Sheikh to someone's brother who worked in marketing at Unilever. One of Aisha's friends was telling a story about his family's maid, a refugee from the Sudan who had been living on the roof of their house.

"I just wish—"

I didn't finish the sentence, but she knew where I was going.

"If it makes you feel any better, he doesn't talk about it with anyone."

I looked down at a plate of empty pistachio shells, then out over the edge of the roof. Below us, the lights of the city bled into each other like far-off conversations, interrupted only by the empty blackness of the Nile.

"It's always easier to pretend," Aisha said, following my gaze, "for everyone."

"Yeah," I said. "I guess you're right."

There was a double meaning to her comment. But I didn't make the connection until a few days later, when we were all out to dinner at Uncle Hassan's favorite restaurant, a fancy Lebanese place in Mohandessin with white tablecloths and crimson-vested waiters. Toward the end of the meal—the table covered with half-eaten plates of hummus, baba gha-noush, kibbeh, and stuffed grape leaves—my uncle started asking me, in his clunky businessman's English, what I thought of the young women at the table next to us.

"They seem nice," I said.

"Really nice," Uncle Hassan insisted.

"Yeah," I agreed, brushing a pile of crumbs into my hand, "really nice."

I had come out to Aisha a few months earlier—right after I told my mother and Bill—and I think Aunt Basimah might have suspected something. But I didn't intend to tell my father or Uncle Hassan, at least not for the time being. I wasn't sure how they would react and didn't want to stress out my father.

Although, of course, that's exactly what ended up happening.

"What?" Uncle Hassan pressed, sensing my lack of enthusiasm. "Egyptian girls aren't good enough for you?"

"He's too much in his studies," Aunt Basimah interjected. "You should have a little fun, Yusuf. You're on vacation."

Aisha did her best to change the subject.

"What's that spice?" she asked, taking another bite of the kibbeh. "Cinnamon? Maybe nutmeg?"

But Uncle Hassan wouldn't let up.

"You're on vacation," my uncle said. Leaning in far too close, he put his hand on my forearm. "If you want, Yusuf, I know some nice girls."

"I don't want any nice girls," I said, and pulled away.

"Well, what do you want?"

He dangled the question in front of me like a flashy lure. And I knew in that moment I had a choice. I could continue hiding, I could continue protecting them, and myself. Or I could lay it all out on the table and hope for the best. In the silence that followed, I took a sip of water, put my glass down, and looked directly at Uncle Hassan. He raised his eyebrows, waiting for a response, and I felt a chill wash through me.

When it came down to it, the issue wasn't really who I slept with. If I got a girlfriend for show and went around with guys on the side, everything would be fine. That was the standard operating procedure in Egypt, at least as far as I understood it. The transgression was in the act of confession.

"Boys," I said, in the calmest voice I could manage. "I want some nice boys."

At that point, my father, who had been watching the entire interaction in silence, rose slowly from his seat and laid his hands flat on the table. He gave his brother a look of disgust, then turned and, swaying slightly from a radiation treatment earlier that week, walked toward the bathrooms.

A few minutes later he came back, lowered himself into his chair, and dabbed at his lips with a napkin. He didn't say anything and neither did anyone else. We ate dessert, then drove back to the apartment, my father and Uncle Hassan silent in the front seat while Aunt Basimah went on about her great-aunt, who had married a Lebanese man and lived in Beirut for more than forty years before she was killed by a car bomb intended for a PLO leader who bought croissants every morning at the bakery down the street from her apartment.

"My dad can be such a fucking asshole," Aisha said, once everyone else had gone to bed. She kicked the foot of her desk. "You sure you're okay?"

"Yeah," I said, staring at my hand, "I think so."

There was a tingling in the tips of my fingers, and my

breath felt shallower than usual. Other than that, I was okay. I hadn't been disowned. No one had thrown any plates or made any angry proclamations. There wasn't even any overt disapproval. But that next morning when I sat down next to my father, the couch cushion between us felt like a brick wall. We spent the following week in tense silence. I went out a few times with Aisha and her friends, bought some touristy knickknacks from Khan el-Khalili. Then I flew back to Boston and started my internship.

A couple of weeks later, Aunt Basimah called to give me an update on my father's health.

"He sends his love," she said at the end of the call.

"Is he there?" I asked. "Can I talk to him?"

"He's asleep," she said, a little too quickly. "But he said, he wanted me to send his love."

It was like that all summer. Every time I talked to Aisha or Aunt Basimah, at the end of the call I would ask to talk to my father, and every time he was either sleeping or too tired or not feeling up to it. He sent his love. He asked after me. But he could never talk. Aisha said he just needed some time and eventually I was able to convince myself that everything would work out. One day he would call and everything would go back to normal. But of course Aisha was wrong. You can never go back to normal.

When, at the end of August, he finally had the strength to talk, our conversation was limp and stilted. We were like two old college roommates whose lives had taken us in different directions. We talked about the weather and the news, Uncle Hassan's business, Aunt Basimah's cooking. He asked about my internship and I told him that one of the stories I had picked out of the slush pile might get published in the magazine.

"What's it about?" he asked.

I tried to describe the story, but ended up getting lost in the different narrative strands.

"It sounds interesting," he said.

It was then—in his polite interest, in the strain at the end of his breath—that I understood. This might be the best I could expect.

Not that it was so bad. During sophomore year, my father's cancer went into remission, and we settled into a new routine, talking once or twice a month on Sunday morning. There was a warmth to those conversations, if not much depth. I told him about the Arabic classes I was taking, my thoughts about applying to graduate school, and, when I got in, the pros and cons of the various programs. We talked about family, politics, literature, and soccer. But we avoided digging too deep, making sure to stay clear of any subjects that might upset the balance of our relationship. In seven years, we never once discussed my personal life. I never mentioned any of my boyfriends or breakups. I didn't really even talk about my friends. And I never once asked how his treatment was going, how he was feeling. I never asked what he was thinking that evening at the Lebanese restaurant in Mohandessin. I never asked him about leaving the synagogue or meeting my mother. I never asked about Ali al-Raqb or the Ezra Scroll. And I never asked him to tell me another story.

3

Mrs. Agnes Lewis and Mrs. Margaret Gibson arrived in Cairo on the Two-fifteen Express from Alexandria. This was how their timetable referred to it, the Two-fifteen Express. Although in actuality the train was rather ponderous. When they finally pulled into Cairo Station—having been delayed by high winds, flooding, a faulty track switch, and a fugitive cow ruminating in the middle of the tracks—it was already well past dusk. Agnes's pocket watch showed 7:25, more than three hours behind schedule.

Taken alone, the travails of the Two-fifteen Express would not have been especially irritating. But the twins had been traveling for six days straight, without proper rest or sanitation, and they were both feeling rather crabby. Fifteen years ago, they might have reveled in the adventure of it all—the Channel passage, the train across France, the boat trip from Marseilles. Fifteen years ago they might have overlooked the fleas and the damp and the motion sickness. They might have brushed all that aside as soon as the looming hulk of the Citadel came into view. But this was not fifteen years ago. It was the first month in the year of our Lord 1897. They had turned fifty-four just a few weeks earlier, and felt every aching year of it. No matter what might happen, whether they found their documents or not, this would most likely be their last trip to Egypt.

Agnes alighted first, followed by Margaret, and they stood side by side at the edge of the platform. From a distance they were indistinguishable, both women of distinction, both wrapped in furs, both squat and sharp-eyed with stringy gray-brown hair wrapped in a loose bun. Closer scrutiny would reveal Margaret's mole, the creakiness of Agnes's gait, and a slightly different shade of green in the eyes. For all intents and purposes, however, they were perfect replicas of each other, an august pair of British widows fringed with the scorch of Presbyterianism.

Undisturbed by the tumult of the platform, Agnes and Margaret took in the arc of the station's new steel ceiling and the useless clack of the arrival board. Green-turbaned pashas brushed past half-naked stevedores and dusty fellaheen laden with great bags of cotton. Two or three dark-veiled women haunted the edges of the crowd, slipping through a brigade of British tourists tromping, no doubt, to Shepheard's Hotel, lunch at the Gezira Club, and a steam packet down the Nile. With a subtle tilt of her chin, Agnes indicated an old Nubian porter smoking a cigarette next to the newsstand, and they crossed the platform toward him.

"Excuse us," Margaret said, using her most mellifluous Arabic. "We have ten trunks on the Two-fifteen from Alexandria, all marked with the names Lewis and Gibson. We would be exceedingly gratified if you were to convey them to our carriage outside."

The man hesitated for a moment to examine them more

closely. Then he extinguished his cigarette on the bottom of his sandal and set off to collect their things.

"They're fragile," Agnes called after him, but he did not appear to hear.

Once their trunks were loaded and the porter paid, the carriage driver set off down Clot Bey Street toward the Hotel d'Angleterre. He took the long way, as Margaret requested, through the Ezbekiyya Gardens.

"It is a slight detour," she said, in anticipation of her sister's objections, "but so much more pleasant. Don't you agree?"

"Yes," Agnes said, softening into her seat. "I do."

For there was nothing quite like riding through the gardens at twilight. The shadow of overhanging palms, the warm night air, the scrape of carriage wheels on gravel, it all brought back that same girlish excitement they had felt on their first visit to Cairo so many years ago. Under the yellow flicker of gas lamps, the old city appeared to be nothing more than an outline, a quaint sprinkling of minarets against the darkness. And when their hotel appeared, rising up between a hedgerow and the gently arched frond of a palm, it looked like an enormous pink cake.

This was not their first stay at the Hotel d'Angleterre, but in the past few years its decor had changed considerably. The lobby had been draped in heavy teal curtains and someone had seen fit to adorn the room with paintings of typical Egyptian scenes, as if to imply that the Nile, the pyramids, Mount Sinai, and the Colossus of Abu Simbel were all waiting there on the other side of the wall. As they followed the bellhop across the lobby, the sisters both glanced at a party of package tourists huddled around the grand fireplace, drinking cordials and talking excitedly about the high quality of perfume to be found in the Khan el-Khalili. Margaret gave them a quick smile, pleasant almost to the point of inviting conversation, but not quite.

"Your room, please," the bellhop said, after leading them up the staircase. Agnes stepped up to the threshold of Room 327 and leaned in to get a better look.

"Your room," the bellhop offered again, stiffening his arm to indicate that they should enter before him. The sisters exchanged a glance and Agnes stepped back into the hallway.

"Unfortunately," she explained in Arabic, "this is not our room. We asked for a north-facing room with two queen-sized beds and a bath. This room faces south and, I may be mistaken, but I do not see a bath."

The boy looked to Margaret, who nodded her agreement.

"Please," he said in English and, holding up his index finger, rushed back down to the lobby.

A few minutes later, he returned with the concierge, a large man with the aspect of an overripe and somewhat bruised tropical fruit. Arriving at the threshold of Room 327, he wiped his forehead with a handkerchief and looked inside.

"The ladies' room is not to their liking?"

"The room is nice enough," said Agnes. "Unfortunately, it is not the ladies'."

While Margaret explained that they had requested a room with a north-facing view, two queen-sized beds, and a bath, the concierge sucked at his mustache and watched his fingers walk around a circle of prayer beads.

"There is one room I can offer," he said, "on this floor, very large, facing north, with two queen beds."

Room 322 was across the hall. And indeed, it was quite a bit larger than 327, with a north-facing view, two queen-sized beds, and a claw-foot tub in the bathroom.

"Of course," the concierge said, when he saw that the ladies found their new room to be satisfactory, "this room is somewhat more expensive."

"Of course," Margaret agreed, placing a hand on her sister's forearm.

Traveling throughout the Near East, often without the fortification of male companionship, Agnes and Margaret had, over the years, developed a nose for swindlers and a stomach for bargaining that matched even the most tenacious of shopkeepers in the Khan el-Khalili. Not that they needed to be frugal. Their dear father had left them enough money to be happily fleeced for the rest of their lives, and then some. For the twins, thrift was a point of pride. And moreover, every pound saved was another pound they could give to charity. In a very real sense, this smarmy concierge was attempting to divert funds away from the assistance of war orphans, the rescue of ancient documents, and the establishment of a new Presbyterian Synod in Cambridge.

"We will gladly pay the price we agreed to last month," Margaret said. Reaching into her handbag, she produced a letter from the owner of the hotel, detailing the terms of their agreement. "Seventy piastres a night, I believe."

"Yes," the concierge said, without looking at the letter, "seventy piastres a night, plus taxes and tips."

• • •

After their trunks had been brought up and a round of bak-sheesh dispensed to everyone the least bit involved with the endeavor, Agnes lay down for a moment while Margaret bus-ied herself making certain all their luggage had arrived in good condition. Between them, the twins had ten steamer trunks. Four were filled with various dresses, petticoats, shoes, furs, hats, and other sartorial items required for a journey that would take them from the dining room of Shepheard's Hotel to the wilds of the Sinai Desert. Two trunks were crammed with dictionaries, Bibles, lexicons, travel accounts, and sundry other books essential to the identification of ancient manu-scripts. One trunk contained all the foodstuffs and medicines they knew they could not procure in Cairo. Another held their tripod, two hundred photographic plates, and the camera it-self, a traveling half-plate from Fallowfield. There was a trunk filled with the chemical reagents and other conservation equipment they would need for their trip to St. Catherine's. And the final trunk contained those items that Mrs. Schechter had asked them to deliver to her husband: a respirator, its at-tendant spare parts, quinine, and a large magnifying glass.

Once certain everything was in good condition, Margaret unpacked their chess set from the second library trunk and began arranging the board on a small side table. She was nearly finished setting up her own pieces when the bellhop knocked and slid a note under the door.

"A letter?" Agnes asked, raising her head from the pillow to see what Margaret was holding.

"From Dr. Schechter," Margaret confirmed.

The twins had come to Cairo to assist Dr. Schechter in obtaining a cache of documents currently housed in the attic of a synagogue in the old city. They had originally planned to travel with him. However, at the last minute they had been detained in Cambridge by an urgent piece of business related to the establishment of the Presbyterian Synod, and everyone agreed that it would be best for Dr. Schechter to go ahead without them, so that he might begin securing the necessary permissions from the Jewish community. Given the exigencies of travel and the sorry state of the postal system in Egypt, they hadn't heard from him since he left Cambridge, nearly a month earlier, and they were eager for his news.

"Will you read it?" Agnes asked.

Margaret glanced over the note, written in Dr. Schechter's broad and rather hasty scrawl, then seated herself on the edge of the bed and began reading aloud.

After the requisite salutations, welcoming them to Cairo and asking after their journey, Dr. Schechter informed the twins that they would be very happy to hear of his progress with Rabbi Ben Shimon. He was looking forward to discussing these matters in detail that following evening, when he hoped they would be able to join himself and Miss de Witt for dinner.

"One supposes that Rabbi Ben Shimon is the Chief Rabbi of Cairo," Agnes said, once her sister was finished, "but who on earth is Miss de Witt?"

"I have no idea," Margaret said, "though it does appear that Dr. Schechter has been rather busy."

"Not surprising."

"Not at all."

Agnes and Margaret had known Dr. Schechter for years. They were of the same set in Cambridge and often saw each other at Dr. Taylor's house. In addition to their shared interest in biblical scholarship, there was another unspoken bond between them as well: the somewhat bitter knowledge that, in spite of their many scholarly accomplishments, the three of them would always be relegated to the outskirts of Dr. Taylor's circle and none of them would ever be allowed to join the permanent faculty at Cambridge, Dr. Schechter because of his religion and the twins because of their sex. This knowledge did not encourage a deeper relationship, however. If anything, it did the opposite. Occasionally, the twins had Dr. and Mrs. Schechter over for tea, as part of a larger group, but their connection with him had never progressed much beyond this initial stage of congeniality and shared resentment, at least not until recently.

One afternoon that past spring, Agnes and Margaret had invited Dr. Schechter over to look through a pile of documents brought back from a previous trip to Egypt. In their initial perusal they had found more than a few intriguing manuscripts, including a fifteenth-century prayer book and a clump of what looked to be ancient incantations of some sort. When they had described the documents to him a few days earlier at Dr. Taylor's house, Dr. Schechter had been rather excited. Seeing them for himself, however, he seemed unimpressed. Shuffling through the general hodgepodge of ancient letters and business contracts, he paused here and there to smile politely or read a few words aloud. His gaze didn't rest on any item for more than a moment until, at the bottom of the pile, he came upon a seemingly unremarkable leaf from an early Hebrew codex. After staring down at it for a full three minutes, Dr. Schechter asked whether he might remove the fragment for further inspection. When he returned, later that afternoon, he was in a state of what could only be described as hysteria. The fragment, he had said, once he was able to calm himself, appeared to be a leaf from the original Hebrew version of Ecclesiasticus.

The sisters exchanged a glance.

"The original Hebrew?"

"I believe so," Dr. Schechter said.

The implications were tremendous. If authenticated, the fragment would establish a reliable source text for Ecclesiasticus and might even prove Dr. Schechter's theory about the language of its composition. But what excited him most was the idea that there might be more where this had come from. The condition of the fragment, its size, and the paper on which it was written, all these things led Dr. Schechter to suspect that this leaf from Ecclesiasticus was, as he had put it, but a single petal in a great field of wildflowers. Hands trembling so much he could barely drink his tea, Dr. Schechter had tried unsuccessfully to explain the Jewish prohibition against discarding Torah scrolls, prayer books, and any other papers that might contain the name of God, how most congregations buried these documents in a special section of the graveyard, but some chose to gather their godly texts in an attic or storeroom, known as a geniza, until they could be disposed of properly.

Despite his incoherence, the reason for his excitement was clear. Somewhere in Old Cairo there was a synagogue, the attic of which was filled with ancient manuscripts that hadn't seen the light of day in hundreds of years. If they were able to secure these documents and bring them back to Cambridge, it would be among the most significant discoveries of the past twenty years, with profound effects on liturgy, linguistics, and biblical scholarship. But they needed to act quickly. For if Agnes and Margaret had been able to purchase this fragment from a common manuscript dealer, it meant that others would be able to buy them, too. Someone with access to the synagogue—a member of the Jewish community, or perhaps one of its employees—was selling the documents on the black market and, without their speedy intercession, this treasure trove of manuscripts would soon be dispersed to the four winds.

Agnes and Margaret had reason to believe that the synagogue might also contain an even greater treasure: the Ezra Scroll. That very morning in fact, on their journey from Alexandria to Cairo, Margaret had stumbled upon a passage in a seventeenth-century travel account, suggesting that the ark of the Ibn Ezra Synagogue possessed *a recess containing a copy of the Mosaic law, written in the very hand of Ezra the Scribe himself, of happy memory*. Upon reading those words, she had let out a small yelp of joy and showed the passage to her sister, who responded in a similar manner. The very notion of the Ezra Scroll—a perfect copy of the Hebrew Scriptures written thousands of years ago by the prophet Ezra—was enough to make one's skin goose with anticipation. If it truly existed, if they found it, if they were able to bring it back to Cambridge, the implications truly could not be greater. It was an idea almost too delicious to ponder. An indisputable source text for the Old Testament, without hint of error or innovation, the Ezra Scroll would be the greatest archeological discovery of the century, if not the millennium. Their names—Mrs. Agnes Lewis and Mrs. Margaret Gibson—would be known to history for years to come and, more importantly, the scroll would serve to establish the true word of God, a perfect and unimpeachable copy of the Hebrew Bible without intermediary or innovation.

And so there they were, in Room 322 at the Hotel d'Angleterre, tired and somewhat irritable, their bones aching from nearly a week of travel. They were both rather anxious to begin the search, but at the moment their exhaustion took precedence.

"Are you hungry?" Agnes asked, and Margaret shook her head.

"Not especially."

"Then I can see no reason why we shouldn't avail ourselves of sleep."

"No," Margaret agreed, "neither can I."

After finishing their nightly exercises, they washed up and changed into their sleeping gowns.

"Would you mind, Meggie?" Agnes asked as she rolled onto her stomach.

"Of course not, Nestor."

In the trunk devoted to foodstuffs and medicines, Margaret found a small bottle of the specially formulated ointment that, although smelling of opium and chili peppers, did a great deal toward alleviating the pain of her sister's rheumatism. Rubbing the ointment into her palms, she unbuttoned her sister's gown and began applying a coat of it to her naked back.

It was just the two of them, and so it had been for some time. Margaret's beloved husband, Mr. James Gibson, had passed away after only three years of marriage, and Agnes's dear Samuel had died less than five years later. This wasn't the life they had imagined for themselves—no husbands, no children, no domestic interests—but it was a life well lived, in the pursuit of knowledge and the general well-being, and they both took some comfort in knowing that their husbands would have been proud of their accomplishments. They had their causes, supported their church, wrote letters to *The Times,* and, when they weren't traveling around the Near East, searching for ancient manuscripts that might shed light on the origins of their faith, they spent most of their days in quiet contentment, reading or studying Arabic grammar in the parlor. Like any partnership, theirs was a negotiation, a carefully constructed edifice of favors and moods. They had disagreements, of course, but in large part they got on remarkably well. For each knew the other's thinking as well as her own.

At that particular moment—Agnes lying on her stomach and Margaret rubbing the ointment into her sister's back—they were thinking, as they often did, of their beloved father. He had been dead now for years, but they could both very clearly recall him, bent over his writing desk, rebuking them for an excessive display of pride, praising a well-wrought translation.

Where would they be without the guidance of his steady

and sometimes chastising hand? It was he who had given them the gift of a proper education, he who had sparked the light of their faith, he who had instilled in them the importance of hard work and a curiosity about the world beyond Glasgow, Edinburgh, and London. For although he disapproved of female education in general, he had seen their promise early and resolved to school them himself, beginning when they were five with Latin and Greek, then moving on to Hebrew, Arabic, and Aramaic. Six days a week, from breakfast until dinner, Agnes and Margaret had worked side by side, diligently translating Cicero, Exodus, and Ibn Sina. Their dinner conversations were primarily of an instructional nature, but every night after the table was cleared and the dishes washed, their father would read aloud to them from the *Odyssey* or the *Arabian Nights*. And as they drifted off to sleep, the sound of his voice filled their dreams with wooden ships, great marble palaces, magic lamps, and dark caves overflowing with treasure.

That following evening—after a mostly pleasant day spent reading, strolling through the gardens, and making inquiries with their friends at the antique book market—Agnes and Margaret took a carriage to Dr. Schechter's hotel.

"So good to see you," he said, leaping up from his chair as they entered the lobby.

With his wild hair and his great silver beard, Dr. Schechter looked as if he would be more at home among the monks of Mount Sinai than the tourists milling about the lobby of a modern hotel.

"It is so very good to see you both," he went on. "I must apologize for not writing earlier. But we have been having quite a bit of excitement here. I have been making great strides with Rabbi Ben Shimon, great strides."

For the past six months, the already somewhat frantic Dr. Schechter had been a man possessed, muttering to himself on King's Parade or in the stacks of the Cambridge University Library, unwashed and disheveled, looking for all the world like a madman. Being in Cairo apparently hadn't done much to calm his nerves, though it did look as if he had bought himself a new suit.

"We have some exciting news," he told the twins, "very exciting."

"We?" Agnes glanced at the rather pretty young lady with whom Dr. Schechter had been sitting.

"Excuse me," he said with a slight blush. "Please allow me to introduce Miss Emily de Witt, from Girton College. Did I not mention I had a student along to help with the transcriptions?"

"I can't say I remember anything about a student," Agnes said. "But then again, I can hardly remember the name of my own dog."

Margaret smiled for her sister.

"It is a pleasure to meet you, Miss de Witt."

"The pleasure is all mine," she said, and gave a slight, but very winning, curtsey.

"We have some exciting news," Dr. Schechter repeated as he led them into the dining room of the hotel. "I have been making great strides with Rabbi Ben Shimon."

It was slightly vexing how Dr. Schechter spoke about the

project. Over the past few months, he had assumed de facto ownership over the expedition, referring to the documents as "my find" and repeatedly thanking the sisters for their assistance. Of course, they had enjoyed more than their share of accolades a few years earlier, after their discovery of the codex at St. Catherine's Monastery. Agnes had been invited to address the Royal Asiatic Society, and Margaret's account of the discovery was praised in newspapers around the world. Many said it was one of the most significant such finds since the Codex Sinaiticus. But fame was only a by-product. If their experience—uncovering the codex, bringing it home, having their names briefly trumpeted about—had taught them anything, it was to remind them of what their father had often said. The text was what mattered, not the author. The true purpose of their work, of any scholarly endeavor, was not recognition. It was the steady accumulation of knowledge, the illumination of an ancient textual variant, the revelation curled upon itself in a dusty palimpsest.

"Great strides," Dr. Schechter said again.

Unable to contain himself any longer, he dove into a dramatic account of his time in Cairo, detailing a series of meetings with the Chief Rabbi and other notable members of the Jewish community. There was a Mr. Bechor, a Mr. Mosseri, and three or four others who, along with Rabbi Ben Shimon, constituted an informal governing council. Knowing something of the Oriental character, Dr. Schechter had invested most of the past two weeks in fraternization, drinking coffee, smoking cigarettes, and touring around the city. At times, he had to admit, it all seemed like nothing more than a grand diversion. Then, three days ago, his hard work had paid its dividend. Rabbi Ben Shimon had granted them full access to the geniza and intimated that he would support the idea of safekeeping the entirety of the collection at the Cambridge University Library.

"What does he want in exchange?" Agnes asked.

Having dealt with all manner of Egyptians, from Bedouin camel traders to Coptic patriarchs, she had a difficult time believing that Rabbi Ben Shimon would give up such a valuable cache of documents without compensation.

"Nothing," Dr. Schechter said, "at least not as far as I can tell. Rabbi Ben Shimon understands the great scholarly value of the geniza documents and I have been able to convince him that they will be well looked after in Cambridge. He is a lovely man and very learned. When you meet him, I am sure you will agree."

"I am sure we will," Margaret said, though she shared her sister's suspicions. In their experience, the shrewdest of characters were often those who seemed, at first, to lack an ulterior motive.

"I've visited the synagogue twice," Dr. Schechter said, redirecting the course of conversation. "And truly, the geniza is beyond anything I could have imagined."

Pausing to cough while the waiter served their dinner— beef Wellington for the ladies and, for the gentleman, a kosher meal provided through the generosity of the governing council—Dr. Schechter went on to describe a vast battlefield of paper, books, and letters, dust everywhere and all of it mashed together without any order whatsoever. Most of the documents held little scholarly interest—business and marriage contracts, deeds, the proceedings of the religious court—but there were gems to be found amidst the rubble, gems of a most astonishing nature. In just two visits he had already uncovered a number of invaluable documents: a page from a fourteenth-century Passover Haggadah and the first half of a letter written by the great poet and scholar Samuel ha-Nagid.

"Samuel ha-Nagid," Agnes marveled, but before she could formulate a question about the letter, Dr. Schechter was overcome by another fit of coughing.

"It's the geniza," he said. "I've never seen such dust."

He continued coughing until Miss de Witt handed him a glass of water.

"We left your respirator at the front desk," Margaret offered. "If we had known the need was so urgent, we would have brought it with us."

Agnes glanced at Miss de Witt, who was watching Dr. Schechter with a concern that bordered on excessive familiarity.

"Mrs. Schechter sent along a few other things as well."

"Thank you," Dr. Schechter said and, recovering himself, steered the conversation back to the geniza. "All that filth, it makes one feel less like a scholar than a housemaid, dusting out the attic of History."

"We are eager to help in whatever capacity you deem most useful," Margaret said. "As you know, my sister and I are not above dusting, and our Arabic is quite passable."

"It's quite good, really," Dr. Schechter said, missing her irony entirely. "But first, we must secure Rabbi Ben Shimon's permission to remove the documents. He has agreed in principle, but such things take time."

"If you think it would be at all possible," Agnes put in, "we would be thrilled to visit the synagogue."

They were both rather curious to see the geniza for themselves. They had come halfway around the world. And, after hearing Dr. Schechter describe its contents, they felt an even greater urgency to get on with their work, securing the geniza and protecting these invaluable documents from whoever was selling them off.

"Yes, of course," Dr. Schechter said. He paused for a moment and tapped the side of his head, like a schoolboy trying to recall the exact wording of a difficult recitation. "The only trouble is, Mr. Bechor offered to take us all out on a tour of the city tomorrow. He is an important member of the governing council. Perhaps we can visit the synagogue the following afternoon?"

As much as they wanted to get on with their work—and as little as they wanted to be led around on a tour of a city they had visited nearly a dozen times—the twins knew better than to refuse an invitation from an important member of the governing council. So they agreed, reluctantly, to meet that next morning in the lobby of their hotel.

After dessert, the twins bade Dr. Schechter and Miss de Witt a good evening and took an open carriage back to their hotel. It was a dark night, clear and cold, and the stars shone like inflamed grains of sand.

"She is rather pretty," Margaret said after a few minutes of silence.

"Certainly not who I imagined when Dr. Schechter said he was bringing along a research assistant."

"Maybe she has some Hebrew."

"I doubt she has much of anything, apart from her charms."

Margaret let this bit of nastiness dissipate before she spoke again.

"And Rabbi Ben Shimon," she asked, "what do you suppose he wants?"

"Money," Agnes said, troubling a loose flap of the seat next to her. "It's usually money, isn't it?"

"Nine times out of ten."

"Or maybe a political favor, protection from the vagaries of Abbas II."

"Perhaps he doesn't care about the documents at all," Margaret speculated. "Perhaps he thinks they're nothing but rubbish and we're fools for chasing after them."

"Or maybe he does care, very much, and truly believes they will be better cared for in Cambridge."

"Which they will be."

"It doesn't really matter, does it? So long as he's willing to grant us the necessary permissions."

"And soon," Margaret added.

"And soon."

They were silent for the remainder of the ride, thinking about Rabbi Ben Shimon and Mr. Bechor, the possibility of the Ezra Scroll and Dr. Schechter's unfortunate willingness to trust in the good intentions of others. Being granted access to the geniza was certainly something, but there was still a great deal of work to be done. The twins were both quite certain now that there was a leak in the geniza. Someone was selling off the documents piece by piece and whoever it was—a member of the governing council, the synagogue watchman, Rabbi Ben Shimon, or someone else entirely—the twins wouldn't stop until the documents were removed to a safer location. Until then, until the proverbial bird was in their hands, the geniza would continue to be parceled out and sold in the stalls of the antique book market. One of the greatest discoveries of the century, thousands of potentially invaluable documents, would be dispersed among the curiosity cabinets of pleasure tourists who couldn't tell the difference between Syriac and Aramaic.

4

THE DUTIES OF the night watchman were relatively simple. Six times in the course of the night, al-Zikri explained, Ali was to walk the perimeter of the synagogue. Three times, he was to inspect the courtyard, the ritual baths, and the prayer hall, including both the women's section and the attic storeroom. In between rounds, he was to sit in front of the main entrance with a charcoal brazier. The governing council had also provided a wooden stool and a blanket, though al-Zikri cautioned against using the latter.

"With a blanket it is easy to sleep."

Ali mumbled his understanding and al-Zikri put a hand on his shoulder.

"Come, I will show you inside."

Circled with prayer mats all pointing toward a raised wooden pulpit, the interior of the synagogue was lit with the flicker of a dozen lanterns. Uncertain what to make of the unfamiliar space, not sure where to step or how much to lower his voice, Ali followed al-Zikri around the prayer hall, nodding along with his explanations of various architectural features. Moonlight filtered through the windows above the women's section and illuminated the carved wooden mashrabiyas that al-Zikri said depicted the stories of Noah, of

Joseph, and of Moses. It gave Ali some comfort to see those familiar prophets on the walls of the synagogue.

"We have the same stories," he said.

"Same stories"—al-Zikri smiled—"same God, you could say, only a different name."

Ali nodded, though he didn't entirely understand. Did the Jews pray to the same God he did? If so, what was the difference between a Muslim and a Jew?

A few steps later, al-Zikri paused in front of a large wooden cabinet topped with an ornamental lamp. This was the ark, he explained, the resting place of the Sefer Torah. Ali examined the doors of the ark, the intricate geometric designs carved around them and, at the center, a few letters luminescent in mother-of-pearl.

"Sefer Torah," Ali repeated.

"It is our holy book," al-Zikri said, "like the Koran."

"May I see it?"

"One Sefer Torah can take as long as a year to complete," al-Zikri said, answering the question by avoiding it. "At the end of its life, we bury the scroll in a special section of the graveyard."

After viewing the ark, Ali and al-Zikri climbed down to the ritual baths, then back up to the women's section, a narrow gallery that looked down on the dais in the middle of the prayer hall. At the far end of the women's section there was a square opening just below the ceiling. Securing his lantern between his teeth, al-Zikri climbed up the ladder that led into the opening and motioned for Ali to follow.

"You only need inspect the geniza three times a night," he

said, as he climbed down into the chamber. "But it is very important that you remember to do so."

Although it was empty, except for a few mounds of what appeared to be discarded documents, the room was suffused with a sense of significance. Ali thought to ask about the purpose of the space, the piles of paper, and that strange tingling awareness he felt in his fingertips, but before he could formulate a question, al-Zikri turned to leave.

"If you hear anything suspicious, anything at all, don't hesitate to wake me."

"I won't," Ali said.

With that, he began his first night as watchman of the Ibn Ezra Synagogue. Squatting under the arch of the main entrance, he stared out into the emptiness of the cold courtyard. His only companions were the frogs croaking in the distance, the steady gaze of the moon, and a furtive cat skulking along the north wall. Unaccustomed as he was to the movements of the night, he had no way to gauge the passage of time. He tossed pebbles toward the well marking the site where Pharaoh's daughter was said to have plucked Moses from the water, hummed a tune to himself, and stared at the flicker of the lantern flame until his eyes blurred. After what seemed an appropriate amount of time, he stood and slipped into his sandals. Tracing the perimeter of the courtyard, he held his lantern up to see behind the trunks of date palms and in the dark corners around the well. He imagined where he himself would hide and illuminated all these places. Next, he inspected the interior of the synagogue, the murky subterranean baths, and the women's section.

The geniza was his final stop. Warm still in the middle of

the night, it was completely black but for the opening above him and the shaft of yellow falling from his lantern. As before, there was a charge in the room, a strange feeling coursing down to the tips of his fingers. Taking a cautious step toward the middle of the room, he lifted his light to its far corners, bathing the piles of paper with a dull radiance. Ali thought he glimpsed the note from Abu Saad to the governing council, stained along the top with his own blood. But before he could look more closely, he heard something rustling near the back of the room.

Ali caught his breath, stood stock-still, and listened intently to the darkness. When he heard it again, he crossed the room and made his way along the wall until the roof sloped down and he could no longer stand. He swept the back of the room three times with his lantern before discovering the source of the rustle. Hidden in the rafters, just below eye level, was a nest of kittens, all the same light-gray color. Ali went over the perimeter again, but the mother was nowhere to be seen. After considering the situation for a few moments, he made a basket of his galabiya, climbed out, and carried the kittens downstairs. Ali's new home was more than big enough for himself and his new companions. In the corner of the main room, next to his bedroll, he made a nest for the kittens using the remains of an old blanket. He fed them leftover bread soaked in water and went back to his duties.

Ali made five more rounds that night. Although he was exhausted, the cold and the excitement kept him awake as the stars wheeled across the great blackness of the sky. And when the first light of day slipped between the palm trees, al-Zikri came to relieve him. He asked how everything had gone, and Ali said there was nothing to report. He didn't remember the kittens until he heard them mewing in their nest next to his feet, by which time he was already in bed, reveling in his good fortune, slipping rung by rung, farther and farther into the hard-earned sleep of a working man.

As the days and weeks went by, Ali grew ever more accustomed to his life in Fustat, to the world of the Jews and the inverted shape of his days. He enjoyed the contemplative solitude of his schedule, watching over the synagogue when the city was asleep and sleeping when the sun rose. Most days he awoke just after noon to the sound of children playing in the street. After washing, he prayed, prepared himself a pot of tea, and warmed a plate of ful or a bit of dinner from the night before. Then he fed the kittens and set out for his daily walk around Fustat. Cutting through the mostly Coptic neighborhood around the old Babylonian Fortress, he might buy a few vegetables at the produce market or some bread at the bakery al-Zikri had recommended. On days he felt particularly flush with money, he would get supper from one of the vendors whose pots—fragrant with the murky tang of molokhia or the smell of beef stew with vegetables—crowded the entrance to the produce market.

When he finished with his shopping, Ali usually made his way to a narrow street occupied primarily by textile workers. Beyond the tentmakers, tailors, and embroiderers there was a small fabric shop owned by Ephraim ibn Shemarya, which, for reasons no one could recall, had become a gathering place for some of the synagogue's more notable members, a kind of informal council meeting. Ali first came upon the conclave entirely by accident, trying to find a shortcut home from the produce market, and Ephraim had insisted that he sit down for a glass of tea.

In the weeks that followed, Ali discovered a more direct route home, but he often found himself stopping by the fabric shop, to sit, drink a glass of strong sweet tea, and listen to the men discuss the news of the neighborhood, of Fustat, Qahira, and the larger world. From time to time, one of the men would direct a question at Ali, but for the most part he just sat and listened.

With time, Ali came to understand many things about the community that employed him. As much as he learned, however, many aspects of Jewish life remained mysterious to him. He knew the Jews sprinkled their prayers throughout the day, and he often observed them pause to mumble a benediction over tea or a piece of bread, but he had only the vaguest grasp of when and why they were obliged to pray. He did not fully understand the purpose of the Sefer Torah, or why it was kept locked away in an ark, and any questions he asked about the ritual baths were met with laughs and bawdy insinuation. The Jews' most perplexing ritual, however, was their practice of discarding papers in the attic storeroom next to the women's section. Even after Ephraim explained their belief that documents containing the name of God should not be discarded like common trash, Ali still had a difficult time understanding why they would keep such papers in the attic, and he often wondered about that tingling sensation he felt when he was in the room. But he knew it was probably best to keep his questions to himself, to do his job, and to let the Jews be Jews. He would learn the answers to these questions, and many others, soon enough.

Almost exactly a month after Ali took up his position at Ibn Ezra, the renovations to the synagogue were completed. Finally, after many months of praying elsewhere, the members of Ibn Ezra would have their own space, and just in time for the Jewish New Year. All week the neighborhood buzzed with preparations. New clothes were made, visiting rooms were swept, and the air smelled sweet with fresh-baked bread. The exterior of the synagogue was scrubbed and scrubbed again; the windows above the women's section were washed. The tapestries were taken out, beaten, and rehung. A new wooden podium was installed in the center of the prayer hall, a gift from Abu Saad, and the lamps were filled with oil. Ibn Kammuna's eldest son had been given the honor of reading from the Sefer Torah, and his reading would be followed, it was said, by a rare exegesis by Shemarya the Pious.

On the morning of the New Year, Ali forced himself to stay awake. Stroking one of the kittens in his lap, he sat on the front steps of his house and watched the men of Ibn Ezra stream through the courtyard, dressed in their finest clothes and faces beaming with the possibility of the new year. Ali listened to their prayers, and when Ibn Kammuna's son chanted from the Sefer Torah, he felt his chest swell with something like pride. Although he was still very much a Muslim—did his best to pray five times a day, and believed with all his heart that there was no God but God, that Muhammad was the seal of the prophets—Ali had come to see himself as a part of this community. When you protect something, no matter what it is, it becomes your own.

After the service, the congregants spilled out into the courtyard, the men discussing the many merits of Shemarya the Pious's exegesis while the women tended to the children. Ali was watching one of his kittens play around the edge of the well in the corner of the courtyard when a slender and unadorned wrist reached down to scratch it between the ears. The owner of the wrist, Ali saw, was no older than himself, and the fine cut of her cloak suggested that she was the daughter of a wealthy merchant. Balanced on the cusp between childhood and marriage, she kept to her spot near the well, every so often acknowledging the greeting of an older woman or gently chastising an unruly child. He had never seen her before, he was sure of it. How could he forget those lips, that gentle curve of forehead? Yet somehow her face seemed familiar.

Ali knew that it was not seemly to stare, but he could not bring himself to look away. He was about to rise—to remove himself physically from the temptation of watching her—when she turned slightly and looked him full in the face. Recalling the moment later, Ali could see her nose and her perfect sloping eyebrows, but he could not remember the color of her eyes. They swirled in his memory, from green to blue to hazel, like the reflection of sunlight on water. What he did remember—very distinctly—was that feeling of fate, like a lightning bolt striking the earth. And when she demurred, turning her attention back to the kitten, it was as if she had severed the nerve running between his eyes and his heart.

That night Ali did his best to stay focused. He prepared himself an especially strong pot of tea and was even more attentive than usual on his rounds, stopping every so often to listen to the darkness and shining his lantern behind rocks too small to conceal even a cat. Still, it took everything in his power to keep his mind from drifting back to his beloved, the young woman who had, just a few hours earlier, graced the courtyard he was charged with protecting.

Ali knew well that the bastard son of a Muslim water carrier would never be able to marry a wealthy and beautiful young Jewess. He knew this, yet his stomach still roiled. He could not shake the sliver of a chance that she felt what he felt, that the force of their gaze had meant something to her as well. All week, he was suffocated by the agony of his own desire. He wanted very much to tell someone, but knew nothing good could come of such an admission. So he kept his thoughts to himself, repeating again and again the words of the Prophet Muhammad, who had said so wisely, *He who is in love and hides it and remains chaste is a martyr*. Ali took great comfort in these words, in the idea that the Prophet understood exactly what he was feeling. More comforting, however, was the knowledge that his beloved would return to the synagogue in less than ten days, to observe the Day of Atonement.

When that morning finally came, Ali sat on his steps and watched the Jews stream into the synagogue. He followed along with the now somewhat familiar sound of their prayers, and that evening, when the mournful bleat of the ram's horn sounded, its stutter and piercing cry felt like a sound inside himself. At last the doors of the synagogue opened and the courtyard filled with somber white robes gleaming silver in the moonlight. Ali inhaled, repeating the words of the Prophet to himself as he gripped a pebble so hard it broke the skin.

He did not see her at first. And then there she was, less than ten paces away, as beautiful as she had been on the New Year. This time, however, his beloved refused to look anywhere but at her own feet. She must have sensed him watching her. How could she not feel the heat of his gaze? Ali wanted to shout, to wave his arms above his head and profess his love to everyone assembled. Fortunately, he was able to control himself.

All night she avoided his gaze. Then, as the crowd began to thin, a lock of her hair came loose from her head covering. When she raised her hand to tuck it back, she glanced up in Ali's direction and held him in her honey-colored eyes. It lasted no longer than a breath, but the very fact of the glance confirmed Ali's most ardent hopes. She remembered him. Why else would she look so pointedly in his direction? And if she remembered him, was it not possible that she had been thinking of him? Ali dropped the pebble he had been holding and shut his eyes. When he allowed himself to open them again, he saw that she was talking with Amram ibn Shemarya. For a moment he thought that perhaps the two had been recently betrothed, but the truth was much worse. When she left the courtyard with Amram and the rest of his family, Ali understood that his beloved was none other than the youngest and most beautiful daughter of Shemarya the Pious.

Those next few weeks were a muddle. Ali continued with his rounds, his walks to the produce market, and tea outside Ephraim's fabric shop. He did his best to maintain some order in his life, but he could not control his thoughts, and when he slept he dreamt of his beloved, waiting by the well or sneaking through dark streets in her pale nightclothes, dreams so real he felt they must be true, if not in this world then another.

Even so, the days continued to pass. The Nile receded and young spoonbills molted their stripes. When autumn was fully upon them the Jews began to prepare for Sukkot, the Feast of the Temporary Dwellings, and Ali helped al-Zikrī build a tentative structure of sycamore and muslin in the middle of the courtyard. All over Fustat and all around the world, al-Zikri explained, Jews were raising similar structures in their fields and courtyards and the open spaces where one normally did not dwell. On the first night of the feast, which al-Zikri said would last for an entire week, Ali watched Ibn Kammuna shake a narrow palm branch in four directions while the rest of the council recited a series of prayers. The men then passed around a large yellow fruit and shared a meal beneath the structure. Doctor Mevorakh invited Ali to join them, but he demurred, not wanting to disrupt the celebration.

For four days the Jews of Fustat ate and prayed in their

temporary dwellings without incident. Then, on the morning of the fifth night, Ali woke to the sound of al-Zikri speaking urgently to Ibn Kammuna in the courtyard. A number of the structures had been damaged, al-Zikri said when Ali came outside. Shemarya the Pious's dwelling had been completely destroyed, as had the structure outside the Babylonian synagogue.

"Keep your eyes open," al-Zikri told Ali later that night as he handed over the watch. And he did.

During his second round, as he was emerging from the prayer hall, Ali saw the sputter of a shadow near the front entrance of the synagogue. Extinguishing his lantern, he crouched behind the well in the corner of the courtyard. In the moonlight, he could see the outline of three boys about his own age. Two of them were carrying sticks and the third had a rock. Listening to their muffled laughter, Ali felt the cold clench of fear in his throat. He knew that hiding was the cowardly thing to do. But wasn't it safer, he asked himself, to let the boys do their business and tell al-Zikri that he was inside the synagogue when it happened? As Ali watched the boys approach the temporary structure in the middle of the courtyard, he stilled his breath and thought of his beloved, imagined her standing there next to him. What would she think of him cowering behind the well?

Without thinking, without considering the danger of what he was about to do, Ali leapt out from behind the well and, waving his arms, shouted in the high wavering voice of a ghost or a djinn. After a beat of silence, two of the boys ran off. The third, the one with the rock, stood stock-still for a moment. Then he turned, threw his rock in Ali's direction, and ran after the others. Ali felt the rock graze his forearm, but he didn't realize he was bleeding until al-Zikri appeared a few moments later.

"What was that?" al-Zikri asked. Then he shone his lantern on Ali's arm. "What happened?"

"I scared them," Ali said, pressing down on the cut with the cuff of his galabiya. "I jumped out and shouted, and they ran."

Over the next few days, many people came by to thank him and hear the story from his own mouth. Ibn Kammuna brought a package of sweets flavored with rosewater, and Doctor Mevorakh gave him a container of the finest tea, but Ali was happiest to see Ephraim and Amram ibn Shemarya. Although they did not give him any tokens of gratitude, they brought with them the knowledge that their youngest sister had heard the story of his courage. And that was the best gift he could imagine.

When the Feast of the Temporary Dwellings was over, al-Zikri told Ali to take the night off, in appreciation of his hard work. Ali didn't think twice about the offer. He didn't wonder why he was being given that particular night off, nor did he consider who would watch the synagogue in his absence. He simply wiped his brow and thanked al-Zikri for his kindness, grateful for the chance to take a longer walk than usual.

After his midday prayers, Ali changed into a clean robe and set out. With no particular destination in mind, he wandered the streets of Fustat, always aware of the possibility, slim though it was, that he might chance upon his beloved. A left turn near the market of the wood-carvers led him to a dead end, and eventually he emerged into a small passageway shaded by the branches of an olive tree. He had no idea where he was, but the heavy layering of light reminded him of the metalworkers' market where his uncle Rashid had worked for many years.

"Ali."

For a moment Ali thought he had heard the sweet voice of his beloved; then he recalled that he had never actually heard her speak.

"Ali. Over here."

When he turned, he saw that the source of the whisper was a man, standing in the doorway of a tiny shop. The man was no taller than a child, and although he did not appear to be particularly old, his hair and beard were white as clouds. Above the door of the shop was a placard engraved with the name Hasdi il-Sephardi. The sign announced no title or trade, nothing but this name and a single Hebrew letter in a circle.

"Come," he said, ushering Ali inside.

Hasdi il-Sephardi's shop was dusty and disheveled, about the same size as the front room of Ali's house and heavy with the smell of sulfur. A low wood counter at the back was covered with clay amulets, strips of parchment, scales, and casks of various sizes. A chair next to the door held a stack of books and a small reed cage filled with what appeared to be a family of frogs. As he stepped inside, Ali felt a tingle of awareness in his toes and the tips of his fingers, that same mysterious charge he felt in the synagogue attic.

"Is this . . . ?" Ali began, then he stopped himself, not sure how to phrase the rest of the question, or whether it was something he should be asking in the first place.

He knew little of the ways of magic, but he knew enough to be cautious. He had heard stories of young women inhabited by djinn, children transported to distant lands, and grown men wandering through vast deserts of the mind. Magic was not to be taken lightly, for all the magic in the world was, in one way or another, derived from the names of God. By rearranging letters, rewriting or transposing them in new ways, magicians were able to harness a small bit of the names' divine power.

"I see you are troubled with love," Hasdi said.

"What?" Ali was shocked that this man he had just met could so easily see the torment within him.

"Who is it?" the magician pressed. "What is her name?"

Ali took a step back and nearly knocked over the pile of books on the chair behind him. He knew that he could not reveal the identity of his beloved. The very sound of her name on his lips would be a scandal, one that would most likely cost him his position as watchman, but the thought of unburdening himself—even to a stranger, especially to a stranger—gave him a sense of relief he hadn't felt for months.

"There is someone," Ali said finally.

Hasdi laughed.

"No need to be coy. I know who it is. I can read it on your face."

Ali turned toward the cage of frogs, croaking weakly near the entrance of the shop.

"With a simple charm, I can make her fall for you."

Ali swallowed and let his mind wander along the path it

had so often trod. She would live with him in his small house next to the synagogue, and every afternoon he would wake to her smile. He wanted more than anything to make this dream a reality, but at the same time he worried the charm might harm his beloved.

Just the other day, Doctor Mevorakh had told the men outside the fabric shop a story about an older Coptic woman he had treated. When he saw her, Doctor Mevorakh said, her eyes were yellow and her hands gripped in tight fists. Her children said that she had been shaking and feverish for days. He tried every medical cure available, but had no idea what was afflicting the woman until, on his way out the door, he tripped over an amulet covered with Coptic and Hebrew letters. As it turned out, she had been struck by black magic intended for her neighbor.

"It is a mild spell," Hasdi said, as if reading Ali's thoughts, "and there is no cost. I enjoy helping young couples in love."

Before Ali could think of another reason to refuse, Hasdi began rummaging through a shelf behind the counter. He produced a small scrap of fabric along with a shard of clay. Mumbling to himself, he wrote a Hebrew letter at each corner of the fabric, wrapped it around the shard, then tied the entire charm with a length of string.

"Take this," he said, handing it across the counter. "Keep it with you at all times. Soon you will become irresistible to your beloved, and maybe to a few other women as well."

"But I—"

"If it is not successful, come back in a week and I will give you something more powerful."

As Ali made his way back to the synagogue, he felt the

sharp edges of the charm rubbing through his pocket. He had done nothing wrong, he told himself. He had fallen in love, lost his way, and accepted a gift from a stranger. He had acted entirely without malice or premeditation. He had not sought out or requested the amulet. He had merely accepted it and agreed to keep it in his pocket. Ali knew that such acts—premeditated or not—could lead eventually to much larger transgressions, but for the moment at least he slept soundly.

Later that same night, Ali woke to a strange humming in the near distance. Although it was his night off, he did not hesitate to rise from his bedroll and check to see where the sound was coming from. Pulling on his galabiya, he grabbed his lantern, and went outside. There was no one in the courtyard. The front door of the synagogue was closed, and the only light came from the moon, hanging pale yellow above the tops of the palm trees like an upside-down fruit. Ali held his breath and listened into the darkness. A low rhythmic hum seemed to be coming from the alley behind the synagogue. In all his nights on guard, Ali had never heard such a thing. It was dense and almost otherworldly, on the edge between sound and feeling.

Standing on the front steps, Ali thought about how he might later describe this moment in a story, the courageous watchman preparing himself for an encounter with the unknown. He imagined the Shemarya brothers relating the story to their sister. Then he touched the charm in his pocket, lit his lantern, and crossed the courtyard.

Pausing just inside the main gate, Ali could hear the humming quite clearly, along with the footfalls of four, maybe five men. Or perhaps, he thought, they were not men at all. Steeling himself, he swallowed, stilled his breath, and pushed the gate open with his foot. At the other end of the alley, near the entrance to the women's section, was a collection of figures all dressed in white robes and turbans.

"Stop," Ali said with as much threat as he could muster. "Who goes there?"

There was a muffled whisper amongst them, and then one stepped forward, his palms out in a gesture of peace. Ali raised his lantern.

"Do not be concerned," the man said as he stepped into the light. It was Ephraim ibn Shemarya.

"It's a holiday," said another voice, which sounded very much like Doctor Mevorakh. "Simchat Torah."

"You are a good watchman," Ephraim said, smiling to himself. "We thought you would not hear us."

Ali hesitated for a moment and looked up at the men. One of them, toward the back, was carrying a large luminous object, the same size and shape as the Sefer Torah he had seen on the New Year. It was as big as a sack of flour and pulsing with a watery glow, like moonlight on silver.

"Go back to sleep, my son," Doctor Mevorakh said. "There is no need for concern."

Ali extinguished his lantern and watched the men disappear, one by one, into the synagogue, all of them humming a soft melody as they processed. When the man with the scroll entered, he shut the door behind him and Ali went back to bed, gripping the charm tightly in his hand as he drifted off to sleep. He was a good watchman. It was true. And yet he couldn't help but feel that, by accepting this charm, he had betrayed the very people he was charged with protecting.

5

SUMMER IN CAIRO is an angry and vengeful god. Even
at six in the morning, even with the fan on high and
the AC unit whirring full tilt, I could feel the heat of the day
seeping in through the walls. The sound of traffic drifted up
from the street below and, lurking at the edges of the room,
there was a sharp incendiary smell like kerosene or burnt
trash. I stayed in bed for a long while that morning, trying to
get back to sleep, staring up at the water stain on the ceiling,
letting myself ease into this new space.

"It's perfect for you," Aisha had said when she described
the apartment to me over the phone.

I could see what she meant. On the third floor of an old
villa in Garden City, the apartment had an air of faded glam-
our, a kind of romantic decay, like an old movie star gone to
seed. There were two bedrooms, ceilings as tall as an ele-
phant, and a formal dining room complete with French doors
and a frosted-glass chandelier. It had a bidet, wainscoting in
every room, and a heavy stone balcony looking out onto a
quiet street overhung with carob trees. This was where I
spent most of that first morning in Cairo, sitting out on the
balcony with my tea and a package of crackers I had found at
the back of the otherwise empty refrigerator, watching the

sun rise through a hazy curtain of smog and thinking how strange it was, actually being there.

It had all happened so quickly. A few days after the package arrived, on my way back from lunch with a friend near campus, I had paused outside a travel agency on College Avenue and, as I stared at one of the antique postcards hung in the window, the idea had presented itself—*Why not spend the semester in Egypt?*—just like that. Before I could think any better of the plan, before I could question my motives or the cost of a last-minute plane ticket halfway around the world, I walked in and told the woman at the front desk to book me on a flight to Cairo. I didn't know what I was looking for, where I would live, how I would pass my days. But I had faith that I would figure something out, that this decision, rash as it might seem, was the right one.

Not that a semester in Egypt was such a radical proposition. When your friends are all graduate students, you get used to the comings and goings of the academic life. A semester at the Indian national archives, a summer of Spanish classes in Guatemala, a year teaching in Rome: it all blurred together after a while. Boundaries were porous and bodies moved across them with ease. Once things got rolling, it was almost too easy, packing up my life and leaving it all behind. My friends thought it was a great idea. Devon said he might try to visit on his way back from a conference in Madrid. And Analise, she even had a name for what I was doing.

"Wrestling the grief," she said, "that's what my therapist called it. It's an important stage."

Even the stickiest of logistics went off without a hitch. My landlord didn't mind me subletting to the Romanian biochemistry student I found standing next to the bulletin board outside International House. Aisha said she would try to find me a place to stay. And my adviser, Steve, couldn't have cared less.

"Sounds great!" he wrote, responding to a four-paragraph email I had spent much of the morning composing. "Keep me updated."

Over the next few days, as I went about the various errands I had to complete before leaving town—buying traveler's checks, filing for a leave of absence from school, getting vaccinated for typhoid and rabies and hepatitis A—I could already feel my life in Berkeley beginning to slip away. I had lunch with friends, went out to drinks, and took a last run in the hills above campus, but none of it seemed real. The Craftsman bungalows all lined up with their weathered shingling, stained glass, and sunflowers in front-yard raised beds, the Gore and Nader signs as far as the eye could see, my friends, the stack of books I was supposed to be reading, the article I was supposed to be revising, the Albatross, Zachary's, the little Thai restaurant down the street from my apartment: the entire city was soft at the edges and fading from view.

When people asked me what I was going to do in Cairo, I didn't say anything about my father or the package or Mr. Mosseri. Instead, I told them that I wanted to work on my Arabic, see family, maybe look into new angles of research. And by the end of the week, by virtue of constant repetition, these justifications had calcified into a sort of reality.

The only person with any questions about the plan was my mother.

"Cairo?" she said. "You really want to spend the semester in Cairo?"

"I think it will be good for me," I told her. "You know, the mourning process, wrestling the grief. Plus, I've been wanting to work on my Arabic."

"Do you think it's safe?" she persisted. "I mean, it wasn't so long ago they killed all those tourists in Luxor."

"Mom," I said, my voice taking on that familiar adolescent whine. "You know that's not what it's like."

Although she hadn't been back for more than forty years, although she always made sure to emphasize that she was an Egyptian *Jew* and had spent most of her childhood in Paris, my mother had been born in Cairo and still very much identified as Egyptian. She planted molokhia in our backyard, read *Al-Ahram* online, and drove the twelve hours to Los Angeles twice a year to stock up on spices. All of which, she reasoned, entitled her to whatever opinions she might have about Mubarak and the Muslim Brotherhood.

"I'll be safe," I said, and left it at that, not wanting to get into an argument about terrorism or corruption or the decline of Egyptian culture.

"I know, it's just—"

She didn't need to say anything else. I knew where she was going. It was always the same story. When she was ten years old, my mother and her entire family had been expelled from Cairo—along with the rest of the foreigners and Jews—kicked out of a city they had lived in for more than a thousand years. She had been forced to leave her friends, her teachers, and the only home she had ever known. Which was why, for her, any discussion of Egypt always came back to the same thing: us vs. them. You couldn't trust "them," whoever they might be. And right or wrong, "we" had to stick together.

In the past, I might have tried to push back a little, poke holes in her oversimplistic binary. I might have pointed out that identity didn't have to be so immutable and that, although she was kind enough to include me in her "us," I was equally one of "them." But I knew it would be easier to just change the subject.

"I talked to Steve yesterday," I said, playing to her perennial interest in the details of my academic life. "He said it shouldn't be a problem, taking my prelims at the end of spring. He thought it was a great idea, actually, going to Cairo."

"I just want you to be happy," my mother said after a long pause, the implication being that, regardless of what Steve or anyone else might think, regardless of what I was hoping to find, going to Cairo wasn't a good idea and it certainly wasn't going to make me happy.

And maybe she was right, I thought, watching Garden City tilt into morning. Maybe I was just running away from my problems. Maybe I was putting myself in danger. Maybe I was sacrificing my graduate career, such as it was, to chase after ghosts that would never give me any answers, at least not the ones I wanted. Maybe it was a bad idea.

I set the empty mug down next to me and glanced at the little blue cell phone Aisha had given me. It was almost seven already and below me, the neighborhood was coming to life. A knot of older men were smoking shisha on wooden stools next to a bright green newspaper kiosk, and across the street a couple of squat black-and-white taxis idled in front of a cheap hotel called Pharaoh's Palace. In a way it didn't matter whether my mother was right, whether I had made the right decision or the wrong one. Because either way, there I was.

By the end of that first week in Cairo, I was beginning to understand the shape of my neighborhood. There was the little café around the corner, the elementary school across the street, and a grocery store two blocks down that stocked peanut butter and Marmite for the diplomats who lived nearby. If you walked too far in any one direction, you were bound to run into either the Nile, Qasr el-Einy Street, or one of the heavily fortified compounds—the U.S. embassy, the British embassy, the Ministries of Tourism and Petroleum—that separated Garden City from downtown. By the end of that first week, I had gotten used to the heat and the pollution, the big hotels, the neon billboards, and the buzz of taxis swarming around Tahrir Square. My Arabic had started coming back. Aisha took me to a used-furniture market near Ramses Station and I bought an electric kettle at a shiny two-story department store on Talaat Harb Street. But as much as I was beginning to feel at home again in the city, I still didn't know anything more about the package that had brought me there.

It was there on the coffee table, waiting for me every morning when I woke. And every afternoon when I got back to the apartment—after a trip to the grocery store or lunch downtown with Aisha or wandering around the neighborhood looking for an ATM that would accept my debit card—it was still there, waiting. Occasionally, if I wasn't too tired, I would sit down on the living room couch, lift the presentation case up from its nest of newspaper, and hold that ancient scrap of paper in my hands, tilting it toward the light as I ran my thumb along the edge of the glass and tried to imagine my father in his armchair, inspecting this very same object.

At first, it had been the words that interested me most. But with time, I began giving more and more thought to the grammar of the thing itself, that dull reddish stain across the top of the page, the weave of the paper, the faded brown tint of the ink. For every object had its story; every key or rock or piece of glass made its own meaning as it moved through the world, from pocket to hand, closet to shelf, attic to kitchen table. And somewhere, beneath those words, hidden in the space between the letters, was the story of the object itself, the thread of its passage through the centuries, from father to son, father to son, until eventually it found its way to me.

What it signified, where it came from, why my father had sent it to me, these questions remained unanswered. I had tried calling the number on Mr. Mosseri's business card at least half a dozen times. But every time I called I got the same recorded message telling me the number in question was no longer in service. When I searched online, at the dusty Internet café around the corner from my apartment, the only Claude Mosseris I could find were a wholesale fabric dealer in Paris and a banker buried in the Bassatine cemetery outside Cairo.

My family wasn't much help, either. When I showed them the package—that first Sunday after lunch at their apartment—none of them quite knew what to make of it. Uncle Hassan said he thought the scrap of paper might be from the attic of the Ibn Ezra Synagogue. And when Aisha tried to read the Arabic side of the note, she could only make out a few isolated phrases, not nearly enough to make any sense of it.

"I don't think this is Arabic," she said, and passed it to her father, who puzzled over the words for a few minutes before giving up.

"What about Mr. Mosseri?" Aunt Basimah asked as she placed a platter of baklava in the middle of the table.

"Yes," Uncle Hassan said absently, glancing at Mr. Mosseri's business card. "He is a good man. And he was a great friend of your father's. I think he is the one who should know about this piece of paper."

"Do you have his number?" I asked. "The one on his card doesn't work."

"He was at the funeral," Aisha offered and Uncle Hassan nodded.

"We grew up together, in the old neighborhood."

But neither of them knew how to get in touch with him.

"What about my father?" I persisted. "He never mentioned anything about any of this? Nothing about the package or this piece of paper?"

Uncle Hassan shook his head.

"We were very close, your father and I. We lived together, worked together, shared our meals. But when it came to the synagogue, there were some things he could never tell me. I was the second son, you know, and in our family, that was everything."

Uncle Hassan rubbed the back of his head and loosened the gold band of his watch.

"Of course," he added, "I did quite well for myself."

It was true. Without connections or capital—in a country that ran on relationships and bribes—Uncle Hassan had turned his father-in-law's corner store into a produce distribution empire that sold tomatoes, cucumbers, and eggplants to nearly every hospital and school in the city. He drove a new Mercedes and sent his daughter to the best schools. But in spite of all this, he said, he was still the younger brother, and in the al-Raqb family the first son was the one who mattered. The first son was the watchman.

"Do you think . . ." I began, trying to find the right words. "Do you think there might be something else?"

Leaning back from the table, Uncle Hassan folded his hands over his stomach and glanced up at the ceiling. The shadow of a thought passed over his face. But he shook it off before it could settle.

"Something else?"

"Maybe in my father's room?"

He glanced down the hall in the direction of the small room where my father had lived for more than twenty-five years. Then he reached across the table and plucked a particularly gooey piece of baklava off the platter. As he chewed, he seemed to be making a calculation of sorts, brother divided by nephew, the privacy of the dead minus the curiosity of the living.

"It's worth a look," Aisha said. "Don't you think?"

"I suppose so," Uncle Hassan agreed, though he didn't seem entirely convinced.

"I'll just be a minute," I said, standing up from the table before he could lodge any objections.

"It might be stuffy," Aunt Basimah cautioned, readjusting

the edges of her hijab. "No one's been in there since I cleaned it. After—"

She took a step with me down the hall, then stopped herself and let me go on alone.

Earlier, Uncle Hassan had asked if I wanted to visit my father's grave that following Sunday. I had evaded the question, mumbling something vague and noncommittal. I knew I wasn't ready to visit his grave. It was too soon. But his room, that was something different, a vestige of his life rather than a monument to his death. And who knew what I might find in there? An address book perhaps, a half-written letter, a few scattered notes to himself?

As I opened the door, hand still on the knob, I felt my heart snag and time collapsed around me like a circus tent. Here was that yellow-flowered wallpaper, the chrome clock above the dresser, the blue-green Persian carpet. I could almost see him, sitting there on his bright orange armchair in the corner of the room, listening to the radio, slipping his shoes off at the end of the day. I could see the lonely imprints of his slippers on the carpet next to the bed, feel the scratch of his sweater, smell that faint potpourri of cigarette smoke, body odor, and cologne.

After standing in the doorway for a moment, I stepped inside, ran my hand along the bedspread, looked in the closet, and opened a few of the dresser drawers. I didn't know what I was looking for. Regardless, there wasn't much of interest: a few shirts, a stack of old VHS cassettes, a ballpoint pen on top of the nightstand. I looked under the bed, flipped the radio on and off. Then, as I was about to leave, leafing through one of the old paperbacks on his dresser, I found a faded newspaper clipping—used as a bookmark or maybe hidden away for safekeeping—a short article accompanied by the picture of a squat bald man holding a Torah scroll. *A leader of Cairo's Jewish community,* read the caption, *Mr. Claude Mosseri, standing next to the newly refurbished Ibn Ezra Synagogue.* Someone, most likely my father, had made a small question mark next to the scroll, as if this picture might be the answer to a question he had been pursuing for some time.

Uncle Hassan was right. Mr. Mosseri was the one to answer my questions about the package. He was the one who would know what that scrap of paper meant to my father and why, of all the things he might have sent me, he had sent me that. But Mr. Mosseri was not an easy person to find. Aside from a disconnected phone number, the newspaper clipping, and a few of Uncle Hassan's childhood memories, the only thing I knew about him was his address, 72 Gamal al-Din Street.

Unfortunately, there were six different Gamal al-Din streets in Cairo, fourteen when you included all the variations on the name, like Gamal al-Din Afifi or Gamal Izz il-Din.

"I bet it's this one," Aisha said, after lunch a few days later at her favorite koshari restaurant. She pointed to a small winding street in Garden City, a couple blocks from my apartment, then turned the map around so I could see it.

"What about this one?" I asked, turning to the page for Dokki.

"Could be," she said as she flipped to the map of Heliopolis. "Or maybe this one?"

There was no reason to think Mr. Mosseri lived on the Gamal al-Din Street in Garden City or the one in Dokki or the one in Heliopolis. But I had to start somewhere, and it might as well be down the block. So, that next morning, I walked up Qasr el-Einy Street to the Canadian embassy and took a left on Gamal al-Din.

If you closed one eye, you could imagine how the street might have looked a hundred years earlier, a wide looping avenue lined with saplings and great stone villas built to the taste of newly rich industrialists, a few blocks from the Nile and a short carriage ride from downtown. These days, the street was home to the Indonesian embassy, a police substation, the Happy Child English Language Nursery School, and a handful of old villas that had been chopped up into single-family apartments. But no number 72.

The only thing between number 74 and number 68 was a narrow alley occupied by a stainless-steel lunch cart.

"Excuse me," I said to the man behind the cart. "I am looking for Mr. Mosseri."

I handed him Mr. Mosseri's business card and he inspected it for a moment before passing it to the man sitting on a wooden stool behind him.

"Mr. Claude Mosseri," read the man on the stool. "Seventy-two Gamal al-Din Street."

"He was a friend of my father," I added.

The men both seemed sympathetic to my search—especially when I told them that my father was Egyptian and had recently passed away—but neither of them knew any Mr. Mosseris. Nor did the proprietor of the produce market on the corner, nor the owner of the newsstand in the middle of the block. The doorman of 74 Gamal al-Din Street said there were no Mosseris in the building. Still, he suggested, I should leave a note for the superintendent, just to be sure. It was a stab in the dark, but I didn't have many other options. So I borrowed a pen and paper from a copy shop down the block and composed two notes in my best Arabic handwriting.

> Dear Sir,
> My name is Yusuf al-Raqb.
> I am searching for Mr. Claude Mosseri.
> If you know him, please call me. My phone number is
> 018 736 2583.
>
> > Thank you,
> > Yusuf

I gave one of the notes to the doorman of 74 Gamal al-Din Street and the other I put in the mail slot of the dentist's office next door. Then I went back to the lunch cart, bought a few half-moons of pita filled with ful, taamiya, fried eggplant, and pickled vegetable, ate them, and walked back down Qasr el-Einy to my apartment.

"Did you find him?" Aisha asked when I called her later that afternoon.

"There wasn't even a seventy-two," I said, and she laughed.

"On to the next."

Over the course of the following week and a half, as August slipped into September and the carob trees outside my apartment began dropping their fruit, I visited Gamal al-Din streets all over Cairo, in Giza and Abbasiya, Nasr City, Heliopolis, and Imbaba. I crisscrossed the city in taxis with ripped-up plastic seats and pasted-on decorations. I walked when I could. I rode the subway. And I pushed my way onto rattling multicolored buses packed with middle-aged men, families, and the occasional older woman with a cage full of chickens. Sometimes I wandered the surrounding neighborhood for most of a morning. Other times, I only stayed a few minutes. But I always left behind a note, slipped under the door of 72 Gamal al-Din Street or one of the buildings nearby.

It was exhausting at times, struggling through the traffic and the pollution and the heat, walking up and down this seemingly endless string of Gamal al-Dins. The neighborhoods began to bleed together, all those piles of trash, concrete, and rebar, the faded political banners hanging between buildings, the children in blue-and-white school uniforms chasing each other past wooden carts piled high with overripe produce, the grease-stained small mechanic shop next to a corner store next to a restaurant serving roast chicken cooked on an open rotisserie.

But there were the occasional flashes of promise. I met an older man at a café in Agouza who said he went to primary school with someone named Mosseri. In Nasr City I ate lunch with a security guard outside a bank who told me that there was a Mr. Mosseri who lived next to his mother. And every so often, as I made my way to one Gamal al-Din or another, I came upon a barbershop or a little café that, for no particular reason, reminded me of my father. Looking through the glass, I would imagine him sitting upright in a green vinyl barber's chair or playing backgammon at the far corner of a café. One day I saw him riding a motorcycle across the Qasr el-Nil

Bridge. A few days later he was smoking a cigarette outside a government building. I knew it wasn't really him. Still it gave me some comfort, that feeling of being watched over. And every time I saw him—drinking tea with a police officer or maneuvering a pickup truck through traffic—I knew I was headed in the right direction.

In retrospect, I can see how lonely I was, going from neighborhood to neighborhood, searching for answers to questions I wasn't fully able to articulate. Sure, I had lunch every so often with Aisha and her friends. I went over to Uncle Hassan and Aunt Basimah's for Sunday dinner. I talked to my mother on the phone. I sent cheery mass emails to my friends, layering my impressions of the city with humorous anecdotes and the occasional somber reflection on wealth disparity. But most of the time I was alone.

During those first few weeks in Cairo—as I wandered around the city looking for the right Gamal al-Din—my most regular and sustained interactions were with the doorman of my building, the bawab, Abdullah. He was always there, when I left in the morning and when I came home in the afternoon, eating his dinner, drinking tea, or smoking a cigarette with one of the taxi drivers across the street. Occasionally, he would ask me a question about my day and once or twice, I shared a tea with him on the front steps of the building. I waved to him and we exchanged greetings. But I didn't think much about him and, for the most part, our interactions were limited to small talk and jokes.

All this changed one afternoon when, coming home from

a particularly dusty Gamal al-Din Street out by the airport, I found him in the lobby of the building, sitting in the doorway of the tiny closet where he slept, legs crossed and eyes shut in contemplation of the Van Morrison song coming from a little tape player at his feet. He wasn't conventionally good-looking. But there was a certain charm in the disorder of his features. And when he opened his eyes, at the end of the song, the directness of his smile caught me off guard.

"Will you help?" he asked, rearranging himself to make room for me in his closet. "With the words? It is a very difficult song."

"Play it again," I said and squatted down next to him.

We listened a second time, then a third, trying to catch the words before they melted into the honk and shout of the street. The fourth time around, I could make out a few more phrases—*met them face-to-face outside . . . living with a gun*—enough to get the basic thrust. There was a bar fight, a fugitive, some unintended consequences. Maybe that was all we were supposed to know. Maybe it was our job to sketch in the empty spaces, to make meaning from what we had been given.

"It's difficult to understand," I said, when he asked about a particularly confusing line.

"Difficult to understand," Abdullah said, "but not difficult to feel."

"Yes," I said. He was right.

As we listened to the next song and the next and the next, I stared at the wall above him, careful not to move, not wanting to lose the charge of our proximity, that feeling of warmth and the sharp yeasty smell of his body. This was his bedroom,

I thought as he leaned over me to retrieve the tape case. It was his living room, and who knew what else, a few square feet of space, furnished only with a nest of blankets, a couple of pillows, the tape player, and a gilt-framed piece of Arabic calligraphy. I had no idea where he kept his clothes and toiletries, where he went to wash himself or brush his teeth. I literally could not imagine the most basic components of his life.

"Linden Arden," he said, reading from the back of the tape case. "Who is he?"

I shook my head. "I don't know."

"You are not very helpful," he teased.

I took the case from him and looked at the cover. A shaggy-haired Van Morrison sat alone in a bright green field, flanked on either side by Irish wolfhounds. It was another world, as different as you could imagine from this closet a few blocks from the Nile.

"Where did you get this?" I asked.

"My friend Gerrit," he said, "from Rotterdam. He gave me the tape, many years ago when he came to visit Siwa."

Abdullah paused significantly, letting the question of Gerrit hang between us.

"You know Siwa?"

I had heard of Siwa, could maybe point to it on a map, a lonely oasis out there in the middle of the desert, near the border with Libya. Beyond that, all I knew about it was the story of Alexander the Great following a flock of birds across the desert to visit the Siwan Oracle.

"The sweetest dates in all of Egypt," Abdullah said.

"Is that right?"

He smiled and took the case back from me.

We sat there for most of the evening, listening to Van Morrison and watching the building's residents file in with their packages, their children, their black plastic shopping bags. All of them nodded and greeted us. A few asked Abdullah if he could come up later and check on a leaky faucet or a malfunctioning air conditioner. But none of them seemed to think twice about the two of us huddled up together in the closet listening to music.

As dusk filtered in through the front door, Abdullah told me about growing up in Siwa and moving with his family to Cairo when he was seventeen. The plan had been for him to take pre-veterinary classes at Cairo University while his mother cleaned houses and his father worked as a bawab. But halfway through the program his mother got sick, and he had to take over the bawab responsibilities from his father, who started driving a taxi.

"It's not so bad," he said, anticipating my sympathy. "I read, listen to music. I watch the people come and go."

"I guess not," I said, staring out the empty doorway.

Growing up, I was always slightly embarrassed by the idea that my father had been a watchman. I pictured him as a security guard at a bank or a fast-food restaurant, a gun for hire in a phony uniform, not quite heroic enough to be a policeman or a firefighter. But sitting there with Abdullah, chatting with the residents as they filtered into the building, I began to see the quiet dignity of the position. A watchman was more than just a guard. He was the spirit of the place, the embodiment of the building in human form.

"Do you know what this is?" Abdullah asked, pointing at the wall behind me.

I followed his finger to a framed piece of Arabic calligraphy just above my head.

"No."

"It is a saying of the Prophet Muhammad," he said. " 'Be in the world like a traveler, or like a passer-on, and reckon yourself as of the dead.' "

I stared at the calligraphy, trying to make out the tangle of letters, trying to understand what he was getting at, what he wanted to tell me.

"Are you very religious?"

It was a silly question, simplistic and a step or two removed from what I actually wanted to ask. Still, he took it at face value.

"I believe in God," he said. "But there are some things I don't agree with."

"Okay—"

As I shifted, trying to formulate the next question, I realized that one of my legs was asleep. I had been sitting in that same position for most of the evening.

"My leg," I said, as I stood up and leaned against the wall, flexing to get the blood pumping again. "It's asleep. Pins and needles."

I stood there for a moment, massaging my own leg.

"I should probably be getting to bed myself."

Abdullah looked up at me, reached over, and squeezed my calf, just under the spot where I had been massaging.

"Thank you for your help with the song."

"Good night," I said, but I didn't move.

We stayed like that for a good two minutes, me standing over him, his hand on my leg, neither of us moving, not even looking at each other.

Everything was telling me to go for it, to lean down and kiss him. But I knew well enough to hold back. I knew things worked differently in Egypt, that platonic touching was normal, that even the most homophobic of men wouldn't think twice about walking down the street holding hands with a friend. In Egypt, gay wasn't something you were, it was something you did. It was an act, or many acts, not an identity. All of which inclined me to mistrust my intuition, to restrain any irrevocable advances until I was sure of Abdullah's intentions.

"I really should be getting to bed," I said eventually.

"Yes," he agreed, and he placed the empty tape case next to my foot. "I will see you soon, I hope."

In the days that followed, Abdullah and I began spending more and more time together. I brought him dinner from the hummus and ful restaurant down the block. We smoked shisha on the front steps of the building, drank sweet black tea, and watched the neighborhood pass by. I told him about my father, Mr. Mosseri, and the various Gamal al-Din streets I had visited. I told him about the waiter who insisted on paying for my lunch, to give me strength, and the group of kids who followed me down the street yelling "Co-ca-Co-la, Co-ca-Co-la." But I didn't say anything about the package my father had sent me—the impetus for my search—in part because it was too complicated to explain and in part because I knew that the package would lead to the synagogue and, if I told him about the synagogue, I would have to tell him about my mother's family, which would mean telling him I was Jewish. Not that I necessarily thought it would be an issue, my being Jewish. But with all the other uncertainties between us—the question of his intentions, the significance of that Arabic calligraphy on his wall, the unavoidable power imbalance inherent in our respective positions—I thought it would be easier to avoid all of that, for the time being.

Meanwhile, those other uncertainties were beginning to dissipate. Or maybe it would be more accurate to say that they were subsumed by something else. Abdullah wasn't the type of guy I usually went for, and maybe that was a good thing. We almost never talked about ideas. I don't even think he knew that I was a graduate student. But there was an ease to our interactions that I can't remember with any of the brash, hyperintellectual guys I usually dated. As we spent more and more time together, drinking tea and smoking shisha on the front steps of the building, we began to develop little patterns and jokes. Those seemingly accidental brushes—his hand against my arm, his knee settling in next to my ankle—became more and more common. And one day, an unseasonably cool afternoon in the middle of September, the tension finally broke.

I had spent most of that morning searching for one of the last Gamal al-Din streets on my list, a wisp of an alley near the southern tip of Zamalek, and when I got back to the apartment I was feeling particularly frustrated.

"Are you okay?" Abdullah asked when he saw me coming

up the stairs. I must have looked upset, because he stood to offer me his stool.

"Yeah," I said. "It's just—"

I had thought it would be easy. I would find Mr. Mosseri and he would answer all my questions. Just being in Cairo, I had thought, would help me understand my father, the package, and all the stories crowded inside. The pyramids and the Cairo Tower, the murky taste of tap water and the prickle of sunburn at the back of my neck, all these things would combine to give me some visceral understanding unavailable to me in California. But, of course, that wasn't how it turned out.

"I don't know," I said, letting my head fall into my hands. "I don't know what I'm doing here."

Abdullah didn't respond, but I could feel the weight of his hand on the back of my neck and his thumb working into my shoulder.

"You are trying," he offered after a long silence.

"But what difference does it make, if I can't find Mr. Mosseri?" I said, sitting up. "What am I doing? Wouldn't it be easier if I just went home?"

While he considered these questions, Abdullah moved his hand to my knee, as if that were its natural resting place.

"Sometimes it is most important to look," he said, his thumb kneading slowly into my thigh. "And for me—"

He paused to find the right words, his lips moving slightly as they tried out the various sounds. Before he could say anything else, I put my hand on the back of his neck and— without thinking, without considering the potential consequences, without even looking back over my shoulder to see if there was anyone coming down the stairs—drew him toward me.

I felt his pulse quicken under my fingers. But when I leaned in, he moved his hand to my chest and gently, unmistakably, pushed me away.

"Not here."

"Come upstairs, then."

"Not now," he said. "I can't leave my post."

"When?" I asked.

"Soon."

Later that night, I woke to the sound of someone jiggling the front door of my apartment. For a moment, I thought it might be an intruder, a drunk neighbor, or a policeman come to arrest me for "obscene behavior." But then the lock clicked, the door swung open, and with a breath of footsteps, Abdullah was at the edge of my bedroom.

"I thought you couldn't leave your post," I teased.

"Tonight I can," he said and he pulled the galabiya up over his head.

He came on strong out of the gate—gripping, grunting, pulling my hair—then slowed at his peak and crumpled beside me. It wasn't at all how I expected. There was no hard shell of closeted reticence, no unschooled tenderness transformed to sweaty passion. And afterward, there was none of the awkwardness I had anticipated.

When I came out of the bathroom, I found him sitting on the salmon-colored velvet couch in the middle of my living room, wearing my Santa Cruz T-shirt and a pair of my blue-

and-green-striped boxers. He had his feet tucked under him and was examining the presentation case, which I had left out on the coffee table.

"What is this?" he asked.

There was no malice in his voice, no suspicion or accusation, nothing but pure curiosity. And yet, seeing him there on my couch, I felt a pinch of anxiety in my chest.

"That?" I said as the fear spread into my extremities.

How was I supposed to know that he was who he said he was? He could be anyone, a fundamentalist, an agent from the Ministry of the Interior. And now here he was, sitting on my couch, asking me questions I didn't know how to answer. Even if I did know how to answer the questions, even if he was who he said he was, I wasn't sure I wanted to tell him I was Jewish. I heard my mother's voice, saying what she always said. *You can't trust them. We have to stick together.* I tried my best to think up a lie, an easily believable story that wouldn't eventually lead back to the synagogue, to my mother's family, and all of that. But in the end, in spite of the fear, the truth was what came out.

"That's the reason I came to Cairo," I said, sitting down next to him.

He held the case for a moment in the bowl of his hands, then he opened it carefully, and trailed his fingers along the glass protecting the paper inside.

"You came here for a piece of paper?"

"It's more than a piece of paper," I said and he looked down at it again, to make sure he hadn't missed anything.

"To me it looks like a piece of paper."

As I explained the importance of this particular paper, as

far as I understood it—the Arabic phrases Aisha had been able to decipher, my father's connection to the synagogue where Uncle Hassan thought the paper might have been found—Abdullah removed it from its velvet lining and carefully examined both sides. He stared down at the Hebrew side for a long while, then looked up at me. The implications of it all were beginning to settle across his face.

"This is Jewish?" he asked.

"Hebrew," I corrected. "It's from a synagogue, in Old Cairo."

He nodded, though he still seemed somewhat confused.

"Your father, he was a Jew?"

"No," I said.

I did my best to explain, how my father was Muslim but worked as the watchman of a synagogue, how he met my mother, who is Jewish, in the courtyard of this same synagogue, before she left Cairo, how—depending on whom you asked, depending on how you thought of it—I was either Jewish or Muslim, or both. Though the truth was, I didn't feel especially connected to either. Aside from a few weeks of Jewish camp when I was younger and a couple of trips to the mosque that summer I spent in Cairo, I didn't have much experience with either faith.

"Maybe . . ." I said eventually, still struggling to explain. "There are some stories my father used to tell me, about the synagogue where this piece of paper came from."

"Yes," Abdullah said, "tell me a story."

When he was comfortable, his head on the armrest of the couch and his feet in my lap, I began, telling him about the great line of al-Raqb watchmen, stretching down through the years from father to son, father to son. When I came to the end, to the package, Mr. Mosseri, and the newspaper clipping I found in my father's room, Abdullah was silent, watching the soft glow of the sunrise through the curtains. He seemed to be formulating a response, thinking through the sentence in order to get it right.

"I want to help," he said finally. "I think I can help you find Mr. Mosseri."

"What do you mean?" I asked and he sat up, rearranging himself on the other side of the couch.

"This scroll," he said, "in the attic of the synagogue, tell me more about this."

6

WITH MORNING, A dusty red light spilled over the Muqattam Hills and filled the floor of the valley between the Citadel and the pyramids. Warming the stone of the medieval city, it lingered among the pillars of the Ibn Tulun Mosque, climbed its spiraling minaret, and spun out over a quilt of streets and stone and cotton fields to the hazy rise of the pyramids. While her other half slept, Agnes sat in the blue wingback chair next to their northerly window, contemplating the chessboard and watching the city fill with color. She usually woke a few minutes before her sister and relished the protective quiet she felt during that early sliver of morning. It made her think always of those first few minutes alone in the world, before she became a sister, a twin, before their mother died; before her life became their life, and her thoughts their thoughts.

As if in response to this sentiment, Margaret opened her eyes and lifted her head, taking in the unfamiliar angle of dawn. A thread of spittle connected the corner of her mouth to the pillow, like a fish hooked to the line of sleep.

"Up long?"

Agnes shook her head and they watched the rest of the sunrise in silence. The light was different here. How could it not be? How could this sun, under whose rays Moses and

Saladin and Ramses had walked, be the same one they knew from Cambridge? The light was of a stronger weft, and stubborn, refracted as it was through sand and dust and five thousand years of history. Perhaps this persistence of light was what disposed the Egyptians toward its absence, the gloomy shadows of the veil and the cold black humidity at the center of the pyramids. Perhaps the strength of the light was what inspired that peculiar Jewish practice, burying sacred texts or secreting them away in the attic of the synagogue. How had Dr. Schechter put it? *The contents of the book go up to heaven like the soul.* The past in Egypt was never too far from hand. Always present, always lurking in some attic or at the bottom of a forgotten chest. The entire country was a sort of reptilian palimpsest. Beneath each skin lived another, waiting for the right reactive agent, the right traveler to uncover it.

Agnes waited until the bottom of the sun lifted itself over the horizon; then she broke the silence.

"Check."

"What?"

"You're in check."

Margaret craned her neck to see the chessboard. It was a close and tangled bout, as their games always were. Agnes had attacked first, but Margaret hung back, drawing her sister in with the patience of a spider.

"That was foolish, Nestor."

"How do you mean?"

"Move my bishop to Q2."

Agnes made the move, and when she did, she saw her foolishness.

"Blast."

They were both silent for a long while, examining the board as they dressed and readied themselves for the day.

"Let me think on it," Agnes said as they walked downstairs.

"You're far too eager to check, Nestor."

"And you, Meggie, are far too eager to gloat."

Dr. Schechter and Miss de Witt were seated near the fireplace at the far end of the lobby, talking to a petite and somewhat dandyish Egyptian man. Presumably this was Mr. Bechor, the industrialist from the governing council of the Jewish community, the one who had insisted on taking them on a tour of the city. At first glance, he appeared dignified and well-groomed—a proper effendi, with his fez and light-gray three-piece suit, his delicate hands, and a mustache so thin one could hardly see it at certain angles—but not without a pinch of the brash self-assurance one typically associated with the newly rich. Standing, he had Margaret's hand at his lips before Dr. Schechter could begin the introductions.

"Such an honor," he said, holding Margaret's gaze for a moment before moving on to her sister. "I have heard so much about you from Dr. Schechter."

Although he was the shortest among them—his shiny bald spot about level with the bridge of Agnes's nose—Mr. Bechor seemed accustomed to upturned glances. Once he was finished with his greetings, he let his gaze sweep from Margaret and Agnes to Miss de Witt.

"Three beautiful women," he exclaimed; then he turned to lead them outside to his carriage, an elegant dark-blue-and-silver Landau coach the likes of which Margaret and Agnes hadn't seen for years.

After instructing the driver in a dialect that seemed to be a mix of North African Arabic and Hebrew, Mr. Bechor saw to it that Dr. Schechter and the three beautiful women were comfortably seated.

"I have arranged a rather pleasant itinerary," he said. "First, a panorama from behind the Citadel. Then lunch at the Gezira Club."

He glanced at the twins and they indicated their approval. They had no choice. Mr. Bechor, Dr. Schechter had told them, was a key member of the governing council, and should be appeased at all costs.

"After lunch, I thought we might visit the site of the new synagogue, on Adly Street, very close to your hotel in fact. Then if we have time, we can stroll through Garden City and take in the new mummies at the museum."

At the mention of mummies, Margaret's face lit up, genuinely.

"My sister is quite enamored of mummies," Agnes explained, and Margaret confessed that it was true.

"I don't think I'll ever get over the sheer thrill of it, seeing the remains of a person who lived so many thousands of years ago."

"They remind me of cats," Miss de Witt put forth. It was the first time she had spoken all morning, and she seemed anxious to make a good showing. "Don't you think, with their little noses and tiny wrinkled lips?"

When no one responded, she straightened her posture and looked around the carriage, first at the sisters and then across to the men.

"Of course, it could be a fancy."

"No, no, you're right," Dr. Schechter said, coming in late to her defense. "I think I would like to be mummified myself. That is, if my religion didn't prohibit such things."

While Dr. Schechter held forth on the topic of Jewish burial practices, their carriage emerged from the shadow of the old city and began its climb to the Citadel.

Mr. Bechor's panorama was located on a small rise behind the fortress. And, one had to admit, it was quite stunning. The chalky white Muqattam Hills rose up behind them and, less than a hundred yards from where they stood, the minarets of the Muhammad Ali Mosque looked like the smokestacks of a great ship preparing to set out on the ocean of humanity. After pointing to the Ibn Tulun Mosque, Birkat al-Fil Square, and the Abdeen Palace, Mr. Bechor launched into a long string of details about the mosque below them, the enormous cost of its construction, the height of its minarets, and the weight of silver in its domes.

"The tower," he said, pointing to a flamboyant brass clock tower in the corner of the courtyard, "was presented to Muhammad Ali by the French king Louis Philippe I, in exchange for the obelisk in Paris's Place de la Concorde."

According to Mr. Bechor's logic, this exchange of gifts proved that Egypt was on equal terms with the great European powers and that, within a few short years, the birthplace of civilization would surpass those upstart backwaters. He continued on in this nationalistic vein as they climbed back into the carriage and rode across the city to the Gezira Club, making more than a few rather preposterous claims about British rule, Ismail Pasha, and the construction of the Suez Canal. In Mr. Bechor's opinion, European colonialism had helped spur Egypt along the road of modernization, but the system had long outlived its usefulness.

"In twenty-five years," he predicted, "Egypt will be a fully independent nation, with a modern economy and a democratically elected prime minister."

"Wouldn't that be wonderful?" Agnes said as pleasantly as she could manage.

"Wonderful," Margaret whispered as their carriage passed through the gates of the Gezira Club, "if not particularly likely."

One had to admit that the city had changed a great deal in the past twenty-five years, and much of it for the better. Whatever one thought of Ismail Pasha, one could not deny that he had succeeded in building a modern European city alongside the medieval core, a modern Cairo complete with gas lamps, pleasure gardens, and municipal water. Even the Gezira Club seemed different. The palm trees and polo grounds were greener than they remembered, and the clientele was decidedly more Egyptian. Everywhere one looked, there was another well-coiffed businessman with an expensive three-piece suit, a fez, and a sheepish yet somewhat cunning grin.

Leading them through the front doors of the club and down the entrance hall, past potted fruit trees and red-coated waiters floating about with drinks on stainless-steel trays, Mr. Bechor paused every few steps to greet a friend, a business partner, or a club employee, bestowing upon each a variation of the same handshake, back pat, and double kiss. Winking his way past the maître d', he directed his party to a semicircular banquette at the back corner of the restaurant. A few moments later, a team of waiters brought drinks along with an assortment of appetizers for the table. This was followed by roast pigeons for the ladies and a mixed grill for the men.

Once the food was properly praised and the meal begun, Agnes saw fit to raise the topic she had been holding to herself all morning.

"Dr. Schechter tells us he found some very interesting documents in the geniza of the Ibn Ezra Synagogue."

"Mrs. Lewis is quite the scholar," Dr. Schechter added by way of explanation. "Perhaps you have heard of the codex at St. Catherine? It was she who uncovered it."

"Yes," Mr. Bechor said and he pursed his lips as if trying to recall the name of a distant cousin who had once asked him for a loan. "I do remember that story. Wasn't there something about the document being used as a butter dish?"

Agnes took a sip of water to cover her scowl. That infernal story—the idea that she had discovered the codex at breakfast one morning, when she noticed ink seeping into her butter—would follow her to her grave. It was truly preposterous. Why would the monks of St. Catherine use their manuscripts as crockery? They didn't even use butter. They used olive oil. And yet, that was the story that stuck in people's minds. People did not remember their hard work or ingenuity, the weeks in the desert, poring over ancient manuscripts. They did not remember the months of transcription or Margaret's book or Agnes's speech to the Royal Asiatic Society. They remembered the butter dish.

"She found it at the back of the monastery library," Margaret answered for her sister, "which is why we were so intrigued by Dr. Schechter's descriptions of the geniza."

Mr. Bechor listened carefully to the end of Margaret's sentence; then he smiled and squeezed a lime into his drink.

"Very true," he said, and, as if continuing along the same strand of conversation, he turned to Miss de Witt. "I do hope you are enjoying your pigeon. It is a specialty of our cuisine."

Miss de Witt touched her napkin to her lips.

"Yes," she said. "I am enjoying it all very much."

While the girl praised the dish, Agnes opened her mouth slightly, waiting for a chance to raise the subject again, to insist on a proper discussion of the documents that had brought them halfway around the world. But, feeling her sister's hand on her knee, she reconsidered her approach. They had dealt with such men before, ministers and masters of industry who shied away from discussing matters of consequence with the fairer sex, and they knew that, for the most part, it was best to handle them indirectly. This was especially important with someone like Mr. Bechor, who knew little about the details of their work and yet, by virtue of his position, was indispensable to its success.

"It is a rather delicate preparation," Agnes said finally. "Is that bergamot I taste?"

After a short discussion of Egyptian cuisine, the remainder of lunch was taken up with talk of the British schooling system, the University of Cambridge, and the possibility that an educated Levantine businessman—such as Mr. Bechor—might send his sons to study there. He and Dr. Schechter had discussed these questions before, it seemed, at length, so most of Mr. Bechor's queries were directed toward the twins. As the conversation progressed, it became clear that he regarded them as gatekeepers of the university, whose advocacy would suffice to secure admission for his son.

They were attempting to disabuse him of this notion—telling him that, while they were friends with a number of professors at the university, they did not hold any official position there—when the headwaiter approached their table with a note. Apparently there was some urgent piece of business at Mr. Bechor's sugar factory, in light of which the afternoon portion of the tour would have to be suspended. He promised, however, that they would complete their itinerary the following morning, if everyone so desired.

"It is a rather unfortunate situation," Dr. Schechter said after Mr. Bechor left, "that of his son."

Glancing at Miss de Witt, he went on to describe how Mr. Bechor's eldest son, Marcel, had been found a few weeks earlier in unnatural congress with the younger son of Ibn Ezra's watchman, Mr. Muhammad al-Raqb. It was a scandal of enormous proportions, and Mr. Bechor believed that the only solution was to send Marcel off to study in Europe. Dr. Schechter had offered to write a letter to the trustees of the university, and he suggested the twins might do the same, if they saw fit. It went without saying, of course, that such a letter would greatly further their efforts to secure the geniza documents.

"Of course," Margaret said, "we are very happy to do whatever we can to help."

It was a rather small favor to ask, compared to the great value of the documents, and Margaret was inclined to write the letter as soon as they returned to their hotel. For her part,

Agnes thought they might use the letter as a bargaining chip. Moreover, there was something about Mr. Bechor that bothered her. Later that afternoon, as they finished the chess match back in their room, Agnes attempted to locate the source of her suspicions, wandering back over the course of the day, from lunch at the Gezira Club to the Muhammad Ali Mosque and the carriage ride across the city. After cleaning up the board—Margaret won handily—they both sank into their chairs and, with the same pensive scratching of the chin, considered the many connections among Mr. Bechor, Mr. Muhammad al-Raqb, their sons, Rabbi Ben Shimon, and, of course, the very pretty, very solicitous Miss de Witt. The more they considered, the more certain they were that one of these people, or perhaps two or three, were responsible for the geniza leak. And the more they thought about it, the more their suspicions began to circle around the watchman of the synagogue. Whether he was the mastermind of the theft or merely an accomplice, Mr. al-Raqb would need to be involved in some way or another.

The next morning at breakfast, Agnes was buttering her toast, paging through a two-week-old copy of *The Times,* and trying to puzzle a way out of her sister's modified French Defense, when the concierge handed her a note from Dr. Schechter. It seemed that the business at the sugar factory was more complex than Mr. Bechor had originally anticipated, and he would be unable to accompany them on the remainder of their tour. On Friday, Dr. Schechter sent over another note, regretting that neither he nor Mr. Bechor would be available that afternoon, as they needed to prepare for the Jewish Sabbath. Saturday, of course, was the Jewish Sabbath itself, and Sunday was the sisters' day of rest. All of which meant that they would not be able to visit the synagogue until Monday at the earliest, a highly irritating turn of events, but not one without a certain advantage.

After breakfast, the twins took a carriage directly to the antique book market and spent the remainder of the day trolling from stall to stall, asking sharp questions and buying up everything they could before the market closed for the evening. The next morning, they went out again and, by the end of the day, they had succeeded in visiting each of the market's hundred and thirty-four stalls. All told, they purchased six crates full of documents, all of them coated with the same thin white dust Dr. Schechter had described. They had done everything they could to staunch the flood, but they were no closer to the source of the leak. When pressed about the provenance of the documents in question, the vendors had all replied with the same halfhearted shrug, acknowledging the validity of the question while foreclosing the possibility of an answer. And, what was more, the twins knew that their purchases would only further inflame the market. Unless they secured the geniza soon, its contents—including, perhaps, the Ezra Scroll—would be scattered to the winds of obscurity. Each passing day meant still more invaluable documents removed, sold, and forever lost.

They were particularly relieved, then, when they received word Sunday evening from Dr. Schechter, indicating that he had finally persuaded Mr. Bechor to accompany them inside the Ibn Ezra Synagogue.

"At last," Agnes said, tapping the cover of her book. "At long last."

The next morning, as they rode through the narrow dirt streets of Old Cairo, past crumbling mausoleums, stray cats, and tumbledown shacks, Margaret reached over to squeeze her sister's hand. It was clearly a very poor neighborhood, but there was such history here.

"The Hanging Church," she said, pointing to their left, "and there's the Church of St. George."

The twins took no small pleasure in the dark gravity of Coptic architecture, and it was always comforting to remember that this Christian community predated the arrival of Muslims in Cairo by many hundreds of years. That morning, however, there was no time for churches. A few hundred feet past the Church of St. George, they disembarked at the front gates of the Ibn Ezra Synagogue, where Dr. Schechter and Miss de Witt were waiting with Mr. Bechor.

"Very few Jews still live in Old Cairo," Mr. Bechor said as he noticed the twins looking at an old woman begging next to the front gates. "But the building retains a great historical and spiritual significance."

Before entering the building itself, Mr. Bechor took them around the synagogue complex, pointing out the newly planted palm trees, the housing for the poor, and the well in the corner of the courtyard where Moses was said to have been taken from the Nile.

"And here," Mr. Bechor said, fluttering his fingers to indicate a small stone structure at the opposite end of the courtyard, "is the residence of our watchman, Mr. al-Raqb."

Just then, a tall and grizzled man wearing a thick gray

galabiya stepped out of the house and crossed the courtyard toward them. He had a somewhat reticent aspect, like an elm tree without leaves. But beneath this wariness, one could see also the spark of his intelligence.

"Mr. al-Raqb will be happy to show you inside the synagogue," Mr. Bechor said after exchanging a few quick words with the watchman. "I, unfortunately, must attend to some rather urgent business at the sugar factory."

The sisters exchanged a glance as Mr. al-Raqb nodded in assent and motioned for the remaining party to follow him inside. This would be a good opportunity to test out some of their suspicions. And, moreover, it was a relief to enjoy the building without the constant chatter of Mr. Bechor.

The interior of the Ibn Ezra Synagogue was laid out like many oriental houses of worship. The men's pews circled around an ornate pulpit at the center of the room, while the women's section looked down from a ring of balconies above. Mr. al-Raqb mumbled a word or two into his great rust-colored scarf as he led them around the edge of the room toward the ark, a dark wooden cabinet trimmed in a sumptuous gold leaf that glowed with the flicker of gas lamps.

"This is where the community keeps its Torah scrolls," Dr. Schechter explained; taking control of the tour, he directed their attention to a stack of boards leaning against the wall. "And these humble planks once formed the border of the previous ark, dating back at least to the thirteenth century."

"This is all rather fascinating," Agnes said when Dr. Schechter was finished explicating the text inscribed on the board closest to them, "but not the reason we came to Cairo."

She then turned to Mr. al-Raqb.

"My dear sir," she said, using her most formal Arabic, "could you please show us to the geniza? You know where that is, I assume?"

Mr. al-Raqb continued to inspect the back of his hand for a few moments before raising his gaze to Margaret.

"You are welcome," he said and he nodded at a narrow flight of stairs leading up to the narrow gallery where the women of the community were relegated.

The entrance to the geniza, this attic storeroom they had come halfway around the world to see, was nothing more than a hole in the wall at the far end of the women's section. An old wooden ladder leaned in over a few broken lamps and a hand-painted sign that read—in Hebrew, Arabic, and French—"Ibn Ezra Elementary School." Without a word, Mr. al-Raqb held the ladder and extended his hand, palm up, as if inviting them into his home.

Dr. Schechter began to speak, but before he could get a word out, he was overcome by a fit of coughing.

"Shall I go first?" Miss de Witt asked cheerily.

The twins agreed that it would probably be best.

"Would you mind taking my picture?"

Miss de Witt handed Margaret her Kodak, then scrambled up the ladder. At the top, she posed for a snap, after which she disappeared down the other side of the wall.

"Come on in," she called, pulling her chin up over the bottom edge of the hole. "The water's fine!"

"Very well," Margaret said, and she passed the camera to her sister.

After testing the strength of the ladder and making certain that both Dr. Schechter and Mr. al-Raqb had turned the other way, she proceeded to climb. Upon reaching the top, she maneuvered herself backward over the ledge and, with a few tentative scoots, found the ladder on the other side of the wall. It took a few blinks to pierce the woozy, dreamlike quality of the attic, but once she did, Margaret saw the magnitude of their discovery.

The room was piled floor to sill with texts, an ancient graveyard of manuscripts discarded willy-nilly and protected by a thick layer of fine white dust. Who knew what was hidden in there? In a thousand years of books, deeds, magic spells, and marriage contracts, they might uncover a letter from Saladin, a new chapter of the Muqaddimah, an unknown variation of the gospels, a new work by Maimonides or Plato or Judah Halevi. Even the more commonplace documents were not without their importance. One might not find much of interest in a particular letter or contract. But, compounded by a thousand years, the debris of daily life became the stuff of History.

There was something else, too. Beneath the paper and the dust, the wood beams and the cobwebs, Margaret felt a strange tingling awareness in the tips of her fingers. As she moved toward the back of the room, the dark corner where the oldest documents seemed to reside, the sensation only grew stronger.

"Nestor," she called out, "you must see this for yourself."

Margaret waited a few moments for a reply, but there was none.

"Let me see if I might be able to convince her," Miss de Witt said. She climbed the ladder, then pulled herself back through the entrance.

Once Miss de Witt was gone, Margaret crouched down to examine some of the documents near the front of the attic. As she did, she noticed the imprint of a footstep in the dust and an empty space from which a pile of documents seemed to have been recently removed. So it was true. Someone was pillaging the geniza. They had assumed as much for some time, but this physical evidence sent a fresh rush of anger bubbling up her throat. Who knew what knowledge those stolen documents might contain, what scholarly puzzle they might help solve?

As Margaret repositioned herself to examine the shoeprint more closely, trying to recall the shape of Mr. al-Raqb's footwear, she noticed a relatively small fragment near her left foot. It appeared to be quite old and was stained across the top with a brownish-red cloud of what appeared to be ancient blood. It looked to be a letter, or perhaps two. One side of it was covered in Arabic script and the other contained a few lines of Hebrew.

"Astounding, isn't it?"

Margaret looked up and saw Dr. Schechter climbing down into the attic storeroom, his back to her as he maneuvered himself to the floor.

"Yes," she replied, somewhat too quickly and, without thinking, she slipped the fragment into the folds of her dress. "One rather loses a sense of time in here."

"My thoughts precisely," Dr. Schechter said as he brushed the dust off the front of his pants and turned to face her, "my thoughts precisely."

✦ ✦ ✦

Originally, the twins had planned to stay on in Cairo for ten days. Their intention had been to finish up with the geniza business, then set off for the Sinai and St. Catherine's. However, as the date of their intended departure approached, they agreed to postpone the Sinai portion of their trip for at least another two weeks. There was no question, really. They were on the verge of a major discovery, at least as important as Troy, the underground caverns of Jerusalem, or Grenfell and Hunt's rubbish dump at Oxyrhynchus. They could not leave Cairo until the geniza documents—and also, perhaps, the Ezra Scroll—were crated, sealed, and safely on their way to Cambridge.

After discussing the matter with Dr. Schechter, who had himself twice delayed his trip to Palestine, they concluded that their next step should be to seek removal of the documents to a more secure location. Dr. Schechter suggested that he put forth the request alone, in a formal meeting with Rabbi Ben Shimon, and the twins concurred. Although they had more experience in such matters, Agnes and Margaret knew their presence would hardly improve the chances of approval.

"It is a highly delicate matter," Dr. Schechter wrote to them a few days later, "always teetering on the brink of success."

He spent the better part of that week attempting to secure the Chief Rabbi's approval. Meanwhile, the twins had more than enough to keep themselves busy. They paid a visit to the Coptic patriarch, and Margaret visited the mummies at the Egyptian Museum with Miss de Witt. For the most part, however, they spent their time in their room, going through the documents from the antique book market, or in the lobby of their hotel, Agnes brushing up on her Arabic while Margaret sifted through their prodigious collection of Egyptian travelogues, trying to discern the significance of the fragment she had removed from the geniza.

As far as she could tell, the fragment comprised two notes, both of which made reference to a young Muslim boy, Ali, who had been recommended for the position of watchman of the Ibn Ezra Synagogue. From the context, she suspected that the notes were part of a longer exchange, between the adviser of an eleventh-century caliph, al-Mustansir, and a prominent member of the Jewish community, a scholar named Shemarya the Pious.

"It's remarkable," Margaret said, looking up from the fragment. "The attic was filled with documents like this, piles of them, and every one a story."

"But no Ezra Scroll?" Agnes asked.

The longer the twins spent in Cairo, the more enamored they had become of the scroll's possibility. They were happy to have found the geniza, of course, but the Ezra Scroll, that would truly be a groundbreaking discovery.

"No," Margaret said. "Not that I could see."

"Though of course one wouldn't expect to find it lying out in the open."

"No," Margaret agreed and she turned back to the journals of Jacob Saphir, a Lithuanian traveler who was said to have discovered the geniza.

That following morning, as she was paging through the same book—looking for the section in which Saphir described peeking into the dark closet that housed the Ezra Scroll—

Dr. Schechter appeared, entirely unannounced, wearing a newly pressed brown suit. Without a word of greeting he sat down, crossed his legs, and smiled.

"My ladies," he said, "we have permission."

After accepting their congratulations, he went on to regale them with the story of his week, the incessant coffee and cigarettes, the long late meals and trips about town. He had spent most of Wednesday drinking at the club with Mr. Bechor, and Thursday he accompanied the Chief Rabbi on a tour of the pyramids. That very morning, the three of them had sealed the deal over tea at Mr. Bechor's residence. Rabbi Ben Shimon had even provided them with a letter of permission, in case anyone questioned their authority. Dr. Schechter produced the letter from his breast pocket and handed it across the table for inspection.

"There is one thing," he remembered. "Mr. Bechor asked whether you might be willing to write that letter, on behalf of his son."

"We will be happy to," Margaret said, intercepting a look from her sister, "whatever we can do to advance the cause."

"And then, of course," Dr. Schechter continued, fiddling with the buttons of his jacket, "we will need to rent a room in which to store the documents."

The twins had known from the first that there would be, at some point, a request for funds. There always was, and it was always somewhat disheartening. Not that they begrudged giving. Quite the contrary. Agnes and Margaret very much enjoyed the practice of philanthropy. What bothered them was the constant focus on the material. If one dwelt long enough in the realm of money, as they had, one began to see the entire world through a golden screen. Every building or professor, every book, painting, every good deed or good idea could be traced back to a lump of gold. And then, of course, neither of them wanted to be treated like a dotty rich old aunt.

"Have you spoken to Mr. Montefiore?" Agnes asked.

"Or Dr. Taylor?" Margaret added.

It was well known among their circle at Cambridge that Mr. Montefiore helped supplement Dr. Schechter's salary, and that his trip to Cairo had been endowed through the generosity of Dr. Taylor. Being, however, an exceedingly private person, at least when it came to money, Dr. Schechter did not like to discuss his benefactors.

"They have both been rather generous," he said, pausing for a moment as if to better consider their generosity. "But I am not sure they would fully understand the importance and immediacy of the geniza, not quite as well as you."

He looked up at the space between them, to see how this line of reasoning was settling.

"Surely Dr. Taylor would understand," Agnes said, for surely he would.

"I should think also that it would be best at present to keep the matter confined to the three of us," Dr. Schechter said.

"And Miss de Witt," Agnes added.

Margaret smiled and put a hand on her sister's wrist. There was no need to make Dr. Schechter squirm. They all knew where the discussion would end.

"How many rooms do you expect we will need?"

"Two," he said, "two or three. I've spoken to the manager of my hotel and he indicated that he would be able to provide the rooms at a discounted price."

"Let us speak to our concierge," Agnes offered. "I think we might be able to extract an especially good price from him."

Dr. Schechter was clearly not comfortable with the idea of housing the documents at the Hotel d'Angleterre—and thus ceding physical control of the geniza manuscripts to Agnes and Margaret—but he knew when not to push.

"I thank you," he said, rising from his seat with a small bow. "Knowledge thanks you, as do generations of future scholars."

"Yes, well," Agnes said, "I, for one, am glad to get to work."

Early Monday morning—after reserving a suite across the hall and purchasing the crates they would use to transport the documents from the synagogue to the hotel and on across the water to the Cambridge University Library—the twins met Dr. Schechter and Miss de Witt outside their hotel. None of them had slept well the night before and all four were silent as they rode south along the water toward Old Cairo, the fog hung thick as cream over the Nile.

As they disembarked in front of the synagogue, Miss de Witt broke the silence.

"Well, hello there," she cooed, bending down to pick up a tiny light-gray kitten mewing for its brood. "Are you lost?"

"Do not touch that filthy creature," Agnes said, and the girl jerked up as if stung.

She had not intended such a sharp rebuke, but she knew that it was in Miss de Witt's best interest. What had Dr. Taylor always said? In Cairo, pigeon is a delicacy, dogs are shunned, and cats are filthy as sewer rats. It sounded like a riddle, but it was really nothing more than the truth. Every great city had its pest. Istanbul had its dogs, London its rodents, and Rome its pigeons. In Cairo the species of nuisance was *Felis silvestris catus,* the common house cat. The city pulsed with thousands of the vile little puss-eyed creatures, hissing and mewing, huddled together in dank alleyways, and digging through piles of garbage. One could not go around handling such animals. It simply was not sanitary. Still, she should not have spoken so sharply.

"What I meant," Agnes said, but before she could find the proper words of apology, Mr. al-Raqb appeared and swept the kitten aside with his foot.

"Good morning to you all."

"A morning of light," Margaret replied, hoping that the traditional stream of greetings might draw the watchman out of his shell.

"A morning of flowers." Mr. al-Raqb smiled, continuing the chain.

"And to you a morning of cream."

"Mr. Bechor has informed you of our agreement?" Dr. Schechter asked once he was quite certain the greetings were finished.

The watchman nodded and welcomed them into the courtyard with an open arm. With the same motion, he attempted to shoo away a gathering crowd of dirt-streaked, dark-eyed children. Some of them were rather young and a few looked to be on the verge of manhood, but they all had the same hungry and somewhat pitiful expression.

"Solomon," Miss de Witt entreated, "do you think we might be able to use the assistance of these boys?"

They were not begging. For the most part, they seemed curious, wondering at the foreigners with their strange clothes and their crates. But one could also see that they would not turn down a coin or a crust of bread.

"I rather think we could," Agnes said, pitching her agreement over Dr. Schechter's mumbled objections.

Miss de Witt smiled quite unabashedly and so did Agnes. In a single stroke, she had given Miss de Witt a gift far better than a dozen apologies, agreeing with her rather good idea to hire the boys while ignoring her excessive familiarity with Dr. Schechter.

"In either case," Dr. Schechter said, "I would like to get to work as soon as possible."

"Very well," Agnes concluded and turned to Mr. al-Raqb. "I think eight will do."

It was agreed that Dr. Schechter and Miss de Witt would oversee the boys packing crates in the courtyard, while Agnes and Margaret volunteered to manage the geniza side of the operation, so long as their lungs held up. Seated on low stools in the middle of the room, they directed the flow of documents with a series of sharp commands and hand motions. The boys soon fell into the rhythm of the work, hauling load after load up the wall, down the ladder, and into the light of the courtyard, their hands and faces accruing a ghostly paste of dust and sweat as the day progressed. Dr. Schechter had expected the job to take at least two days, but with the help of the boys, they were finished by late afternoon.

"Done and sorted," Margaret called out and her voice echoed off the walls of the nearly empty attic.

"But no Ezra Scroll?" Agnes asked.

Margaret shook her head—she had been thinking precisely the same thing—and they both looked around this dusty room that had, for nearly a thousand years, held a mountain of discarded documents. It was stripped nearly bare now, a hull of its former self. And yet, the room still pulsed with a twinge of the electricity Margaret had felt before, when it was full.

That same tingling feeling was with them as they climbed down the ladder and found the carriage outside, fully loaded with crates.

"I believe it would be best," Dr. Schechter suggested, "if Miss de Witt and I were to ride back with the first load while the two of you stay behind with the remainder."

"That is an excellent idea," Margaret said with a quick glance at her sister.

Without Dr. Schechter and Miss de Witt around, they would finally have the opportunity to talk frankly with Mr. al-Raqb.

"Yes," Agnes agreed.

After the carriage left, the watchman asked Agnes and Margaret if they would like some tea. Neither of them was particularly thirsty, but they had learned long ago never to refuse an offer of food or drink. To do so was a grave insult and, moreover, such invitations were often a prelude to further conversation.

"Very much so," Agnes smiled and, without a word, Mr. al-Raqb disappeared into his house.

A moment later he returned with three stools, a small

charcoal stove, and a clay pot. They sat on the stools and watched in silence while he prepared and poured the tea.

"May God grant you health," he said as he handed them their glasses.

"Health to you," the twins said in unison, and they raised the dark sugary tea to their lips.

Agnes and Margaret had a number of questions for Mr. al-Raqb, but they waited for him to speak first.

"My father was a watchman," he said finally, "and his father and his father, too. For nearly a thousand years."

Margaret nodded and took another sip of tea. She had suspected that Ali—the young Muslim boy indicated in the fragment she had removed from the geniza—might be related somehow to the current watchman.

"I cannot read," Mr. al-Raqb continued. "I cannot write. I know nothing of these papers in the attic. But I do know that many other people are interested."

"Many people are interested," Agnes repeated, watching Mr. al-Raqb's face for a reaction, "and many people want to buy them."

He nodded again, in confirmation, the anger in his face as clear as the fading day. The geniza leak, it seemed, troubled him as much as it did them.

"Can you tell us who?" Margaret asked.

"It is not for me to tell."

"We are prepared to offer you a very sizeable reward for the information."

"It is not for me to tell," he repeated.

Margaret looked into the bottom of her glass and swirled the last remnants of tea.

"Do you know the Ezra Scroll?" she asked, taking a slightly different tack. "They say it is hidden in a dark closet, guarded by a snake."

A flicker of recognition shot across the watchman's craggy face; then he looked up at Margaret, making direct eye contact for the first time in their conversation.

"There is no snake."

"But the scroll," Agnes persisted, "the Ezra Scroll. Is it here in the synagogue?"

Mr. al-Raqb regarded her over the rim of his glass, pursed his lips, then shook his head once.

"You have been to the cemetery?" he asked. "Bassatine? You know, they bury papers there."

"And books?" Margaret persisted. "Scrolls?"

The watchman squinted, as if trying to see the outline of his reply in the sun falling below the walls of the Babylonian Fortress.

"My father showed me this scroll when I was small," he said, "but they moved it when they rebuilt the synagogue. It is not where it once was."

The twins exchanged a quick glance.

"Do you know where it is now?" Agnes pressed. "Is it in the cemetery?"

"That is all I know." Mr. al-Raqb refilled their glasses. "I have told you what I know."

By the time they finished their second glass of tea, the carriage had pulled up to the main gate of the synagogue; Dr. Schechter leaped out with a smile.

"Ready for the next load," he said.

Rising from their stools, Agnes and Margaret thanked Mr.

al-Raqb for his hospitality and promised that his kindness would be repaid. They helped Dr. Schechter as well as they could with the loading, then joined Miss de Witt in the carriage.

"Quite a nice man," Agnes remarked to her sister.

"Did he say anything of interest?" Miss de Witt asked.

"No," Margaret said, "not particularly."

"Well then," Dr. Schechter exclaimed as he climbed into the carriage. "We have reason to congratulate ourselves. The only remaining obstacle is the Egyptian Customs Authority."

As they rode, Agnes and Margaret both looked out the window of the carriage. A pale yellow stretch of sky lay atop the water like a layer of sponge cake. They certainly did have reason to congratulate themselves. After two long weeks of work, the geniza documents were safe from thieves and poachers and the pull of the black market. There was still the Ezra Scroll, of course, and the question of who was responsible for the leak. But for the moment, they were content to bask in the not-insignificant accomplishment of securing their documents.

7

FOR A WEEK and a day, Ali kept Hasdi il-Sephardi's charm with him at all times. Clutching it in his pocket and rubbing the edge of the string, he could feel its magic balanced at the edge of his perception like a low hum. But as much as he believed in its power, there was no way to know whether the amulet was truly working. At some times, he was sure he could feel his beloved burning for him. At others, he pictured her going about her daily chores, completely unaffected by the charm. After eight days of this with no results—at least not as far as he could discern—Ali decided to seek out stronger magic.

Finding Hasdi's shop again proved to be much more difficult than Ali had imagined. At first, he tried retracing his steps through the wood-carvers' market, but no matter what path he chose he found himself back where he had started. He asked a few shopkeepers nearby if they might direct him to Hasdi il-Sephardi's shop, but most had never heard the name and those who had merely shook their heads. After searching for the better part of the afternoon with no success, Ali sat down to rest near a food stall selling taamiya and ful. He was weighing the coins in his pocket against his hunger, when he felt a hand on his shoulder.

"Looking for me?"

It was Hasdi. His grip was surprisingly strong, and in the dim light of the alley his wild white hair seemed tinged an unnatural shade of blue.

"Come," he said with a tilt of his head. "My shop is just around the corner."

Cutting through a row of empty stalls, Hasdi led Ali deeper and deeper into the market. They turned left, skirted around the edges of the glassblowers' market, then doubled back and emerged into that familiar passageway shaded by olive branches. Hasdi's shop was exactly as Ali remembered it. This time, however, the reed cage near the door was filled with pigeons instead of frogs.

"The charm was unsuccessful," Hasdi concluded before Ali could say anything. "May I inspect it?"

Turning it over in his hands, Hasdi nodded to himself as if realizing a fatal flaw. Then he threw the charm into the stove behind him. It went up with a quick bright flame.

"You are the watchman of the Ibn Ezra Synagogue."

"Yes," Ali said, for there was no use in lying.

"And," Hasdi said as he disappeared underneath the counter, emerging a moment later with a slightly translucent piece of vellum, "you are familiar with the Ezra Scroll?"

Ali shook his head. He had never heard of the Ezra Scroll.

"In the attic," Hasdi prompted.

He threw a handful of powder into the air and the shop shimmered with a faint silver light. As the light receded, Ali recalled that peculiar incident a week earlier, after the Feast of the Temporary Dwellings. He remembered how he had awoken to the distant sound of humming and found the council of Ibn Ezra gathered in the alley, all dressed in white, and one of them holding a luminous object about the size of a Sefer Torah scroll.

"When you are in the attic of the synagogue," Hasdi continued, speaking slowly and clearly, as one might to a small child, "extinguish your lantern. You will notice one of the panels glowing slightly. Open the compartment and place this piece of vellum inside. Leave it there for two nights, then bring it back to me."

Ali began to ask a question, but Hasdi cut him off.

"You want her to feel for you, the way you feel for her?"

"Yes."

"Then this is what you must do."

Later that night, rubbing the vellum between his fingers, Ali stared into his tiny fire and tried to work out the consequences of what he had been asked to do. He knew nothing about the Ezra Scroll. Still, he sensed something very wrong with the plan. Hasdi il-Sephardi was not a good person; he knew this for certain. And he knew that good magic could not come from bad people. Even so, he told himself, perhaps it was not a question of intentions but results. What could be wrong with a charm that brought him closer to his beloved?

On his third round that night, Ali convinced himself to do what Hasdi had instructed. When he entered the attic of the synagogue, he extinguished his lantern and, after a moment standing in the warm darkness of the room, he saw it. Just as Hasdi had said, one of the wall panels was glowing as if dipped in a faint hoary light. Without the illumination of his lantern it was difficult to miss. Ali stared at the panel for a long while. Then, wiping his hands dry on the front of his galabiya, he picked his way carefully across the attic, over piles of documents and discarded books. When he was less than an arm's length from the glowing panel, Ali squatted down and reached out to touch it. As the tips of his fingers brushed the wood, he felt a wave of energy pulse through him like a sudden rush of blood. It was a feeling similar to that tingling awareness he had noticed on his first night in the attic, only a thousand times stronger.

As Hasdi had said, there was a hidden chamber behind the panel, inside of which was a Sefer Torah scroll. Nestled upright in a bed of pale blue silk, the scroll was luminous and pulsing with slick silver light. Without stopping to think or to question what he was doing, Ali placed the vellum next to the scroll. Then he returned the panel, grabbed his lantern, and left the attic.

When he got back to his post, Ali's mouth was dry and his heart was beating so loudly he thought it was something outside himself. He could still feel the power of the scroll coursing through his body. All at once, he understood why the council was so secretive about the rites he had observed that night after the feast, why Hasdi was so insistent about the execution of the spell. The Ezra Scroll contained a magic so powerful it could not be spoken. And Ali knew that, in meddling with its powers, he had done something terribly wrong. He had betrayed the trust of al-Zikri and the entire council. He had wronged all the members of Ibn Ezra, including his beloved—especially his beloved. As the beating of his heart subsided, Ali felt a great shame settle into the pit of his stomach. And yet, at the same time, a small part of him was happy, smiling at the thought that this new charm might really work.

Two nights later, Ali retrieved the vellum and slipped it into the sleeve of his galabiya. He tried not to think about what he had done, but he could feel it there, pulsing lightly along the inside of his arm. After just two days in the attic, it seemed to have absorbed a small portion of the Ezra Scroll's magic, just as an article of clothing will assume the smell of its owner.

That next afternoon, Ali brought the vellum with him to Hasdi's shop.

"You were successful," Hasdi said, barely able to contain his grin.

Ali nodded and handed it over. Its glow was difficult to make out in the bright light of the afternoon, but he could feel its warmth rushing through his hand.

"Excellent," the magician said, seeming quite pleased as he cut off a corner of the paper.

While Hasdi filled the small triangle of vellum with a snaking line of Hebrew and Arabic letters, Ali let his eyes range over the shop. The cage near the door, he noticed, was occupied now by a litter of black and white kittens. Ali tried not to imagine what would become of these animals. He tried not to think of the frogs and the pigeons that had preceded them.

"Burn this in your fire tonight," Hasdi said, placing the piece of vellum inside a small cloth bag. "And make sure you inhale a bit of smoke."

"Okay."

"This is strong magic," Hasdi continued. "It will not fail you."

"And the rest of the vellum?"

"That is your payment," he said with a chuckle, "a small price to pay for true love, I should think."

A small price to pay for true love. Ali repeated this phrase to himself over and over again as he went about his rounds that night, doing his best to avoid the question of whether love compelled by magic could ever be true. In the darkest hour of his shift, when the night birds ceased their chatter, Ali sat down on his stool and took this new charm out of his pocket. He could see its glow more clearly in the darkness and he felt a subtle warmth where it touched his palm. What he was about to do was wrong. He knew that it was wrong, just as he knew the Nile would flood its banks the following spring. Still, it was a small price to pay for true love.

Ali pictured his beloved, asleep on the floor next to her sisters; clenching his teeth, he placed the charm in the fire. At first, it did not burn. Then the vellum crackled and burst into flames. Instead of smoke, it gave off a shower of light like tiny stars. An uprising of sparks danced along the ridge of the flame. Then, as suddenly as it began, the fire died back to its normal shape. Ali was still staring into the flames, watching the last sparks flicker and vanish, when he heard a voice by the front gate.

"That light," al-Zikri said, looking around the courtyard. "Did you see that?"

"It came from the fire," Ali told him. "I was burning a strange piece of wood."

They both looked into the fire, as if a better explanation might be found there. After some time, Ali spoke again.

"May I ask you a question, al-Zikri?"

He had so many questions—about the Ezra Scroll and

Hasdi il-Sephardi, about magic and betrayal and the price of true love—but these were questions he could not ask. Instead, he asked a simpler one, a question he had been wondering about for some time.

"Why do the Jews put their papers in the attic?"

"It is natural you would be curious," al-Zikri said and, sucking on the bottom of his mustache, he glanced back at the fire.

There was the injunction against throwing away documents that contain the name of God, he explained, which was based on the belief that such papers hold something of God's majesty. Ali nodded. He had heard this before.

"Different synagogues choose different means of disposal," al-Zikri continued.

The members of Ibn Ezra chose to discard their papers in the attic of the synagogue—which they called the geniza—in part for reasons of religious practice and in part because the graveyard, Bassatine, was so far away. As he finished his explanation, Ali began to ask another question, but stopped when he saw what he thought was a fleck of suspicion at the corners of al-Zikri's eyes. They stood for a few moments in silence, then al-Zikri put a hand on Ali's shoulder and turned to leave.

"Good night, Ali," he said. "We will talk more in the morning."

That following afternoon when Ali stopped by Ephraim ibn Shemarya's fabric shop, hoping to continue the conversation with al-Zikri, the men were consumed with a discussion about one of the synagogue's ritual slaughterers, a man named Yakob, who had suddenly taken ill. Doctor Mevorakh said he had never seen such an illness. First came the chills and bloating, then the patient was covered with festering sores that seemed to sap the very life from him. All week, the mood outside the fabric shop was tense. No one talked much, except when Doctor Mevorakh stopped by with an update. Then one morning, less than a week later, Ali was awakened by the sound of wailing. He ran outside and al-Zikri told him the news. Yakob had died.

"There is no power or strength but in God," Ali said and al-Zikri agreed.

"Life is a fickle guest. One never knows when it will depart."

Yakob was a simple man, without money for musicians or professional mourners, but he was well loved. And that night, when the funeral procession passed by the front gates of the synagogue, the dead man's bier was followed by what seemed to be the entire community, all bearing torches and lanterns. Watching the procession stream past, Ali bowed his head, but not so deeply that he would miss his beloved if she walked by. He knew this was a horrible thing to think, but at that point, his longing was beyond his own control.

After the procession had passed, Ali returned to his post and took up his lantern for a second round. Nothing seemed amiss in the courtyard or the prayer hall, but when he climbed down into the attic, he saw that the piles of paper had been scattered, as if by a hungry animal. The compartment that housed the Ezra Scroll had been thrown open, but thankfully the scroll was still there, glowing slightly in its nest of pale blue silk. Raising his lantern, Ali picked his way to the back of the attic, looking for some indication of who or what had caused the mess. When the slant of the roof prevented him from going any farther, he turned. And there, hiding in a dim niche at the front of the room, was Hasdi il-Sephardi, a sack slung over his shoulder and white hair glinting in the yellow lantern light. For a long moment, neither of them spoke. The only movement in the room was the trembling of Ali's hands.

"You do not see me," Hasdi said.

Ali closed his eyes, wanting very much to believe that this was nothing more than a hallucination, but when he opened them again, Hasdi was still there.

Ali took a small step forward and Hasdi raised his hand.

"You will not tell anyone you saw me."

He put a finger to his own temple and Ali felt his head throb in that very spot.

"If you tell anyone you saw me, I will expose you. I will tell them you forced me to cast a spell on her. I will tell them and you will be ruined. Do you understand?"

"Yes," Ali managed through the throbbing. As soon as he agreed, the pain subsided and Hasdi slipped away.

After checking to make sure the Ezra Scroll wasn't damaged, Ali tried to re-form the piles of paper. But no matter how he shaped them, they looked much smaller than they had before. He sat down on the dusty floor of the attic, turned off his lantern, and tried to reassure himself. But he could think of nothing reassuring. If one could make a powerful spell with a piece of vellum left next to the Ezra Scroll for two nights, what might one do with thousands of papers that had lived alongside it for years? He was ruined. He had failed and betrayed the entire community. Shouting into the darkness, Ali kicked a pile of papers, and slapped at the wall until his hands were numb. He had failed in his only task. He had abandoned his post, allowed a thief into the synagogue. And there was nothing he could do to make it better. If he kept the incident to himself, he would be blamed for the missing papers. If he told al-Zikri about the theft, he could only imagine what would happen to him.

All that night and for many days to follow, Ali was consumed with shame and doubt. He continued with his rounds and every day he made sure to stop by Ephraim ibn Shemarya's shop, if only to maintain the impression of normalcy. In everything he did, however, he could feel his insides gnawing away at themselves. He blamed Hasdi il-Sephardi. He blamed the council for giving him their trust. He blamed Yakob for dying. He even began to resent his beloved. Most of all, however, Ali blamed himself. And in his worst moments, he wished that he could go back to Uncle Rashid's house, sleeping on the floor of the pantry, carrying skins of water on his back. It was a hard life, simple and mean, but it was a life he understood, a life he deserved.

8

ACROSS THE STREET from the Mar Girgis Metro station, tucked in beneath the sand-colored stone walls of Old Cairo, was an arched wooden doorway studded with iron bolts. On either side, men were selling bottled water and postcards sheathed in plastic. A pair of silver cats slept in a patch of shade under a broken chair, and a group of children kicked a deflated soccer ball back and forth across the street. I told the taxi driver to let me off there, then bought a bottle of water and made my way through the gate into a narrow alley lined with shops.

"Papyrus," one of the shopkeepers shouted as I walked by. "Best quality."

"No, thank you," I said and continued on past the procession of eager young men hawking tapestries and papyrus, soft drinks, film, perfume, and the same assortment of little trinkets you could find anywhere in Egypt.

According to the map at the back of my *Lonely Planet,* the Ibn Ezra Synagogue was on the other side of Old Cairo, wedged in between the Abu Serga Church and the Greek Orthodox cemetery. It wasn't particularly difficult to find. A right at the Nunnery of St. George, a left at Abu Serga, and there I was.

My father had taken me to visit the synagogue a few times when I was younger, but the building I remembered—a boxy, dull yellow structure looming over the churches around it—looked nothing like the one in front of me. It may have been a trick of memory or some combination of perspective and restoration. Either way, I had to squint to convince myself that this squat whitewashed structure was the same place I had visited as a child, that this was the synagogue where my mother's family had worshipped, the building my father's family had protected for nearly a thousand years, and somewhere in this courtyard filled with sweat-stained tank-topped tourists, talking about dinner the night before and the camel ride later that afternoon, was the exact place where my parents first met.

It had been Abdullah's idea, coming to the synagogue. Even if it was just a tourist attraction, he said, there might be someone there who knew how to get in touch with Mr. Mosseri. He was right—he usually was—it was worth a try. But by that point, I was beginning to lose hope. I had been to all the Gamal al-Din streets in the city. I had left notes, talked to strangers, pressed Uncle Hassan for any memories he might have about Mr. Mosseri or his family. I had called the telephone company; had visited the main synagogue on Adly Street, twice. And that previous week, Abdullah had arranged to take the afternoon off so that he could accompany me downtown to the vast ant farm of Egyptian bureaucracy known as the Mogamma. After nearly a month of searching for Mr. Mosseri, I was beginning to consider the possibility of failure, of packing up and going back to Berkeley. Or maybe I would pick up a few classes at the language school where Aisha taught and drift through the remainder of the year on grammar worksheets and conjugation exercises.

Standing amidst the sunburns and cargo shorts, listening to a group of Australians argue about the ethics of giving money to street kids, I tried to remember some of the stories my father used to tell me, about the various al-Raqb men who had defended the synagogue from harm. I tried to picture my parents as children playing hide-and-go-seek in the spaces behind the palm trees. But any imaginative abilities I might have possessed were eclipsed by the new paint job, the beep of the metal detector behind me, and the tour groups with their matching T-shirts.

"Excuse me."

In the midst of these thoughts, a security guard approached me from behind.

"Excuse me, sir," he said. "You cannot stand here."

In retrospect, it probably would have been wiser to respond in English, to play the bewildered tourist card. Instead, I snapped back in Arabic.

"I can't stand here?"

"You can stand *there*," he offered, indicating the Australians a few feet away. "But not *here*. It is a restricted area."

I took a half step toward the Australians, then stopped. Why should I have to move? Why shouldn't I be able to stand wherever I wanted? If anyone had a claim to this space, it was me. My ancestors had prayed in this building; they had risked their lives to protect it.

I was trying to get this line of reasoning straight in my head, when another more official-looking guard crossed the courtyard toward us. He was wearing a black bulletproof vest and his gun hung loose off his shoulder like a toy that had long ago lost its appeal.

"Can I help you, sir?"

In spite of the gun and a touch of suspicion at the outer reaches of his voice, he truly did seem to want to help.

"Yes," I said, "actually, I'm looking for Mr. Mosseri."

"Mr. Mosseri?"

I reached into my pocket for his card, but there was no need. The very mention of his name was enough. Without another word, this second guard leaped into action, barking orders into his walkie-talkie as he led me to a small stone bench nearby.

"If you don't mind," he said, "we can sit here."

He pulled up a chair, took out a pack of cigarettes, and offered me one as he lit his own with a match.

"No, thanks," I said.

We were both quiet for a moment, watching the tourists file through the metal detector. Then he turned to examine me more closely.

"You are Jewish?" he asked.

"Yes," I said, and he tilted his head to get another perspective.

"To me," he said, ashing carefully into an empty soda can, "you look Egyptian."

"My father was Egyptian," I told him, neglecting my mother for simplicity's sake.

"He is Muslim?"

"He was," I said and, in explanation of the past tense, "He died a few months ago."

The guard mumbled his condolences—*There is no strength or power but in God*—then returned to the matter at hand.

"If your father was Muslim," he explained, "you are Muslim, too."

"True," I allowed, "but Jews pass through the mother. So I'm also Jewish."

The guard considered this paradox for a moment, but he wouldn't concede the point.

"You can't be both," he said. "It is impossible."

Before I could respond, before I could try to refute the impossibility of my ancestry, the walkie-talkie squawked again and the guard exchanged a few words with a gruff voice on the other end.

"You are Yusuf?" he asked me.

"Yes," I said.

There was another quick exchange—something about Mr. Mosseri and maybe his car—then the guard returned his walkie-talkie to its holster.

"Come back this afternoon," he told me. "Five o'clock."

"Today?" I asked.

"This afternoon," he repeated. "Five o'clock."

When I returned to the synagogue—after lunch, a visit to the Hanging Church, and three hours in the Coptic Museum—the sun was beginning to dip below the walls of the old city and the shopkeepers were packing up their wares. All the tourists and the security guards were gone. The Abu Serga Church was closed for the evening and the courtyard of the synagogue was empty except for a short bald man in an elegant blue suit.

"Yusuf!" he exclaimed, holding out his arms to greet me.

I had spent most of the past few weeks trying to find this man—calling him, walking up and down every Gamal al-Din Street in the city, talking endlessly about him with Abdullah and Aisha, searching the Internet, the phone book, the halls of the Mogamma, staring at his business card and the newspaper clipping from my father's room, hoping to uncover some clue as to his whereabouts—and then, just like that, there he was, shaking my hand and kissing me on either cheek.

"Mr. Mosseri."

There was a whiff of gardenia about him and, as he straightened his suit jacket, I noticed a bright orange silk handkerchief glancing from his breast pocket. He had an easy smile, a broad nose, and an elegant, almost courtly demeanor.

"I'm so very glad you came," he said. Then he put a hand on my shoulder and raised his eyebrows to a sympathetic peak. "Your father would be so happy to know you're here."

"Thank you," I said, not sure how else to respond.

He asked me about my accommodations, and was beginning to say something about an Italian restaurant he knew in Garden City, when a realization crossed his face.

"I do hope you haven't been trying to call me."

"A few times," I admitted.

"That card," he said and, in the way he covered his mouth, I could see that he understood exactly what had happened. "I am so sorry, Yusuf. This business with the telephone company, the new exchanges. It really has been quite maddening."

He went on for a few minutes—trying to explain the new exchanges, how the state telephone company had added an extra digit to all the landlines in Cairo, or changed the area code, or something along those lines—then he stopped himself midsentence.

"But here you are," he said. "And I can't imagine you want to hear me go on about our problems with the telephone company. You must have quite a few questions."

"I do," I said, and I did, though I hadn't thought to arrange them in any particular order.

Mr. Mosseri raised an expectant eyebrow, then seemed to change his mind.

"Before we get to all that," he said, "perhaps it would be best to have a quick tour of the synagogue. It really is most magnificent in the daylight."

As we climbed the stairs to the women's section, Mr. Mosseri described the restoration process he had helped oversee a few years earlier and pointed to some of the building's more notable architectural details. The interlocking diamond pattern on the ceiling had been designed by a craftsman whose great-grandfather worked on the previous renovation. And the gleaming red-and-gold ark at the front of the room had been built to the exact specifications found in a century-old architectural plan.

"It's beautiful," I said, and it was.

Looking out on the succession of black-and-white marble arches that suspended the women's section above the main prayer hall, I tried to recall the last time I had been inside a synagogue. Rory Trout's bar mitzvah, maybe, or my grand-mother's funeral in Paris. I couldn't remember exactly, but I knew it had been a long time ago, at least ten years. And wherever it was, it was nothing like this.

"Yes"—Mr. Mosseri smiled—"we are very happy with how it turned out."

He patted the iron railing in front of us, then turned to lead me back down the stairs to the main prayer hall.

"You know," I said before he could continue with the tour, "I was hoping you might be able to tell me something about the—"

I paused, not sure what to call the piece of paper my father had sent me.

"The fragment?" he offered. "Yes, of course."

It was difficult to know for certain, Mr. Mosseri explained, especially with such an old document. But one could be rela-tively confident about the basics: the fragment comprised two different letters, most likely from the middle of the elev-enth century. In all probability, these notes were part of a longer exchange between the chief adviser to the sultan and the leader of Cairo's Jewish community. As for their content, they both mentioned a young Muslim boy named Ali and the question of whether he might be suitable to serve as watch-man of the Ibn Ezra Synagogue.

"Ali al-Raqb?"

"As I said, it is difficult to know such things for certain."

"I thought that was just a story."

"Yes, well," Mr. Mosseri observed, "a story is never just a story."

He hesitated a moment, then continued on in another

vein, describing the fragment's historical and material context, the Jewish prohibition on throwing away documents that might contain the name of God, and how, sometime in the middle of the eleventh century, the Jews of Ibn Ezra began discarding these papers in the attic storeroom of their synagogue. He answered all of my questions, and then some. Still, I got the sense that he was stepping lightly around the edges of the story, that there was some piece of it he was doing his best to avoid.

"When he asked you to send me the package," I said halfway through a story about the papers' dispersal, something about a rabbi and two sisters from Cambridge, "did my father mention anything in particular?"

"How do you mean?"

"Did he," I tried to put it more clearly, "was there any particular reason he sent me the package, any reason he thought I should want it?"

"You know, of course," Mr. Mosseri said, "the fragment, it is quite invaluable. But I suppose you're asking—"

As he paused, trying to find the right words—unsure, it seemed, how much exactly to reveal—I noticed Mr. Mosseri's gaze rest on a squat rectangular opening just below the ceiling of the women's section.

"Is that it?" I asked. "The geniza?"

"It is," Mr. Mosseri conceded.

Not much larger than a bathroom window, the entrance to the geniza was edged in dark wood trim and covered with plywood. If you didn't know what to look for, it would be easy to miss entirely.

"We can't go inside, can we?"

"The geniza?" Mr. Mosseri said, somewhat taken aback. "Oh no, it is quite difficult to access. No one's been inside for years."

"But it would be possible?"

He looked at me a moment, then his expression softened to a smile.

"I suppose it would be."

Without another word, he led me to the other end of the women's section. I could feel my pulse in my throat as he retrieved an old wooden ladder from a pile of construction materials and propped it against the lower lip of the entrance to the geniza.

"There are no lights," he warned, holding the ladder for me as I climbed, "and I can only imagine how dusty it is in there."

At the top, I pushed aside the plywood door, then maneuvered over the ledge and lowered myself down to the ladder on the other side. It took a moment for my eyes to adjust, but when they did I saw that the room was almost entirely empty and the floor was thick with murky gray dust.

Standing there at the edge of the geniza, I imagined it filled with paper, a thousand years of love letters and prayer books, business contracts, deeds, and the occasional shopping list, all muddled together in a great heap of possible divinity. I thought about all the al-Raqbs who had stood in that very place—from the first watchman to the last, from Ali al-Raqb to my father—passing through the attic on their nightly rounds. I thought about all the documents that had settled there and what those pieces of paper meant: a wedding or a new business partner, a death in the family, an unreturned letter from a brother on the other side of the world.

The room was empty, but there were thousands of stories embedded in the space. There was also, I noticed, a charge in the air, a faint prickle of energy. I took a step toward the center of the room and, feeling it even more strongly, remembered what my father had said that afternoon on the Nile, about the scroll hidden in the attic of the synagogue.

It was then, as I tried to recall what exactly he had said—something about the prophet Ezra, rumors of magic, the name of God—that I saw a flash of gray peek out from behind a pile of cleaning supplies. My heart skipped and I jumped back. Then I saw another movement, much closer, and realized it was a cat. The attic was teeming with them, dozens of scrawny little creatures, and all with the same slightly luminous silver coloring.

"We do our best to keep them out," Mr. Mosseri said as he climbed down into the attic, "but it's a losing battle. I imagine they must have found a way in through the roof."

I nodded and watched the cats retreat into the darkness.

"So this is it," I said.

"This is it," he confirmed, "not nearly as grand as one might imagine."

We were both silent for a moment, then Mr. Mosseri clasped his hands together, like a weary host smiling the last of his guests out the door.

"Do you mind," I said, "can I ask another question?"

"Not at all."

There were so many things I wanted to know—about the fragment and Ali al-Raqb, the geniza and my father's time as watchman of the synagogue—but instead I asked the question at the top of my mind.

"My father mentioned something once, about a scroll hidden in the attic."

Mr. Mosseri's smile drooped. He opened his mouth and closed it again, as if paging through a variety of possible explanations. He started to speak, then stopped himself, looked back at the entrance above us and lightly tapped the side of his head, as if to dislodge a vital piece of information.

"Are you free this Friday evening?"

"Yes," I said.

"Perhaps," he said as he produced a large white handkerchief from the inside of his jacket and wiped the dust off his glasses, "you could join us for dinner. I think I might have something that you would be interested in seeing."

After returning the handkerchief to his pocket, Mr. Mosseri turned back to the opening through which we had entered. Knowing well enough not to press any further, I followed him out and, blinking in the shift of light, closed the door behind us.

9

T HE QUESTION OF Bassatine—that is, the question of whether to visit the cemetery and see what they might uncover there—was contested almost entirely in silence. It was less a discussion than a war of attrition. Agnes could not reconcile herself to the idea of disturbing the graveyard, no matter what they might find there, while for Margaret the potential of rescuing invaluable documents from plunder and dispersal trumped any concerns about honoring the dead. Besides, they would not be disturbing any human remains.

In the twenty-four hours following Mr. al-Raqb's revelation that there were documents—including, perhaps, the Ezra Scroll—buried in the Bassatine cemetery, Agnes and Margaret did not exchange more than a dozen words. Neither raised the question; neither so much as whispered the name of the cemetery. There was no need. Each knew what the other was thinking. For the better part of a day, they circled each other silently, bolstering their fortifications, mustering counterarguments, and reading clues into the smallest aberration in routine. An extra dollop of butter at breakfast, an offhand remark about Miss de Witt or Dr. Schechter, anything might reveal the other's hidden assumptions.

Playing white, Agnes moved first.

"How would you like it if someone dug up our graves?"

Margaret set down her book—a collection of travel accounts written by the fifteenth-century rabbi Obadiah de Bertinoro—and looked at her sister, who had just finished her forward bends. Margaret had anticipated this line of reasoning, but did not expect it so early. It could be a trap, but more likely her sister's thinking was clouded by an overwhelming sense of righteousness.

"According to Obadiah," she said, touching the book in her lap, "the documents are buried in an unused section of the cemetery, more than two cubits from any grave."

Agnes sat down on the edge of her sister's bed.

"It still feels wrong."

"Think of it as buried treasure, Nestor. Just imagine. A perfect Torah scroll, written by Ezra himself, four centuries before Christ."

Margaret knew it was unlikely that the Ezra Scroll would be buried at Bassatine. Still, even the possibility was a potent argument.

"Should we place so much weight on Mr. al-Raqb's word?" Agnes asked. "And what about Dr. Schechter? Can you imagine what he would say if we told him we were planning to dig up a Jewish cemetery?"

"I think Dr. Schechter would heartily approve," Margaret said. "But even so, we should probably keep the plan to ourselves."

Agnes exhaled, a sign of impending surrender, then flopped onto her stomach.

"Will you do my ointment, Meggie?"

With a little pressure, Margaret knew she might force her

sister to concede then and there. Experience, however, had taught her to delay such gratifications. It was far better to wait, let old Nestor come around on her own steam.

And indeed, the next morning at breakfast, Agnes raised the topic again. Overnight, her concerns had shifted to the particular. Where exactly was the cemetery? How could they conduct their visit without arousing suspicion? Having already thought through the answers to these questions, and many more, Margaret laid out the details of a plan by which they might visit Bassatine, find the documents, and remove them, all while avoiding detection by Dr. Schechter, Mr. Bechor, and the others. By the end of breakfast, Agnes's fears had been allayed, and together they composed a note to a Coptic fixer upon whom they had relied a number of times over the years.

The next morning at dawn they set out with five donkeys, two empty trunks, a clattering assortment of shovels, and three bulky men, excellent diggers and all—the fixer assured them—very discreet. According to Margaret's Baedeker guidebook, Bassatine was located on the southern edge of the city, sandwiched between the east bank of the Nile and the limestone quarries of the Muqattam Hills. The land had been granted to the Jews in the ninth century, after Ibn Tulun built his palace atop their previous cemetery. When Obadiah de Bertinoro visited the graveyard six hundred years later, he reported that the road was rife with bandits and the cemetery surrounded by empty desolation for miles. In the intervening centuries, a few military installations and quarries had sprouted up, but the area still retained a rather desolate feel. Aside from a family of carrion crows, the only sign of life was a camp of Bedouins, their dark brown tents pockmarking a depression given on the map as Wadi Turah.

Agnes and Margaret did not notice the cemetery—separated from the rest of the desert by a stone wall the same color as the hills behind—until one of the diggers pointed it out. They watched from atop their donkeys as their fixer roused the old Bedouin charged with guarding the graveyard and offered him a cigarette. Anticipating the necessity of a bribe, they had agreed in advance that they would be willing to provide thirty pounds to the guard for showing them the document burial ground, if one existed, and for looking the other way as they excavated it. After half an hour of negotiations, shouting, hand waving, and gesticulation, the guard agreed to abandon his duties for the sum of ten pounds.

"Southwest corner," the fixer said, pointing with his chin as he rolled a celebratory cigarette, "behind the Mosseri plot."

Dismounting, Agnes and Margaret walked through the cemetery while the diggers brought their gear around to the southwest corner.

"That wasn't too difficult," Margaret said, laughing, as she helped her sister over a small iron fence that separated two sections of the cemetery, "now, was it?"

"No," Agnes agreed, and they continued for a few paces in silence, "though I can't help but think. How are we any different from common tomb robbers?"

"Intention," Margaret said, knowing her sister's guilt would be best assuaged by a simple answer. "A good intention makes all the difference."

While the diggers set about their work, Agnes and Margaret established themselves on a stone bench abutting a great marble mausoleum inscribed with the name Mosseri. With a saddle blanket draped over their legs, they watched the diggers' progress in silent anticipation. Their men were clearly not the first to trouble this plot. The top three feet of soil were loose and devoid of documents. Both sisters worried that there might be nothing left. But then, after more than an hour of fruitless labor, one of the men shouted and pointed to a yellowed piece of vellum reaching out of the earth like a disembodied hand.

"Stop," Margaret cried, and she scrambled into the ditch.

The men leaned on their shovels while she brushed sand off the document and scanned its first few lines.

"A marriage contract," she said, handing it up to her sister.

"More rubbish," Agnes sighed.

Having resided for many years under the dark dry press of sandy loam, the contract was remarkably well preserved. Of course, they had not come all the way to Bassatine for a marriage contract. They had not defiled a graveyard for such common ephemera. But its presence signaled the likelihood of more treasure below. Agnes laid out their blanket as if preparing for a picnic and placed the contract at the top left corner. Meanwhile, Margaret directed the diggers to abandon their shovels and continue with hand tools, scooping the soil into tin pails and carefully handing up any papers they unearthed.

They continued on like this for most of the morning. Then, just past midday, the old Bedouin guard ran out of his tent yelling and waving his arms. At first they couldn't understand what he was saying. As he got closer, however, Agnes realized that he was shouting, over and over, the classical

Arabic word for horse—*khayl*—almost identical to the more modern word for pride or arrogance.

A few moments later, the hazy speck on the northern edge of the horizon revealed itself as a horse and rider, followed by two others. At the top of the nearest rise, a few hundred yards away, the leader of the party pulled up his reins and the other two riders did the same. Rummaging around at the bottom of her saddlebag, Margaret found a pair of opera glasses. By the time she had the riders in focus, they were turning back toward Cairo. Still, she was certain she recognized the leader of the group.

"Mr. Bechor."

"Mr. Bechor," Agnes repeated, drawing the name out as she allowed herself a moment of smug moralism.

It was possible that Mr. Bechor had come to Bassatine in order to pay his respects to a deceased family member. Or perhaps he had heard word of the twins' visit and was riding out to confront them. But why, in either case, would he come so far only to turn around? Considering his retreat, and the cemetery's distance from any other conceivable destination, the only possible explanation was the one they had been avoiding for some time. Mr. Bechor was responsible for the geniza leak. He had plundered the attic of the Ibn Ezra Synagogue and sold the documents off piecemeal for his own profit. Now that the geniza documents were under lock and key, he planned to do the same with the papers buried in the Bassatine cemetery.

In retrospect, it made perfect sense. Mr. Bechor had unfettered access to the Ibn Ezra Synagogue. He probably needed the money to fund his son's schooling. Or perhaps he intended to pay off debts related to the trouble at his sugar factory. Regardless, they had their thief.

"Mr. Bechor," Margaret said, waving her opera glasses at the old Bedouin guard. "He's been here before. Hasn't he?"

"Yes," the guard confirmed as he extinguished his cigarette on the sole of his sandal, "every day for a week."

Agnes considered this information for some time before turning to her sister.

"What should we do?"

"The only thing we can do now is keep digging."

It was true. And so, they continued on with their work until the end of the day, until the sun fell behind the rim of salt-colored hills and the men began complaining of their backs. They did not find the Ezra Scroll that afternoon, but they had rescued a crate full of documents from an otherwise precarious future. And what was more, they had uncovered the identity of their thief.

Riding back to Cairo, Agnes and Margaret were both silent, watching the first stars as they considered the many possible implications sprouting from this newfound knowledge. They had their thief—yet, the situation was exceedingly delicate. If accused, Mr. Bechor would most likely lash out, call in favors with the other members of the governing council, and perhaps attempt to derail their entire expedition. If so, one had to hope that he had not recognized them from the top of the dune. For although they felt confident in the virtuousness of their own intentions, one had to admit that, from an outsider's perspective, their actions were not all that different from his. And, unlike Mr. Bechor, they wouldn't be able to fall back on the goodwill of the community. It was, indeed, an extremely delicate situation.

"We cannot tell Dr. Schechter," Agnes said as they entered the city.

"Not yet," Margaret agreed.

Telling Dr. Schechter would require revealing the details of their own trip to Bassatine and, moreover, they could not be certain that he would trust their word against Mr. Bechor's. It would be better, they decided, to sit with the information for a day or two and wait until more concrete evidence arose.

Unfortunately, this was not an option. When the twins arrived at their hotel, they found Dr. Schechter and Miss de Witt waiting for them in the lobby. In all the years of their acquaintance, Agnes and Margaret had never seen Dr. Schechter in such a state. His shoes were muddied and his hair a great tangle of curls.

"You defiled a graveyard?" he shouted and, jumping to his feet, pointed at the crate being carried in behind them. "For what? For paper?"

Apparently, Mr. Bechor had decided to strike first, informing Dr. Schechter of their visit to Bassatine and, thus, setting his word against theirs.

"Solomon," Miss de Witt said somewhat sharply, bringing him back to himself.

She laid a hand on his elbow and he sat down again.

"Now," she continued, soothing him as she might a child, "let us hear what Mrs. Gibson and Mrs. Lewis have to tell us. Surely, they had approval from Rabbi Ben Shimon."

"Did you?" he asked, the question dying to a plea.

The twins shared a glance.

"No," Margaret said. "There was not time for approval. What we did have was good information that the cemetery was being plundered by black-market dealers. In fact, our fixer believes we may have scared some off this afternoon."

Agnes smiled inwardly at her sister's ability to blend the truth with a perfect proportion of easily forgettable lies. Margaret went on for some time, her voice steady as a lion tamer, describing the mendacity of the old Bedouin guard and the unmistakable signs of previous visitors. She did not mention Mr. Bechor. To do so would only play into his plan, setting up a confrontation over Dr. Schechter's trust. Still, she succeeded, by the end of her speech, in bringing the good man back to himself.

"If anyone finds out about this," he said, "it could put our entire project in jeopardy."

"That is a risk," Agnes agreed. "But we decided it was a risk worth taking."

"You should have consulted me," Dr. Schechter chided, needing somewhere to channel his anger. "We should always keep each other informed of such decisions."

Agnes and Margaret agreed that they would, in the future, consult him on all important decisions.

"Speaking of which," Miss de Witt said, "I should think that Mrs. Gibson and Mrs. Lewis would like to join us for lunch next Tuesday with the Chief Rabbi."

"Yes, of course," Dr. Schechter agreed. He clearly had not intended to invite them to lunch, but after his speech on keeping each other informed, he could not very well put them off. "That is an excellent idea."

◆ ◆ ◆

Rabbi Ben Shimon had suggested Shepheard's for lunch and, although neither Agnes nor Margaret would admit as much, they were both rather excited by the prospect of spending the afternoon there, in part because it presented the opportunity to air out some of their better outfits.

"There is nothing like Shepheard's," Agnes said as they ascended the front steps of the hotel, and the sisters both smiled the same private smile, allowing the shadow of the lattice-work portico to wrap them in a feeling of opulence.

Their companions were seated at the other end of the lobby and as they crossed it, they were able to observe the group from a distance. Miss de Witt looked radiant in her yellow day gown. Dr. Schechter was his usual disheveled self. And Mr. Bechor seemed somewhat subdued, his typical self-assurance retracted into scaly calculation. As for the Chief Rabbi, the twins were quite taken with him from the start. Though his long robes and thick gray beard lent him a venerable appearance, one could discern a certain mischievous brilliance in the bright green dart of his eyes. In another context, one might imagine him as a successful businessman or a member of the cabinet.

"Our table should be ready," Mr. Bechor said, interrupting Dr. Schechter's halting introductions. "I told them to expect us at one."

"Excellent," Margaret said, smiling through her teeth while Mr. Bechor took her by the arm and led the group into the dining room.

As they took their seats, Agnes and Margaret noticed more

than a few nearby diners repositioning themselves to better observe the motley group. A couple seated at the next table exchanged a worried glance, concerned perhaps that the Chief Rabbi—with his great beard, dark robes, and turban—would be followed into the dining room by a push of coolies, peasants, and burka-clad widows ululating about the martyrdom of Hussein. Accustomed as they were to such attention, the twins knew the best response was to straighten one's back and carry on without acknowledgment.

"We have arranged for a traditional Jewish meal," Mr. Bechor explained as a team of waiters began placing bowls of molokhia soup in front of them, "prepared according to our dietary laws by Rabbi Ben Shimon's wife."

"That will be lovely," Agnes said, although the truth was that she had been hoping for something more refined.

"Very good," Margaret added in Hebrew. "Delicious."

Once they established a medium of exchange—English and Hebrew, with a bit of Arabic mixed in—the conversation progressed quite smoothly. Rabbi Ben Shimon seemed genuinely interested in the details of Agnes and Margaret's education, as well as the various fruits of their previous excursions to St. Catherine's. They spoke for some time about the Coptic patriarch, who was a mutual friend, and engaged in a heated though entirely friendly exchange about the true location of Mount Sinai. Neither Rabbi Ben Shimon nor Dr. Schechter had actually visited the site, but they both strenuously defended the conviction that Moses received the Ten Commandments at the top of Mount Horeb. Margaret, advancing the view held by most contemporary scholars, argued that the biblical Mount Sinai was in fact the mountain now known as

Mount Serbal. After nearly an hour of general discussion, coffee was served—without the option of cream, as per Jewish dietary laws—and Mr. Bechor brought them around to the true purpose of the meeting.

"I trust everything is well with the geniza documents?"

Mr. Bechor addressed himself primarily to Dr. Schechter, though he allowed for the possibility that one of the ladies might be interested in the conversation as well. Margaret coughed into her fist and did her best to compose herself. What gall he had, asking after the well-being of documents he had, only a few days earlier, attempted to steal.

"Yes," Dr. Schechter said, "very well, indeed. Though I cannot imagine we would have accomplished much without the assistance of Mrs. Lewis and Mrs. Gibson."

Agnes nodded and Margaret allowed a small smile as Dr. Schechter described a few of the documents he imagined would be of most interest to Rabbi Ben Shimon. Then Mr. Bechor introduced the topic they knew must eventually be discussed, the Egyptian Customs Authority.

For much of the past week, Mr. Bechor explained, he and Dr. Schechter had been working to release the documents from administrative purgatory.

"But as you know," Mr. Bechor said, "the customs authorities can be rather difficult when it comes to the matter of removing antiquities from the country. And, given that some of the documents in question are nearly a thousand years old, the entire lot is considered an antiquity."

Although the Chief Rabbi had granted Dr. Schechter the rights to anything found in the attic of the synagogue, the authorities were contending that such rights could not legally be granted without first proving the Chief Rabbi's ownership. There were no records, of course, to prove ownership of documents that had, until a few weeks previous, been regarded as trash. As for the fact that they had been resident for more than a thousand years in a synagogue owned by the Jewish community, this apparently meant nothing.

"Would it be of any help," Rabbi Ben Shimon asked, once Mr. Bechor was finished, "if I were to intercede directly with the authorities?"

"I would hate for you to have to concern yourself with such a quotidian matter," Mr. Bechor said, waving away a waiter who had come to refill his coffee, "and I suspect this might be a question that even your influence might not be sufficient to fully resolve."

Glancing at the Chief Rabbi—who seemed to accept Mr. Bechor's assessment at face value—Margaret set her cup down and crossed her hands in her lap. She could see where this line of conversation was going.

"What is it, then?" she asked. "Baksheesh?"

They had already given Dr. Schechter a hundred pounds for assorted bribes. That, to Margaret, seemed more than sufficient.

"You could say that," Mr. Bechor responded, smiling, "though the customs authorities will want more baksheesh than a bellhop."

He repeated the word—*baksheesh*—like a teacher subtly correcting his student's pronunciation.

"We have been working with someone inside the Customs Authority to help expedite the approval," Mr. Bechor continued, with a subtle turn toward Dr. Schechter. "I spoke with him yesterday and he said he is very close, has almost secured the release of the documents, in fact. It is just that—"

"He needs more money," Margaret interrupted. "He wants more baksheesh."

Not accustomed to having his sentences finished for him, especially not by a woman, Mr. Bechor repressed a flash of anger.

"Yes, that is what he said."

"That is what he said," Margaret muttered under her breath. And everyone expected that the baksheesh would be supplied, without question, through the generosity of Mrs. Lewis and Mrs. Gibson. "Of course that is what he said."

As much as she wanted to lay Mr. Bechor bare, as much as she wanted to unmask him in front of Rabbi Ben Shimon and Dr. Schechter, Margaret knew there was nothing to be gained from such a confrontation. Mr. Bechor had played his move—informing Dr. Schechter of their visit to Bassatine—and now he was waiting for theirs. They had the upper hand and there was no telling how he would respond if they backed him into a corner. All the same, she could not allow him to fleece them any longer.

"How much does he need?" she asked, her voice steady and dripping with sarcasm. "One hundred? Two hundred? Five hundred?"

"I think," Agnes interrupted, "what my sister means to say—"

"No, I mean exactly what I say."

She turned to address Dr. Schechter.

"The truth of the matter is that we do not have much confidence in this approach. Before providing any more money, we would like to pursue a secondary line of attack."

"What is that?" Dr. Schechter asked, with a mixture of skepticism and curiosity.

"We have arranged for a meeting later this week with the Consul-General."

"Lord Cromer?" Dr. Schechter asked, and Margaret nodded.

She placed a hand on her sister's knee, to quiet her objections—for they had not, in fact, arranged such a meeting—then responded to Dr. Schechter's question, raising her voice perhaps more than she intended.

"Lord Cromer," she said and their table, indeed the entire dining room, fell silent at the sound of the Consul-General's name.

10

BEFORE CONSIDERING THE question of Ali's culpability—the question of evidence, motive, and premeditation—the judicial council of Ibn Ezra first needed to establish the nature of the complaint against him. And before considering the nature of the complaint against him, they needed to determine his standing among them. Was Ali ibn al-Marwani a member of their community? Was he a guest, a worker, or some combination of the three? If he was a worker, as Doctor Mevorakh and Shemarya the Pious argued, the dispute could be handled informally. Those who espoused this approach thought it best for al-Zikri to take the boy aside and ask whether he knew anything about the missing papers. If, on the other hand, Ali was determined to be a member of the community, as Amram ibn Shemarya and Ibn Kammuna contended, he would need to be brought before the council and given a proper trial. They all knew, of course, that, as a Muslim, Ali was not bound by the council's judgment. If he disagreed with their verdict, he could disregard it and request another trial in a Muslim court.

"Our only real power is over his salary," Doctor Mevorakh said, "which would lead one to believe that we are acting as the boy's employer, not a judicial body."

"Why rule on anything?" Amram ibn Shemarya interrupted, "if we know that our judgment might eventually be overruled by the caliph?"

The discussion went on like this for some time, bouncing back and forth between the two camps. It was a delicate decision, the fragility of which was only increased by a certain rhetorical incongruity on both sides. The more suspicious members of the council found themselves extolling Ali's importance to the community, while those who advocated for a more lenient approach were forced to argue that Ali was nothing more than a watchman.

The discussion went on late into the night, twirling round and round until finally it was determined that al-Zikri should be the one to decide. He knew the child best. It was he who had discovered the missing papers, he who had connected their theft to Ali's peculiar question a few nights earlier. And it was he who had brought the matter to the attention of the council. If al-Zikri thought the situation called for nothing more than a frank talk, that was how they would proceed. If he thought the full judicial council should be convened, so it would be. Everyone knew al-Zikri was fond of Ali, but they knew also that he would not allow affection to color his judgment.

"If Ali is innocent," he said after thinking on the matter for some time, "his innocence should be proclaimed before us all. If he is guilty, so too should his guilt."

The first Ali heard of the charges against him was the following afternoon, when al-Zikri and Doctor Mevorakh knocked at his front door.

"Your presence is requested at Ibn Kammuna's residence," Doctor Mevorakh said, standing at the top of Ali's steps with his hands clasped behind his back.

Ali sensed something serious was afoot, but he did not ask for any further explanation. After retrieving his sandals, he followed Doctor Mevorakh and al-Zikri through the produce market to the other end of Fustat. Eventually, they stopped and al-Zikri knocked on a huge blue wooden door decorated in tessellated seals of Solomon. This, apparently, was the residence of Ibn Kammuna. As they entered the house, Ali's fears were momentarily subsumed by a wave of opulence. From the top of the narrow marble entranceway, he could see a succession of blue-green and purple tapestries leading to a broad pool of light, which he guessed was the courtyard. Ali waited in the entranceway for what seemed like a long while. Then a servant appeared and led him toward the pool of light.

The courtyard of Ibn Kammuna's residence was larger than the courtyard of the synagogue and much more lavishly appointed. The interior spaces of the house rose up on all four sides, pillars and shaded balconies looking down on a small arbor of shade trees and the perpetual gurgle of a fountain. Between the entranceway and the fountain, sitting silent on a semicircle of cushions, was the entire judicial council of the Ibn Ezra Synagogue. Ali could feel the heat of the sun burning the top of his head as the members of the council regarded him in silence.

"Please be seated," Ibn Kammuna said finally, gesturing to an empty place at the hub of the semicircle.

Ali sat cross-legged on the cushion and stared down at the

fabric of his robe, stretched tight between his knees like the skin of a drum.

"We have asked you here," Shemarya the Pious began, "to answer some questions."

Ali could feel the marble pressing hard against the knobs of his ankles while the great scholar outlined the scope of their concerns: the missing papers, the flash of light, the strange question he had asked al-Zikri. He felt his throat constrict as he waited for mention of Hasdi il-Sephardi and the spells, but Shemarya the Pious ended his speech without raising either of these matters.

"We are not accusing you of any wrongdoing," Ibn Kammuna concluded. "But if you know anything about this, you must tell us."

A silence fell over the group like a heavy muffled blanket. The council, Ali realized, knew nothing of his true offenses. Although he had no desire to lie, he saw their accusations as an opportunity to wipe the slate. It was a chance to confess, even if the crime was not his own.

"It was me," he said after a long pause. "I stole the papers."

Around the circle, Ali saw a wave of pursed lips and furrowed brows. A number of men spoke at once, but Ephraim ibn Shemarya's voice rose above the rest.

"Will you give us a few moments to discuss our judgment?"

"Yes," Ali said, keeping his eyes on the ground as he rose from his cushion.

He turned and was headed back toward the entranceway when he heard the sound of Shemarya the Pious clearing his throat, the very same sound that had saved him a few months earlier from the judgment of the crowd. The room fell silent.

"My son," Shemarya said, "before you leave us, please allow me to ask one question."

Ali nodded.

"Will you please tell the council why you stole the papers?"

"Yes," he mumbled, but in the moment he could not think of a single reason why he would want to steal those papers. He swallowed and tried to begin again. "It was me. I stole the papers."

"Did you?"

Ali opened his mouth, but the words wouldn't come out. A number of the men in the circle exchanged glances.

"If you did steal the papers," the great scholar said finally, "then would you please inform the council of their current location?"

As he looked around the room—from the elder Shemarya and his sons to Ibn Kammuna, Doctor Mevorakh, and al-Zikri—Ali recalled that verse from the Surah of the Cow, the one his aunt Fatimah often repeated when exhorting him to be truthful. *Enter houses through their proper doors. And fear God that you may prosper.* It was time, he decided, to reveal his true self. He was finished with lying and sneaking around, letting his feelings fester inside him like an old pot of stew left out in the sun. He was done with the secrecy and the deception. Whatever the consequences of his actions might be, he wanted to face them.

And so, with an unsteady voice, Ali told the judicial council about his infatuation with the youngest daughter of Shemarya the Pious. He told them about Hasdi il-Sephardi's shop, the charm he had burned in the fire, and his encounter with Hasdi in the attic. As he spoke, sparing no detail of his betrayal, Ali felt as if a rope were unwinding from around his chest. He knew that the consequences would be severe. He could tell as much from the shocked expressions on the faces around him. But whatever his punishment might be, he was glad to finally unburden himself.

"These are serious matters," Ibn Kammuna said when Ali was finished. "We will have to ask you to wait in the hall while we discuss our judgment."

"Discuss?" Amram ibn Shemarya said, rising from his cushion in anger. "What is there to discuss? He betrayed us. He put a spell on my sister. And he freely admits it."

"There is nothing to discuss," Ephraim ibn Shemarya added. "We should put him out into the street and forbid him from ever returning to the synagogue. If he were Jewish and we were Muslim, he would already be in prison."

"What is there to discuss?" Amram asked a second time, and there were a few murmurs of agreement.

Ali kept his gaze fixed to the straps of his sandals. He didn't look up until he heard the voice of Shemarya the Pious.

"My child."

At the sight of the great scholar, his kind face and long white hair wrapped up in his beard, Ali felt sick to his stomach. All the abuse from Amram and Ephraim ibn Shemarya was nothing compared with their father's disappointment. He wanted to beg for forgiveness, to tear his galabiya and prostrate himself in front of the council, but he knew that such a display would not be looked upon with favor. And so, he said nothing.

"This is all very troubling," Shemarya began after a long

silence. "The magic you describe is quite strong indeed. And I will not deny that I am angry. But in such moments of anger, we must be ever more mindful of our capacity for mercy. Let us not forget that we are descendants of Abraham, Abraham who forgave the sins of Abimelech and then prayed to God for his enemy's forgiveness."

When Shemarya the Pious was finished with his speech, Doctor Mevorakh told Ali to wait in the hall.

"We will fetch you when we have come to a decision."

For much of the afternoon, Ali sat in the entranceway of Ibn Kammuna's residence, watching the outline of his face swim through the milky surface of the marble floor. He heard the council's discussion as an undifferentiated stream of sound, punctuated every so often by a shout or silence or a single word bouncing down the hall like a ball from a child's game escaped into the road. After some time, a servant brought a pot of tea and a plate of fruit arranged in a spiral of yellow, white, and red, but Ali could not bring himself to eat. Just the thought of it, the idea of that slick sweet fruit flesh sliding down his throat, made him sick. He stared down at the dark callused soles of his feet and thought of the saying *Paradise is under the feet of the mothers*. It seemed true enough. But then again, what did he know of mothers? And if paradise was under their feet, what was under his own soles? Nothing but worn leather and dirt, fitting for the bastard orphan son of a water carrier.

Darkness was beginning to assemble when a servant returned and led Ali back into the courtyard. Without raising his eyes, he seated himself on the edge of his cushion. Shemarya the Pious was the first to speak.

"You have committed a grave offense."

"A number of offenses," Amram put in.

"You colluded against us," Shemarya continued as if he had not heard his son's interruption. "You lied to us. You defiled our holiest of objects. And on top of all this, you bewitched my youngest daughter."

Judging from Shemarya's choice of words, it would seem that the charm had worked. Ali tried to put this thought out of his head. He tried not to imagine his beloved pining for him. He tried to focus on what Shemarya the Pious was saying.

"What you have told us will allow us to restore the afflicted child."

At this, the great scholar devolved into a fit of coughing. When he had subdued the cough, he took a calming breath and tried to begin again. But, overcome with emotion, he could not bring himself to speak. Eventually, he nodded to Ibn Kammuna, who took up the remainder of the judgment.

"One could make the case that you did not know what you were doing, that no one explicitly told you not to do what you did, that you did not have the sense to know it was wrong. It is not a strong case, but it can be made."

Ibn Kammuna paused and looked around the circle.

"We are not pleased with your conduct. But we do value your honesty and hard work. We are also aware that this is your first infraction. Our tradition teaches us to be pliant as a reed, not hard like the cedar. And so, we have decided to grant you clemency, on a conditional basis."

Ali released his breath.

"If you would like to continue in your present position,"

Doctor Mevorakh said, "you must make two vows. First, you must agree to find a wife."

"When a man marries," Ibn Kammuna said, "all his sins are forgiven."

The rest of the council nodded, and Ephraim ibn Shemarya added an aphorism of his own.

"He who has found a wife has found happiness and obtains favor from the Lord."

"You are a good boy," Doctor Mevorakh continued. "But you have the restlessness of a boy. We will give you two months to correct your ways. If, by the end of that period, you have not found a wife, we will be forced to search for a replacement."

The doctor allowed the first half of the sentence to sink in before moving on.

"In addition to finding a wife, you must forget everything you know about the Ezra Scroll. You will never speak of it. You have never seen it. You have no knowledge that it exists. The same should also be applied to your dealings with Hasdi il-Sephardi."

Ali opened his mouth to ask a question, but Ibn Kammuna interrupted him.

"Hasdi is dangerous, but his is the magic of schoolboys. We will see that he is banished from Fustat. Even so, you must never speak of him again. Is that clear?"

"Yes."

"You should also be aware," Ephraim ibn Shemarya added, "that this ruling is provisional. There are many among us who would like to terminate your position immediately, but we have agreed to give you another chance. The council will be meeting again in two months to make our final decision. If there are any problems between now and then, I can assure you that we will not be so lenient."

Ali nodded.

"Is there anything you would like to say to the council?" Doctor Mevorakh asked.

There were so many things Ali wanted to say, far too many for a single speech. So he said only that which was most important.

"Thank you."

Ali was indeed very thankful. But as he made his rounds that evening—investigating the silent corners of the courtyard, poking into the empty spaces behind the ark, in the ritual baths, and especially in the attic—he felt his desire gurgling back up again. Even after everything that had happened, a tiny part of him still hoped he might find a way to be with his beloved. He tried to swat these thoughts away. The council had granted him clemency, he told himself; they had given him a second chance. If he wanted to keep their trust and keep his job, he needed to tamp down his longing.

It wasn't until the middle of the night that he discovered a way to force the forgetting. He was finishing up his fourth round, trying not to imagine his beloved's reaction to the events of the day, when he accidentally burnt his wrist on the edge of his lantern. Crying out, he dropped the lantern and splashed his wrist with cold water. Ali often burned himself, but this time he noticed something new. Behind the pain there was also a melting, as if a portion of his worries had escaped through the burn. The next time he thought of his beloved, he pressed his forearm for a few beats against the rim of his lantern and again he felt that same release. Over the course of the night, Ali burned himself nine times, leaving puffy red marks all up and down the underside of his arm. It was painful, but effective. When he woke that next afternoon, he could already feel his yearnings beginning to slip away.

11

Mr. Mosseri's apartment was on a short tree-lined street in Mohandessin, three blocks from the Nile and around the corner from the Tawfiqiya Tennis Club. For some reason, this particular Gamal al-Din Street wasn't included in the index of my map. But once I knew where to look, it wasn't much trouble to find.

"Here it is," Abdullah had said, the morning after my visit to the synagogue.

Pushing his plate aside, he pointed to the bristle of little side streets off al-Sudan.

"Gamal al-Din," I said, reading aloud from the map. "There it is."

I flattened the map on the table and took a bite of my peanut butter–and–Nutella sandwich. There it was, exactly where Mr. Mosseri had said it would be, in Mohandessin, just around the corner from the Tawfiqiya Tennis Club. After weeks of searching, weeks of wandering aimlessly up and down various Gamal al-Din streets in Nasr City, Imbaba, and Heliopolis, I had finally found the right one.

"There it is," I repeated, but Abdullah was already on to the next question.

"When Mr. Mosseri invited you, what did he say he wanted?"

"He said he had something I would be interested in seeing."

As the week progressed, we returned again and again to this question. What was it that Mr. Mosseri thought I would be interested in seeing? I did my best to temper my expectations, to keep my imagination in check. But when I stood there on the sidewalk in front of his building, seeing that address—72 Gamal al-Din Street—carved into the bronze plaque next to the front entrance, anything seemed possible.

"Welcome," Mr. Mosseri said, pulling me into his apartment with a surprisingly muscular hug. "Welcome, my friend. I trust we weren't too difficult to find."

"No. Not really."

"Good," he smiled and, patting me on the back, led me into the dining room.

Seated at the long glass-and-chrome table was a group of older ladies all talking in a mixture of Egyptian Arabic and French. A few of them were smoking. There was a television on in the living room and the table was scattered with little plates of hummus, olives, pickled vegetables, and nuts. When Mr. Mosseri and I walked in, the conversation stopped and a wave of greetings rippled down the table.

"Me and the old ladies," he said, after introducing his mother, Mrs. Shemarya, Mrs. Mevorakh, Mrs. Tunsi, and Madame el-Tantawi. "They won't leave. And I won't leave without them."

"I was so sorry to hear about your father," Mrs. Mevorakh said as I sat down in the empty seat at the head of the table.

"Such a kind man," Madame el-Tantawi put in.

"May his memory be for a blessing," Mrs. Mosseri said, and everyone nodded their agreement.

I thanked them, then turned to listen to Mrs. Shemarya, who was already halfway through a story about the pigeons my great-uncle—her husband's cousin—used to keep on the roof of their apartment building.

"Such a mess," she said. "You've never seen such a mess."

"Is that right?"

"You wouldn't believe it," she said, shaking her head in disgust.

Listening to her go on about my great-uncle and his pigeons, I wondered if perhaps this was what Mr. Mosseri wanted to show me. I had expected something more tangible—a picture of my father or a dusty academic tome about the geniza—but wasn't it also possible that he had invited me over in order to introduce me to this cluster of old ladies who, as far as I could tell, were the last Jews of Cairo? Or maybe I was the attraction, their link to a world that no longer existed.

"Every afternoon," Madame el-Tantawi said, resting a hand on my forearm to get my attention, "your grandmother and I used to play marbles in the courtyard of her father's house. And every afternoon my cousin Yakob watched us from the roof of the house next door. She was a modest girl, your grandmother, a good girl, and she never raised her eyes to him for more than a moment. Still, he watched us every day for nearly three years. Then, on the day after your grandmother's sixteenth birthday, he entered the house through its front door and asked for her hand in marriage."

"So we're related?" I said. "Your cousin was my grandfather?"

Madame el-Tantawi shook her head ruefully and continued with the story.

"Later that same day, while your grandmother and her parents were considering the proposal, my cousin went out to a nice dinner with some friends and, halfway through the meal, he choked on a chicken bone. Died facedown in his own soup."

She paused to serve herself a portion of stewed green beans and chicken, then came around to the moral of the story.

"Life is too short to wait, Yusuf. It is far too short."

"Such a sweet boy," Mrs. Shemarya said, chewing on a mouthful of green beans. "What a shame to die like that, in his own soup."

All night they told stories—about their cousins and their friends, about my grandfather's bravery and my great-grandfather's failed business ventures—talking about the past as if it were another life, which perhaps it was. They asked after my mother and said what a pretty girl she had been. They argued about the quality of the lamb served at a wedding fifty years ago. They talked about crystal and silver, the Gezira Club, British troops, and the Abdeen Palace. Then, toward the end of dinner, the conversation came back around to my father.

"He was a good man," Mrs. Tunsi said. "Even in difficult times, he always had a smile for me, for everyone."

There were a few assorted nods as Mrs. Tunsi segued into a story about how my father chased down a group of neighborhood boys who had set a stink bomb in the ritual baths. When she was finished, Mrs. Mevorakh described an incident involving a family of cats trapped on the roof of the synagogue. Then Mr. Mosseri told a story, from my father's produce salesman days, which ended in him returning ten thousand pounds to a poor fruit vendor who had inadvertently overpaid his account for nearly three years. I had heard most of these stories before—from Uncle Hassan and from my father himself—but hearing them retold from this new perspective, I began to understand what my father had meant to these women, their families, and the community he had served. He was more than just a watchman. He was a friend, a protector, an adviser, one of the linchpins that held the community together.

"I remember when he was a boy," Mrs. Shemarya said after the tea was served, "he and your mother, they were like bread and butter."

As she began the story—describing how my parents first met in the courtyard of the synagogue—the air in the room shifted slightly and side conversations fell silent.

"It was a great scandal," Madame el-Tantawi put in, "a Jewish girl and a Muslim boy, even if he was an al-Raqb."

There were some nods of agreement. Even so, the general consensus seemed to be that the past was past. What mattered was the end result, that their relationship had produced such a fine young man as myself.

"I remember when your father came back from Paris," Mrs. Shemarya continued. "He was so smitten."

"And your mother," Mrs. Mevorakh put in. "They were both so young—"

Before she could finish her sentence, Mr. Mosseri stood up suddenly from the table.

"I nearly forgot," he said as he disappeared down the hall. "Excuse me."

A few moments later, by which time the conversation had digressed into an argument about my grandmother's maiden name, Mr. Mosseri returned with a battered old shoebox and set it on the table in front of me.

"This is what I was telling you about," he said, "what I thought you might be interested in seeing."

The box contained hundreds of letters—pale blue aerograms, mostly—with index cards marking the years from 1958 to 1976. I pulled out a stack and shuffled through them. They were all written in my mother's tiny slanting handwriting and all of them were addressed to my father, Ahmed al-Raqb, Ibn Ezra Synagogue, Old Cairo, Cairo, Egypt. I had never known my father to be particularly fastidious. But apart for the inevitable crusting of adhesive flaps, the letters were in pristine condition, all lined up in chronological order like tiny soldiers of the past.

"After your father left the synagogue," Mr. Mosseri explained, "I found this at the back of his closet in the watchman's house. I tried to give them back to him, more than once, but he said to throw them out. Being a sentimentalist at heart, I couldn't bring myself to follow his wishes. So I put the box at the bottom of a trunk and forgot about it. Until last week, that is, in the attic, when you asked if there might be anything else."

Mr. Mosseri removed his glasses and wiped a fleck of dust from the lens.

"I imagine he would have wanted you to have them."

"Thank you," I said.

I read a few lines of the first letter, sent from Paris to Cairo in 1958. Then I folded it back up, wanting to save the box for later that evening when, sitting cross-legged on the couch in my living room, I could read through the entire story at once.

My mother, Claudia Shemarya, was born in Cairo in 1948. The youngest child in the family, she was, from an early age, particularly attached to her father. Despite the admonitions of those who said that he would spoil her, he allowed her to follow him around the neighborhood, trailing behind him from the café to the bakery to the produce market.

The only place she wasn't allowed was the slaughterhouse, where the men of the Shemarya family had worked for years. There was no question about that. And so, when her father was finished with his morning rounds, when he was ready to go to work, he would deposit her at the courtyard of the Ibn Ezra Synagogue, where the children of the cantor and beadle played together with the al-Raqb boys.

Over time, my mother became inseparable from this little troupe. She was especially fond of the watchman's eldest son, Ahmed al-Raqb, and he looked after her as closely as he would his own sister. The other children said they were in love. And perhaps, in some childish way, they were. But as unusual as their friendship was, no one paid it much attention, in part because they were so young and in part because there were so many more important matters that needed attending.

In October 1956, the president of Egypt, Gamal Abdel Nasser, announced the expulsion of all foreigners from the country. This included British, French, and Italian nationals as well as thousands of Jewish families who had known no other home. It happened slowly at first, then all at once. Businesses were seized, civil liberties were stripped away. Jewish teachers, doctors, and engineers were fired. Some families converted, some went into hiding, some used their connections to stay another year and another. But most simply left. After more than a thousand years living on the shores of the Nile, the Jews of Cairo dispersed to London, Paris, São Paulo, Tel Aviv, and San Francisco.

The Shemarya family left Cairo for Paris in February 1958. Being only ten at the time, my mother didn't understand the world-historical implications of her exile. She only knew that bad things were happening in Egypt, and that France—the cradle of the language she learned in school, the birthplace of those horrible nuns who taught her math and literature— France would be safer. The day before her family was set to leave, she visited her friend Ahmed one last time. She promised to write, and he promised that one day he would visit.

Because the postal service between Cairo and Paris was so unreliable, because one could not expect to receive mail in a timely manner, if at all, my mother's letters read like a kind of epistolary diary, like notes to an imaginary friend from a distant and very different world. *Dear Ahmed,* the first letter began, *I am writing like I told you I would. Paris is exactly like Cairo but much bigger. I have a new school, a new house, and new friends. We eat baguettes with jam every day for lunch and onion soup for dinner.*

In those first few years, my mother's letters were mostly dry and perfunctory. She gave detailed descriptions of her family's new home, lists of books she had read, and long chronicles of disputes between school friends. But as the years passed and childhood turned to adolescence, she began sending longer, more intimate letters, pages and pages of her most personal thoughts squeezed onto a single aerogram. Although they were mostly platonic, these letters verged at times on more romantic territory. *I'm lonely here and it's raining,* she wrote in the winter of 1962. *I think of Cairo almost every day and when I do, I think of you.* She told my father more than once that he was her closest friend. *You are the only person in the world who truly understands me,* she wrote at the end of a two-part letter from March 1963. *If only our circumstances were different. If only.*

By the time my father took over as watchman of the Ibn Ezra Synagogue, in 1965, there were fewer than a thousand Jews in Cairo. Those who remained were subject to an increasingly hostile atmosphere. Jewish businesses were targeted by vandals and the new synagogue, Sha'ar Hashamayim, was defaced a number of times in riots inspired by Nasser's fiery radio speeches. The Ibn Ezra Synagogue avoided defacement if only because it was already in such disrepair. But as difficult as his job was, my father continued to perform his duties with care and devotion, like his father and his grandfather before him.

After the Six Day War, when anti-Jewish sentiment was at a peak, his brother tried to convince him to resign and join him in the produce distribution business. My father must have known that the Jewish community would not be able to support a watchman much longer. Still he rejected Uncle Hassan's offer, in part because of his commitment to the Jews of Cairo and in part, I would like to imagine, because he didn't want to betray his memory of that innocent little girl, Claudia Shemarya, or his image of the young woman she had become. For in spite of her childlike handwriting, there was no doubt that my mother was no longer that same little girl.

Her letters from this period were full of passion, curiosity, and self-doubt, enamored of the world's beauty and overflowing with strongly held, sometimes contradictory ideas about politics, culture, and art. *Yesterday I saw a linden tree,* she wrote, *dripping wet with rain, and I thought of all the workers in the world, so burdened by the weight of history.* At times she seemed to be writing to herself, using the letters as a journal in which she tried to make sense of the world and her place in it. At other times, they read like an intimate conversation between old friends, my mother providing the dialogue for both sides.

You said you want me to send you a picture, she wrote in the fall of 1966, just after her eighteenth birthday, *so you can imagine the person who is writing to you. I understand. I've thought many times about asking the same of you. But I am reluctant to take that step. Why? Because I already have a picture of you, my dear Ahmed—in my mind. It might seem strange, but the truth is that I can see you perfectly, in your words, in the curve of your letters, in the crease of the page on which you write, I can see you better than I could in any picture. Though you must wonder as you read this: Maybe there's some reason she doesn't want to send a picture? Is she hiding something? Fear not, my curious friend. I can assure you that I am very pretty.*

In June of 1968, following an uncharacteristic silence of two months, my mother posted a long letter detailing her

participation in the student revolt that spring. A fervent ide-
alistic barrage covering twelve pages of thick, cream-colored
paper, the letter recounted impromptu lectures, late-night
debates with fellow classmates, ideological skirmishes, and a
particularly powerful experience helping to staff a makeshift
first-aid clinic behind the barricades. *I agree that those who
lack imagination cannot imagine what is lacking,* she wrote. *I
hate de Gaulle with the very fibers of my soul. But after seeing what
I saw that day, I'm not entirely sure violence is the solution.* In addition to her account of the revolt, the letter also alluded to a
profound personal transformation. *I see the world now with
fresh eyes,* she wrote. *We are all connected. I see that so clearly.
Love is more powerful than anything. Try as they might to take it
from us, the possibilities in the bond between two humans cannot be
broken.* What she meant by this, I have no idea. Maybe it was
just cosmic vagueness. Perhaps she was trying to hint at an
affair with one of her fellow revolutionaries. Or maybe she
was trying to express her own tangled feelings about my father. Regardless, the letter seemed to be a turning point, a last
gasp of adolescent passion before she settled into adulthood.

In the years that followed, the flighty romance of her teen-
age years was replaced by a mature self-awareness. She wrote
once a month, updating my father on her studies, the success
of her brothers' kosher meatpacking business, her job as a
secretary at a small law firm, and her thoughts on pursuing a
doctorate in French literature. As she began to think of the
future, her fantasies took on a more practical quality. She
wrote long, detailed descriptions of the life she imagined for
herself, where she wanted to live, how many children she
wanted to have, and so on. Although she was always careful

to allow for the possibility that my father would be included in this future, she also seemed increasingly aware of the potential difficulties in such a union. *If all this dreaming is too much*, she wrote in March 1971, *if you ever want me to just be quiet and get on with my life, to stop sharing all these crazy fantasies, please tell me. Because we both know how hard it would be— with my parents, with your parents, with everyone—and the last thing I want is for you to get hurt.*

In the fall of 1973, three weeks into my mother's first semester as a doctoral student, the Yom Kippur War broke out. A week after the end of the war, she sent a short and somewhat cryptic letter to my father at Uncle Hassan's address in Maadi. *My dear Ahmed*, she wrote, *I hope you know how much I care about you and how much I admire your dedication to your work. That goes without saying, I suppose, but it's worth saying after the week you've no doubt had. You should know also that I'm not the only one who feels this way. You are a good man, Ahmed. No matter what anyone might say, you have no reason to be ashamed. You did the only thing you could have done. And I, for one, think you behaved heroically.* The letter continued on like this for a few more lines. Then, in closing, she suggested that he might come visit her in Paris.

When I first read this letter, I felt a tingle of anticipation at the base of my spine. Here was the turning point, the crux of it all. I knew what happened next. Still, in the moment, it felt unsettled. Flattening the aerogram on the coffee table in front of me, I tried to picture my mother sitting down at a café or a carrel in the university library, tried to imagine what she might have been thinking as she unfolded the thin blue paper and began writing to her childhood friend, that

invisible yet ever-present confidant who was her only remaining link to the city of her birth. She would have been
twenty-five at the time, in her first semester of graduate
school, still living with her parents, and entirely unaware of
how drastically this letter would change the course of her
life. Had she thought about my father that morning on the
Métro, had she already begun to work through the words she
would use to console him, had she decided to invite him to
visit, or had she simply poured her heart onto the page and
sealed it up before she could reconsider? Who knows what
she meant by the offer? In a way, it doesn't matter. Because,
two weeks later, my father was on a boat to Marseilles.

There is no record of the visit except in retrospect, but it
seems to have gone well. When my father returned home
from Paris, there was a letter waiting for him at Uncle Hassan's apartment. *My dear Ahmed,* my mother wrote, *I would
like nothing more than to be there with you now, to greet you upon
your arrival, to spend the night in your arms. But for now this letter must stand in my stead, this letter, the fast-fading memories of
our time together, and the hope that we will see each other soon.*
Two days later, she sent a longer note, recounting certain details of their trip—a movie in the middle of the day, a crêpe
shared in the park, an impromptu weekend in the Loire
Valley—and reflecting on her reaction to something my father said on their last day together. *I don't know why it upset
me so much,* she wrote. *I'm not religious. I don't even know if I
believe in God. Still, I don't think I could ever bring myself to con-
vert, if only because I know how much it would upset my parents.*
Four days later she sent another letter, enumerating how
much she missed him, then another a week after that.

The letters continued on like this for four months. Then, something shifted. In March 1974, she wrote a long ruminative note, filling three aerograms with her thoughts on history and culture, the past and the future, Ibn Khaldun's theory of civilization and Levinas on confronting the Other. *I want to escape the shackles of the Old World,* she told him. *I want a better life, for myself and for my family. More than anything, I want for us to be together. I want to live that life with you. But, my dear Ahmed, my sweet friend, the truth is I don't know how it can happen. I wish it were possible, I wish it were that easy, but with my family, with your family, I just don't know how it would work.* At the end of the letter, she mentioned some difficulties with her parents and asked him to send all future correspondence to her office at the university. She neglected, however, to mention that most important piece of news— and the source, most likely, of the difficulties with her parents: she was four months pregnant with his child.

It's a striking omission, but one can imagine how difficult a time it must have been for her. Her parents can't have been happy, especially not when they found out who the father was, not only a Muslim but a common watchman. One would imagine that all available options were discussed. At the time, abortion was illegal in France, but it wouldn't have been too difficult to go abroad or find a back-alley clinic in Paris. There were also ways to arrange for a discreet adoption, go to Switzerland for a few months and come back good as new. Whatever discussions they might have had—the shattered dishes, the frank conversations, the hushed phone calls to well-connected friends of the family—my mother kept them to herself. And the decision she eventually made, she made alone.

Her next letter was posted eight months later, from Culver City, California. *I am living in Los Angeles,* she wrote. *I dropped out of my doctoral program and I'm teaching French at the university here. The reason I am writing is to tell you that you have a son. His name is Yusuf and he is three months old. I apologize for not telling you earlier and I understand if you are upset that I kept this information from you. Things have been very difficult. So many times I wanted to write, to tell you everything. So many times I imagined getting on a plane to Cairo, taking a taxi to your apartment, and falling into your arms. But I knew that this was a decision I had to make on my own.*

Over the next eight months, her letters were tender and intimate, filled with detailed accounts of my development and descriptions of our life in Los Angeles. *He has your smile,* she wrote a few weeks before I turned six months old, *and when he giggles he scrunches up his nose just like you.* Over time she became more and more open to the idea that they might be able to make a family together. *You would like it here,* she wrote. *It's always warm and you're never too far from the water.* In July of 1975, my mother sent a postcard of the Santa Monica Pier. *I wish you were here,* she wrote, and less than a month later he was.

Her next letter, postmarked at the end of September 1975, was an extended reflection on what seemed to be a less than successful visit. *I'm glad you came,* she wrote, *I really am, because I wanted you to see Yusuf and because it helped me to see what I have known for a long time now but haven't been able to admit to myself, that it could never work between us. This has nothing to do with our fight at the beach or your disagreements with my landlord. It's not because I don't love you. I do. It's not because I don't think you will be a good father. I do. We're just too different, Ahmed. As much as I care about you, the truth is that our lives have taken us in different directions and it's best, I think, to acknowledge that now instead of later.*

At this point, my mother's pale blue aerograms gave way to a stack of letters from my father, all of which were still sealed. They had traveled halfway around the world, from Cairo to Los Angeles, only to be returned, unread, back again to Cairo. Twenty-five years later, they were still unopened. And so, as I read through them, ripping into the envelopes with the edge of my thumbnail, I felt my father was writing directly to me, which in a way he was.

They began as love letters, as promises and dreams. *You are my light,* he wrote in October 1975, *my closest friend and the mother of my child. We are meant to be together.* But as the months progressed, the tone of his letters became increasingly desperate. *We should be a family,* he wrote on my second birthday. *A family is best for everyone. A son needs his father. But also a father needs his son.* By that point, my father had resigned his position at the synagogue. He was working for Uncle Hassan's produce distribution company, beginning to make a new life for himself. Even so, he wrote, *I will leave all this to be with you and Yusuf in Los Angeles or Paris or anywhere you want.*

My mother wrote to him dutifully on the first of each month with a picture and an update on my development. She told him details about her life and even suggested the possibility that he might visit again, to see my development for himself. But she returned all of his love letters unread. It was almost as if she were afraid of how she might react, as if she were still fighting some part of herself that wanted to be with him. Regardless of her motivations for not responding, my father continued writing into the void, twice a month for more than a year. His letters continued on that same stubborn and lonely path, from Cairo to Los Angeles and back, until February 1977, when my mother sent a short note telling him that she was engaged. At the end of that letter, the last in the box, she informed him that she and her fiancé—Bill—were planning to visit her parents in Paris that following spring. *This will be a good opportunity for you to see Yusuf*, she wrote.

Although the visit took place more than twenty years ago, I can still remember pieces of it: the moldy smell of my grandparents' apartment, the white marble stairs outside their building, a visit to the zoo on a rainy day. There are pictures, too, an album of overexposed snapshots my mother kept at the back of her closet. They are mostly of me, wearing brown corduroy overalls and a red-striped long-sleeved shirt, helping my grandmother blow out the candles on a birthday cake. But my father is there, too, smiling on the couch, sitting with me on the floor, playing with a blue plastic truck.

Even without the photographs, I can see his face, his eyebrows, the droop of his mustache. And in the lines of his smile I can begin to imagine how he must have felt, seeing my mother with her new fiancé, sitting with us in the living room of my grandparents' apartment, knowing that in a few weeks the trip would end and we would all go back to our respective homes, as if none of this had ever happened.

◆ ◆ ◆

When I woke up that next morning—having fallen asleep on the couch—I went through the box again and found the letter my mother wrote after my father visited her in Los Angeles, the one ending their relationship for good. *As much as I care about you,* she told him, *the truth is that our lives have taken us in different directions and it's best, I think, to acknowledge that now instead of later.*

"It was so long ago," my mother said when I called her that afternoon. "I remember him visiting. But the letter—"

She trailed off and I stared down at the semitranslucent airmail paper on the coffee table in front of me, my mother's careful handwriting stretched from one edge of the page to the other. It had always been difficult for me to see things from her perspective, to see her as anything but my mother, but after reading through her letters, I was beginning to appreciate what it must have been like, being uprooted at such a young age and then, sixteen years later, leaving her friends and family and starting over again in a new country.

"You said it was something you had known for a long time," I prompted, looking down at her words, "but hadn't been able to admit to yourself."

I had called to ask about the end of their relationship, my father's trip to Los Angeles, what it was that made her think they couldn't work together. But as I listened to her, trying to explain what was going through her head twenty-five years earlier, I kept glancing at that other letter, at the edge of the coffee table, the one in which she invited my father to come visit her in Paris. That was the heart of the matter, the fulcrum on which this story teetered. And more important, perhaps, than the letter itself was the impetus behind the letter, the shameful episode that caused my father to resign his post as watchman. For if he hadn't left the synagogue, my mother wouldn't have invited him to visit her, and if she hadn't invited him, I never would have come into being.

"It was such a long time ago," my mother said when I asked her whether she remembered why my father left the synagogue. "And your father, he wasn't really one to talk about his problems."

"You don't still have his letters, do you?"

"I doubt it," she said. I heard her shuffling through a pile of papers on her desk, as if she thought she might find the letters there, buried under a crust of bills. "I can't imagine I would have brought them with me to Santa Fe."

She paused and I could hear their dog barking in the background.

"Okay," I said. But there was still one thing I didn't understand. "Why did you return his letters? The ones he sent after he visited you in California?"

"I knew it wouldn't work," she said. "Whatever my reasons were at the time, I knew that for sure. And he was so charming. I guess I was worried that if I read any of his letters—"

She trailed off again and we were both silent for a long while, allowing his memory to balance on the line between us, imagining that alternative universe in which she had allowed herself to be charmed.

That Sunday, when I asked Uncle Hassan if he remembered why my father resigned from the synagogue, he scratched his palm against the armrest of his favorite chair and regarded me with a half squint, as if trying to determine the quality of a suspicious tomato. I had been over to their apartment every Sunday for the past month. But aside from that first visit, we mostly avoided the topic of my father. We talked about Uncle Hassan's business and the upcoming American election, Mubarak and the protests in the West Bank. But it was best, we all seemed to agree, not to disturb my father's memory.

"It was his great shame," Uncle Hassan said finally. He glanced down into the bottom of his empty tea glass and frowned to himself. "His great shame."

He looked up at me, to see whether this answer might be sufficient, but he knew it wasn't.

"He should know," Aunt Basimah said as she refilled her husband's glass.

"He deserves to know," Aisha put in.

"Yes," Uncle Hassan conceded. "I suppose he does."

He looked at me and blew across the top of his tea.

"It was his great shame," he repeated, "his greatest shame. But your cousin is right. A son deserves to know his father's pride also with the shame."

And thus, Uncle Hassan began the story.

In those chaotic first hours of the Yom Kippur War, as Egyptian troops marched across the Suez Canal and Syrian tanks rolled into the Golan Heights, my father was at his post in the courtyard of the synagogue. There was nothing unusual to report until late morning, when he heard a commotion on the street that ran alongside the main prayer hall. Through the gates, he saw two plainclothes police officers and a dozen or so angry men from the neighborhood. The officers said they had reason to believe that the Jews were hiding guns in the synagogue and intended to attack the police substation nearby. My father tried to convince the officers that this was clearly nothing more than a rumor. In fact, he told them, it was a Jewish holiday. The Jews were all praying at the other synagogue downtown. Still, the policemen insisted on searching the premises. If my father didn't comply, they said, they would force their way in and arrest him.

Not wanting to jeopardize his own safety and leave the building unguarded at this critical moment, my father unlocked the gates. He accompanied the officers on their search, answering questions about various ritual objects and insisting the entire time that, no matter what might happen between Israel and Egypt, the Jews of Cairo were loyal Egyptian citizens who wanted nothing but to live in peace. For nearly an hour, my father trailed along behind the officers, unlocking doors and making sure they didn't damage or steal anything. After scouring the courtyard, the prayer hall, and the ritual baths, they asked to be shown to the attic.

My father told them that it was empty, that it was dark and difficult to access. But the officers insisted. And so, reluctantly, he raised the dusty ladder and leaned it against the lip of the entrance. All three of them climbed in and the officers raked their flashlights over the room. They turned over an old metal pail and peered inside a wooden crate filled with jugs of bleach. But aside from these cleaning implements and a few broken lamps, the room appeared to be empty.

As they were about to leave, the smaller of the two officers noticed a crack in the wall panels and knelt down to inspect it more closely. As it turned out, the panel was the door of a secret compartment, inside of which was hidden an ancient

Torah scroll. In spite of my father's protests, the officers re-moved the Ezra Scroll and insisted on taking it to the station for further inspection. As they carried it out of the attic store-room and down the stairs to the courtyard of the synagogue, my father tried to reason with them, to convince them that it was only a book, an ancient holy book that shouldn't under any circumstances be removed from the synagogue. But they wouldn't listen.

In a last-ditch attempt to stop them, my father tried to block their way out, standing in front of the synagogue's main gates with his arms crossed over his chest. They told him to step aside and when he refused, the larger of the two officers laid my father out with a single punch. As they left, they spat on the ground next to his head.

"It wasn't his fault," Uncle Hassan concluded. "What else could he have done? Nothing. There was nothing else to do. But even so, he could not forgive himself."

My father blamed himself for unlocking the gates and for not fighting back more vociferously, for allowing the officers to trample on the honor of the synagogue and steal its most valued possession. The day after the war ended, he submitted his resignation. It was accepted, in part because there was no money left to support his position and in part because there were many in the community who blamed him, even if there was nothing he could have done. A few weeks later, dis-traught and unsure what to do with himself, he boarded a boat for France.

"He could not forgive himself," Uncle Hassan repeated. "For many years he was very depressed."

"And the Ezra Scroll?" I asked, recalling the newspaper

clipping I had found in my father's room, the small question mark next to the Torah scroll Mr. Mosseri was holding.

"The Ezra Scroll?"

Uncle Hassan smoothed down the edges of his mustache and shook his head slowly from side to side.

"It was never seen again."

12

IN THEIR GIRLHOOD, it was not an uncommon occurrence—
to wake in half darkness with that hollow feel of doubling
and the persistent image of a horse or a ship or a man with
a hideous nose—but Agnes and Margaret had not shared a
dream for nearly three decades. It felt rather childish, then,
and somewhat unsettling, to be looking across the unfamiliar
light of the hotel room, reaching out for confirmation of what
they both already knew. To think the same thought was normal. They were twins, after all. Given the same set of information, it made sense that they would occasionally come to
the same conclusion. But how could one understand dreaming the same dream?

"I still smell the dust."

Margaret murmured her agreement. She smelled it, too.
She saw the graveyard of paper and books, that storm of souls
rising up to heaven like Judgment Day. It was not a night-
mare. Still, the dream stayed with them both, the smell of the
dust and all those frail souls swirling about it.

"What do you suppose it means?" Agnes asked as they performed their morning exercises.

"Perhaps it has some connection to our meeting."

"Yes"—Agnes smiled into her forward bend—"and we will

202 ♦ MICHAEL DAVID LUKAS

all soon be released from the purgatory of the Customs Authority."

The previous evening, as they were preparing for bed, the sisters had received a very welcome note from Miss de Witt. Her uncle had cabled, she wrote, and said that the Consul-General would be delighted to meet them the following morning at ten if they were able. Neither of them had truly believed the girl when she told them that her uncle might be able to arrange the meeting with Lord Cromer. Still, they were both very happy to be proven wrong.

Now that they had their meeting, they knew it would not be especially difficult to impress upon the Consul-General the great importance of the geniza documents. For inside every colonial administrator was a public schoolboy entranced by the mysteries of the Orient. And once they were able to convince him of the geniza's consequence, Lord Cromer would be able to snip the red tape of the Egyptian Customs Authority with a snap of his fingers. The documents would be released, and all without having to rely on Mr. Bechor or any of his unsavory connections.

"That girl is something," Margaret marveled as she buttoned up the back of her sister's dress.

"Yes," Agnes agreed, leading the way downstairs to the lobby, "though I'm not entirely certain what."

By the time they sat down for breakfast, the dining room was clattering with holidaymakers and pilgrims. The guests of their hotel were mainly British—it was the Hotel d'Angleterre, after all—with some Germans, a smattering of Slavs, and a table of Greek Orthodox priests stopping over on their way to the Sinai. More than a few of the British diners recognized in Agnes and Margaret the markings of a sympathetic tribe and smiled in acknowledgment of their shared origin. A pair of tight smiles allowed the twins to maintain a perimeter around their table without appearing overly disagreeable.

"Nine o'clock," Margaret said when the clock struck the hour, and they rose as one to meet their carriage.

Although their meeting was not until ten, Margaret had ordered the carriage for nine. If one wanted to be punctual in this country, she knew, it was necessary to give the locals a wide margin of error. Of course, she and her sister were both rather excited as well. Lord Cromer did not meet with just anyone. He was a busy man, administering the entire country practically by himself, and they very much valued the time he had set aside for them.

"The British Consul-General's residence," Agnes said as they climbed into the carriage waiting outside their hotel.

"Thirty al-Maghrabi Street," Margaret added.

She had looked up the address in her Baedeker guidebook earlier that morning, so as not to be at the whim of the driver.

"Thirty al-Maghrabi?" the driver asked, somewhat hesitantly.

"Yes," Agnes snapped, "that is what she said."

The driver took them along Abbasiya Street, across the northern end of the medieval city, and fifteen minutes later he brought the carriage to a halt across from a grand, though rather decrepit building on al-Maghrabi Street, clearly not the residence of the most powerful man in Egypt. The façade of the building was streaked with multiple layers of dirt and two of the windows on the third floor were boarded up with wood.

"Thirty al-Maghrabi Street," the driver announced with a halfhearted flourish.

"I do not know where you have taken us," Agnes said, "but this is certainly not the residence of the British Consul-General."

Mumbling something unintelligible to himself, the driver climbed down from his seat and wandered over toward the doorman of the building.

"The Lord has moved," he reported upon his return.

"You know where he currently lives?"

"Yes," he said. "Garden City, next to Qasr el-Einy Hospital."

"How long will it take to get there?"

"Not long."

"Well, then," Margaret said, "we should probably be going."

As they rode back along Abbasiya Street toward the Nile, Agnes and Margaret were both rather agitated by the idea that they might be late for their meeting. And, worse still, there was no one to blame but themselves. They were both silent, watching the city pass until, turning off Qasr el-Einy Street, they stopped in front of the Consul-General's residence, a gleaming white marble building with a mouthful of pillars and a garden far greener than any they had seen for months.

"We are here for a meeting with Lord Cromer," Agnes said to the two smart-looking young men standing guard outside the front gate.

"Mrs. Lewis and Mrs. Gibson," Margaret added, anticipating their query.

"I hope you will not mind a short walk," said the taller of the two, after confirming the meeting in his logbook. "For safety reasons, there is a ban on native vehicles in the driveway."

"Of course."

They knew that this small plot of land was, legally speaking, a piece of the Queen's dominion, but neither Agnes nor Margaret had expected to feel quite so much at home. It was uncanny. In the inhospitable and muggy climes of Egypt, not more than a hundred yards from the banks of the Nile, Lord Cromer had re-created perfectly the feeling of a British country house. Ordered and elegant, the grounds were lined with poplar trees and neatly trimmed hedges. At the top of the drive, the guard passed them to a butler, who led them through the entrance hall and up the main stairs to a small study that resembled nothing so much as the office of a Cambridge fellow. The butler bade them sit, which they did, though a moment later the Consul-General entered through an interior door and they both stood to greet him.

"Mrs. Lewis," he said, "Mrs. Gibson. It is a pleasure to finally meet you."

He was a handsome man, more so than pictures in the newspaper would indicate, with lively blue eyes, a wide white mustache, and a stomach the size of a woman's six months gone.

"The pleasure is ours."

Motioning for them to sit, Lord Cromer lowered himself into the chair behind his desk and crossed his legs.

"How do you take your tea?"

"Light cream, no sugar," Margaret said.

Agnes nodded in assent as another butler came into the room and Lord Cromer asked him to bring three cups of tea, light cream, no sugar.

"I had a crate of Afternoon Darjeeling shipped in last week," he said. "Taylors of Harrogate. It is a luxury, but I am sure you will agree a very important one given the quality of tea available in Egypt."

The twins did agree, very much, on the importance of such luxuries and the sorry selection of tea available in Egypt.

"Now then," Lord Cromer said, crossing his hands in his lap, "old Claude mentioned you are acquainted with his niece, Miss de Witt?"

They both nodded, though this was the first they had heard of old Claude.

"And I understand that you played a part in discovering the Sinai Palimpsest?"

"Yes," Agnes said, for it was she who had discovered it.

Lord Cromer tilted his head from one side to the other, as if attempting to persuade a dram or two of bathwater from his ears.

"Is it true the manuscript was being used as a butter dish when you found it?"

"Not entirely," Agnes said, smiling to suppress a grimace. "It was in a bad state when we came across it. But the story of the butter dish, charming as it may be, was entirely the fantasy of a newspaper editor."

"One would imagine the monks of St. Catherine's don't

have much in the way of butter," Lord Cromer observed. "One would think they use olive oil, primarily."

Agnes smiled at Margaret, acknowledging the astute perception of their host. It was a pleasure to be in the company of someone who understood.

"Precisely."

"In addition to your scholarly pursuits, I understand that you have also been rather involved in the establishment of the Presbyterian Synod at Cambridge."

"Yes," Margaret said. Assuming Lord Cromer did not share their faith, and would not think much of women's involvement in such affairs, she did her best to minimize their role in the synod. "We are very devoted to our church."

As he blew across his tea, his Lordship's gaze drifted, and Margaret could sense his attention wandering toward the stack of papers on his desk. As much as he enjoyed this little chat, the look seemed to imply, it would need to end shortly.

"My Lord, we have a small request," Agnes said, and Lord Cromer pressed his hands together in front of his mouth, indicating that he was ready to consider.

"Miss de Witt's uncle may have mentioned that the Chief Rabbi of Egypt, Rabbi Ben Shimon, recently granted Dr. Schechter and ourselves the rights to the contents of the attic at Ibn Ezra."

"Yes."

"The contents of the attic," Margaret continued, "are really quite astounding. We have not yet had the time to look through all of the documents, but I would venture to say that it will be the most significant such discovery in the past fifty years."

Lord Cromer nodded, to show he understood fully the significance of their find.

"Although the Chief Rabbi granted us permission to remove the documents and transport them back to Cambridge, we have encountered some difficulties in navigating the Customs Authority."

As Margaret spoke, Lord Cromer wrote a few words on the notepad in front of him.

"I will see that the matter is resolved," he said, punctuating the sentence with a rather loud sip of tea. "Now, is there anything else I can do for you?"

Margaret patted down the front of her dress and glanced at her sister, unsure whether this question was a signal of the interview's conclusion or an invitation to continue. There were so many things Lord Cromer could do for them. With a flick of the pen, he could build a school, protect a building, or send someone to prison. With a few words, he could change the course of history. What might Lord Cromer say if they told him about Mr. Bechor, their trip to Bassatine, their speculations about the Ezra Scroll? Margaret's head swam with possibility. But before she could distill the possibilities into a single request, Agnes brought the interview to an end.

"I am sure you are quite busy," she said, and they both stood. "Thank you so very much for your help."

That same evening, as they were dressing for dinner, the twins received word that the documents had been approved for export. Along with this official communication came a personal note from Lord Cromer, in which he thanked them kindly for their visit. The note was accompanied also by a tin of his Lordship's prized Afternoon Darjeeling, which he hoped would serve them well for the remainder of their journey.

Although they had accomplished fully what they set out to achieve—and gotten a tin of Darjeeling to boot—Agnes and Margaret could not help but feel that they had been handled. Perhaps this was how it was with Lord Cromer. One was flattered, stroked, assisted, then shown the door. Either way, the sisters both felt the tang of a missed opportunity. Being in the presence of such power, such decisiveness, gave one a certain intoxication, the sense that anything truly was possible.

Once they had secured the approval of the Egyptian Customs Authority, things began to move rather quickly. Railcars were secured, telegrams were sent, forms were stamped with official seals. Miss de Witt volunteered to accompany the documents—to Alexandria, then on to Marseilles, Dover, and Cambridge—so that Dr. Schechter could go on to meet his brother in Palestine. He had considered changing his plans in order that he might personally deliver the crates to Cambridge, but Miss de Witt succeeded in persuading him otherwise. She had pledged to watch over the crates as closely as she would her own newborn child. What was more, she said, her uncle planned to join her for the second half of the journey.

But before Marseilles, before Palestine, and the Cambridge University Library, before any of this, the crates needed to be packed, labeled, sealed, and delivered to Cairo Station in time for Tuesday's Alexandria Express.

"Shouldn't be too much trouble," Miss de Witt said when

she saw the extent of the task before them. "I quite enjoy packing, myself."

If Agnes and Margaret had retained any doubts about the young woman's character, they were swept aside in those final days of dust and sealing wax. With her cheerful assistance, the work went much more quickly than they had imagined, so much so that they were able to spend much of Monday afternoon in the lobby of the hotel drinking Lord Cromer's Darjeeling.

"I nearly forgot," Miss de Witt said when Agnes asked about some detail of her uncle's travel plans. "I received a note from him yesterday. He inquired after you and insisted that I give you his very best."

"Your uncle," Margaret said, imagining some obscure professor of mathematics whom they invited to dinner once or twice a year, "he is a Cantabrigian?"

"No, he lives in London."

"And he said to give us his best," Agnes repeated.

"Remind us of your uncle's name, my dear," Margaret said, cutting to the point. "I'm afraid we're not as familiar with London as we once were."

"Mr. Claude Montefiore."

She said the name with a hint of question in her voice, but of course they knew it. Mr. Montefiore was one of the richest men in England, and Dr. Schechter's greatest benefactor.

"Surely, Dr. Schechter mentioned who my uncle was."

As Miss de Witt looked from Agnes to Margaret and back, she was overcome with a heavy blush of realization. Dr. Schechter had not mentioned who her uncle was. He had neglected to inform the twins that his young research assistant was also the niece of Mr. Montefiore. If they had known—if Dr. Schechter had told them that Miss de Witt had come to Cairo as an emissary of her uncle—the twins would never have questioned her propriety. But Dr. Schechter was exceedingly private when it came to money and he disliked speaking of his benefactors. So he had left to their imaginations the explanation for Miss de Witt's presence. And what else could they think? There were only so many reasons a young woman would accompany a married man halfway around the world.

"Well," Miss de Witt said, unable to meet their gaze. She touched her neck, stood, then sat back down again. "I cannot imagine—"

All three of them were silent for a long while, Agnes and Margaret embarrassed by the suspicious tilt of their imaginations, and Miss de Witt by her realization of what the twins must have thought.

"Are you planning to be in Cambridge for Easter term?" Agnes said, changing the subject abruptly.

Miss de Witt looked up from her tea.

"Yes, I am."

"We will not be back for another month at least," Margaret continued, "but when we do return we would be very glad for you to call on us."

"It would be a pleasure," Miss de Witt said.

"We are always interested in assisting the education of young women," Agnes agreed, "especially those as promising as yourself."

"Thank you," she said, and after a brief pause Agnes directed the conversation back to the details of the crates' upcoming journey.

It wasn't until later that afternoon, when Miss de Witt went back to her hotel to wash up, that the twins were able to discuss the misunderstanding in private.

"What were we supposed to think?" Margaret asked with a touch of anger in her voice. "Dr. Schechter should have told us her uncle was Mr. Montefiore."

Agnes considered this for a few moments before responding.

"He should have told us," she agreed, "though we also could have asked."

"True," Margaret allowed.

They both looked out the window and were silent as they watched a flock of starlings ducking and diving in formation against the deep blue gathering twilight. Neither of them raised the subject of their own omissions and half-truths, their own transgressions. And in their silence, they agreed that it would be best to keep all that to themselves. It would be best not to tell Dr. Schechter about the Ezra Scroll, the geniza leak, or their suspicions of Mr. Bechor. For there was nothing to be gained by such revelations, and much to be lost. Agnes and Margaret continued watching the birds for a long while, until their swoop bled into the night and they were nothing more than a rustle.

Such was life, speeding ever more quickly toward its conclusion.

"Leaps and bounds," Agnes said. "Leaps and bounds."

They both knew they might not return to Cairo. They knew that the Four o'Clock Mail might be their last train out of Cairo Station, their final trip into the desert they loved so well. They had never ceased to be grateful for the chance to visit Egypt, not to mention Jerusalem, Istanbul, and everywhere else they had been. Most people felt lucky to see Paris or Rome, and they had been around the world many times over. Still, it was difficult not to want more—more trips, more books, more discoveries. It was difficult not to wonder what they might uncover if they stayed on a few more days in Cairo. But there would always be another scroll, another cache of documents, wouldn't there? Sometimes persistence was a virtue, and sometimes it was better to let go.

After some time, Margaret rose and took out the scrap of paper she had removed from the geniza a few weeks earlier.

"I was thinking," she said, after staring down at it for a few moments, "I was thinking that this fragment might make a suitable gift, to thank Mr. al-Raqb for his kindness."

"An excellent idea," Agnes said.

Staring together out the window, into the darkness, their thoughts turned to that final unanswered question, the Ezra Scroll, and they recalled the words of their father's favorite theologian, Hugh of St. Victor.

It is, therefore, a great source of virtue for the practiced mind to learn, bit by bit, first to change about in visible and transitory things, so that afterwards it may be able to leave them behind altogether. The man who finds his homeland sweet is still a tender beginner; he to whom every soil is as his native one is already strong; but he is perfect to whom the entire world is as a foreign land.

The wisest among us, they knew, were those who could accept that God's plan was both infinitely complex and utterly incomprehensible, that the world was full of mysteries whose answers would never be revealed.

13

I N THE WEEKS following his trial, Ali kept mostly to himself. He did his rounds, tended to his kittens, and performed his prayers. On those occasions when he was forced to leave the house—going to the produce market or the bakery—he kept his eyes on the ground and was especially careful to avoid any encounters with members of the judicial council. For although their judgment had been generous, he knew that there were still many who had not forgiven him. And why should they, when he hadn't forgiven himself?

Most of all, Ali was terrified of seeing Shemarya the Pious and his sons, because he had betrayed their trust, but also because he feared that the sight of them might bring back all those feelings he had so painfully repressed. In spite of everything, he could still feel desire lurking at the dark corners of his mind. The very thought of his beloved made the scars on his arm pulse with blood and he knew that the slightest provocation could return him to his prior state.

His only consolation during that period was the patient sympathy of his kittens. On those days when Ali was feeling especially frustrated, he would take one of them into his lap and, scratching it between the ears, he would unburden himself of all his worries and regrets. Although they never responded, Ali felt they understood. They were orphans, too.

Like himself, they were teetering unsteadily on the verge of adulthood, beginning to make their way in the world for the first time. Sitting with them, Ali would often recall the wise words of that other orphan, the Prophet Muhammad. *The worst among you are your bachelors. Marriage is my way; whoever shuns my way is not of me.*

Ali knew he needed to find a wife. The council had given him two months to accomplish this task. But he had no idea where to look and, moreover, he worried that no one would want him as a husband. As the days slipped past, drawing ever closer to the council's deadline, Ali convinced himself there was no solution to his problems. Eventually he became resigned to the idea of losing his position at the synagogue. It would be an appropriate punishment, perhaps what the council had intended all along. He would go back to his uncle's house and live out the rest of his days as a lowly water carrier.

Then, one afternoon less than a week before the date by which he needed to find a wife, Ali decided on a whim to visit the tomb of the great saint Sayyida Nafisa. He did not usually place much stock in the power of saints' tombs, but he needed to do something and by that point he could think of nothing else.

The next morning, after passing the watch to al-Zikri, Ali packed a sack of food and set out toward the tomb. As he passed through the gates of Fustat, he fell in with a stream of pilgrims making their way across the empty plain. There were old men with wooden walking sticks, sick children in their fathers' arms, the wives of wealthy merchants, a donkey laden with marble tombstones, and more than a few pregnant women, all of them journeying to visit the tomb of Sayyida Nafisa. According to Aunt Fatimah, his own mother used to visit the shrine when she was troubled or nervous or in need of guidance. In fact, she had visited just a few weeks before his birth. Ali had no idea what she might have wished for then, but the thought of his mother, pregnant with him and praying at the saint's tomb, gave him no small amount of comfort.

After walking for much of the morning, Ali saw in the distance the outline of a minaret surrounded by mud huts, a scattering of trees, and the makeshift cemeteries of those who wanted to spend eternity next to the great saint. As he drew closer and made his way through the outskirts of this strange village—this city of the dead—he noticed the buildings were all festooned with lanterns and green fabric. All around him, the streets were teeming with beggars and pilgrims, the faithful, the hopeful, the superstitious, and, at the edges of the crowd, a ring of vendors selling food and strips of paper on which one might record a prayer. He overheard two women talking about the festival and realized that he had come to the shrine on the holiest day of its year, the celebration of the saint's birthday. Ali inched through the crowd and before long he was standing in front of the great yellow mosque, inside which the body of Sayyida Nafisa was interred.

The area outside the mosque was thick with supplicants and it took a good deal of pushing for him to reach the entrance. When he did, he removed his sandals, placed them in the pile of footwear, and waded through the pilgrims, sliding his bare toes along the carpet until he found himself less than an arm's length from the tomb itself. Lady of benevolence and miracles, a scholar unmatched in knowledge and piety, Sayyida Nafisa was the great-great-great-granddaughter of the Prophet Muhammad and one of Qahira's three patron saints. Her holiness, people said, bestowed great powers on her tomb. She made barren women fertile and granted great riches to the humblest of men. Ali knelt and laced his fingers through the metal grill that protected the tomb. He was not asking for a miracle. He did not want to be healed. He was not requesting money or a change of station. He only wanted a bit of guidance.

Resting his forehead against the cool metal, Ali offered a prayer to the great saint and to her great-great-great-grandfather, the Prophet Muhammad. He prayed to the one true God, who had so many names—Allah, Deus, Elohim—but could not be divided.

"Ali."

In the midst of his prayers, Ali heard the sound of his own name and, looking back over his shoulder, he saw a young woman standing at the entrance to the shrine. She was unremarkable except that she looked almost exactly like his cousin Fawziyah. Thinking that this young woman might actually be his cousin, Ali stood and tried to make his way back through the crowd. When he arrived at the entrance, she was gone.

It was a frivolous thing to have done, interrupting his prayers in order to chase after this young woman. As he collected his sandals and followed along with the stream of supplicants leaving the mosque, Ali upbraided himself. He had lost his one chance to ask the great saint for guidance. And for what? For nothing but a silly whim. How could he ever hope to find a wife if he couldn't even finish a prayer? Trembling with frustration, Ali sat down under the shade of a rich man's tomb and let his head fall in his hands. When he was finished scolding himself for this particular foolishness, he moved on to a more familiar set of recriminations. He was a liar and a cheat. He had betrayed the ones who trusted him most and squandered what good fortune he had stumbled into. He didn't deserve to be the watchman of Ibn Ezra and he certainly didn't deserve a wife.

Ali raised his head and ran a thumb down the ladder of scars that marked the underside of his arm. As he did, a strange thought occurred to him. It seemed foolish at first, but the more he considered the idea, the more sense it made. On further reflection, his only surprise was that he hadn't thought of it before. It was an elegant resolution to a seemingly unsolvable problem. And was it not possible, he thought, that this idea was, quite literally, the answer to his prayers, that the image of the young woman at the entrance to the mosque had been Sayyida Nafisa's hand guiding his thoughts? In any case, he knew what he was going to do.

Ali walked for much of the afternoon and when he arrived at Bab Zuwayla, the sun was even with the top of the gate. Nodding to the guard, he continued along the wide stone street that ran through his old neighborhood. He took a left at the butcher's, a right at the mosque, and there he was. The doorway to Uncle Rashid's house was smaller than he remembered. Its whitewash was faded and the front step was littered with spent sunflower seeds. Glancing up at a pigeon cooing in the eaves above, Ali swallowed back the sour taste of apprehension and knocked.

"Who is it?"

"Uncle Rashid, it's me. Your nephew, Ali."

"Ali," his uncle sang. Then he shouted into the back room. "Ali the Sheikh has decided to pay us a visit."

"A fine day," Ali said as he stepped into the main room.

"Indeed it is," his uncle replied, making fun of Ali's formal tone.

Ali hesitated, not sure whether it was better to deliver his request standing or sitting.

"Come," his uncle commanded. "Sit down. You need me to tell you everything?"

He sat on one of the cushions near the kitchen and looked around the room. The floor was swept clean of shells, but its walls still smelled of palm wine and old fava beans. Just a few moments in his former home and Ali was beginning to question the wisdom of his decision. He knew he was acting rashly, but this was the only way for him to keep his job, his house, and the life to which he had become accustomed. Moreover, the plan would allow him to deliver his cousin into a better life.

"Uncle Rashid," Ali said finally, "I have come here to ask you a question."

"Then ask."

"I have come," he continued, "to ask for the hand of my cousin Fawziyah."

The moment he said her name, Fawziyah came out of the kitchen with a tray of coffee.

"Did you hear that?" her father asked, grinning a brown-speckled handful of teeth. "You and Ali are going to be married."

She flushed and looked down at her feet to hide the size of her smile. Then she ran back into the kitchen to tell her mother.

"You have made her very happy," Uncle Rashid said. "We were beginning to lose faith in the power of our prayers."

It was, Ali realized, exactly what they had all been waiting for. It wasn't a foolish idea at all. Uncle Rashid raised a glass and together they drank, to grandchildren, great-grandchildren, and so on down the line.

According to the Prophet Muhammad, a married man has fulfilled half of his religion. The remaining half is satisfied with fear of God. And indeed, when Ali woke up the next afternoon, he felt as if he were starting over again in a new life. His feet were sore and his neck had been burnt by the sun, but even these discomforts felt like confirmation of a great good fortune. After a small meal, he washed himself, then put on his best galabiya and walked directly to Ephraim ibn Shemarya's fabric shop. As he approached, conversation stopped and all the men turned to look at him.

"Where have you been?" Ephraim asked.

Ali looked around the circle and, seeing so many of the men who had judged him, he forgot for a moment what it was he had come to say. He opened his mouth and blinked.

"What is it?" Doctor Mevorakh asked. "You look unwell."

"I have some news," Ali said finally. Not sure how best to approach the subject, he jumped right in. "Yesterday I was engaged, to my cousin Fawziyah. We will be married in three days at a mosque near Bab Zuwayla."

"Congratulations," Ephraim said and, after a brief pause, he rose from his seat to shake Ali's hand. "I wish you the best."

The other men in the circle all followed suit. One by one, they stood and shook Ali's hand, each offering his own personal good wishes.

"Two engagements in one week," Doctor Mevorakh remarked, and the rest of the men fell silent.

"Two engagements?" Ali asked, trying not to seem too curious.

"We have been doubly blessed this week," Ibn Kammuna explained after exchanging a glance with Ephraim ibn Shemarya. "Two days ago, my eldest son was betrothed to Ephraim's sister."

Ali swallowed and a twinge of pain shot up his arm. Staring at the embroidered hem of Ibn Kammuna's galabiya, he felt the men in the circle watching him. He knew what he needed to say. But, when he imagined his beloved on her wedding night, reclining on a bedroll in the private chambers of Ibn Kammuna's eldest son, the word stuck in his throat like an unchewed piece of meat. It took a great feat of will for him to force it out.

"Congratulations," he said. Then he shook the hand of everyone assembled, just as they had shaken his.

"A thousand congratulations to both the couples," al-Zikri said, and the rest of the group responded in kind.

"A thousand congratulations."

Ephraim offered Ali a glass of tea and he accepted, if only

because his throat was so dry. He sat in his usual seat by the entrance to the shop and, as he sipped the sweet dark tea, he listened to the men discuss the question of whether a particular fish might permissibly be eaten. No one said anything reproachful and no one looked at him unkindly. Still, Ali felt something was not right. The men all seemed to be aware of his presence, noticing him in a way they had never noticed him before.

"May I ask a question?" Ali inquired in a lull between topics. He hadn't intended to say anything, but once he spoke he couldn't go back.

"Of course," Doctor Mevorakh said. "What's on your mind?"

Ali took a small sip of tea, then set the glass aside and asked the question that had been troubling him for some time.

"Why did you forgive me?"

The men offered a number of sensible explanations, repeating many of the same reasons they had cited previously: that their tradition taught them to be merciful, that they were acting in the model of Abraham, but none of these answers were particularly satisfying.

"Perhaps," Ephraim ibn Shemarya said finally, "I might offer a story."

"The two brothers?" al-Zikri asked.

"The two brothers," Ephraim affirmed and, as the rest of the men settled into their seats, he began.

"There were once two brothers, two brothers as close as brothers could be. They studied together, they ate their meals together, and, when the time came for them to choose a trade, they decided to go into business together. For many years they were very successful. Then one evening the younger brother, Noah, was going through the accounts and found a troubling inconsistency. The next morning, he confronted his brother Jacob, who admitted to stealing the money. Noah was furious, and when Jacob begged for forgiveness he refused. Eventually, it was decided that Jacob would leave the village while Noah continued their business alone.

"In the years that followed Noah had many difficulties, in business and in life. He never married and he lost nearly all his money in a series of shipwrecks. Meanwhile, his brother Jacob built a thriving business, married, and had three sons. This bothered Noah more than any of his own misfortunes. Why should he struggle while his dishonest brother was blessed? The village rabbi said it was God's will. Unsatisfied with this answer, Noah went to the rabbi of a town nearby, who told him that God works in strange ways. Noah was unsatisfied with this answer as well. And so, he decided to wander the earth until he found an answer that satisfied him.

"Noah wandered for years and years, asking the same question of everyone he met. Eventually he came to a distant kingdom, many months' journey from the village of his birth. When he arrived in the capital he asked to speak with the wisest man in the city and was shown to the deathbed of an old kabbalist. Noah told his story to the old kabbalist, and when he came to the end he asked the same question he always asked. Why should he struggle while his dishonest brother was fortunate? The kabbalist was quick to answer, as if he had been considering this same question for some time.

"'When God first created the universe,' he said, 'it was a

universe built on the idea of infinite justice. Each act of dishonesty or violence was accorded an equal punishment. A man stole his neighbor's goat, and his own livestock were stricken with illness. A woman beat her child, and her stew was spoiled. In a short time, however, this universe collapsed under the weight of so much justice. So, when God set out to create the universe a second time, it was built on the idea of infinite loving-kindness. In this universe, each act of dishonesty or violence was accorded equal forgiveness.

"'Does this answer your question?' the old kabbalist asked, and Noah burst into tears.

"'Yes, yes,' he said. 'If only I had the chance to forgive my brother.'

"It was then that the old kabbalist revealed himself.

"'You still can,' he said and, with a smile, he extended his hand. 'Do you not recognize me?'

"At this, the two men embraced and they died in each other's arms."

When he finished telling the story, Ephraim's eyes shone with a brief smile and he poured himself another glass of tea.

"Wonderful," al-Zikri said, then the men all turned toward Ali.

"I think I understand," he said, though he wasn't entirely sure he did.

It was a story about the importance of forgiveness, but at the same time, the ending would suggest that there was, indeed, some justice in the world. Why else would Noah be given the chance to forgive his brother? If nothing else, the story seemed to confirm the wisdom of the second rabbi, the one who said that God works in strange ways.

"Think on it," Ibn Kammuna offered, and Ali said he would.

Ali tried his best to puzzle out an understanding of Ephraim's story. But for the next three days, his thoughts were consumed with the more immediate concern of paying for his impending nuptials. Weddings are expensive, no matter their size, and, since Uncle Rashid had no money or job, Ali had to pay for the entire celebration himself. In addition to the cost of the musicians, alms for the poor, and the suggested donation to the mosque, there were Fawziyah's wedding garments, her henna, and her makeup. Ali bought himself a new outfit as well as new clothes for his aunt and uncle. On top of all this, he paid for the majority of the clothing, bedding, and jewelry in his cousin's trousseau. Ali had asked al-Zikri for an advance against the following month's salary, but even that was not enough. The day before the wedding, Aunt Fatimah convinced him to go back to al-Zikri and request a further advance, to pay for the silver comb that she insisted was a necessary part of any respectable trousseau. He was on his way out the door when Fawziyah spoke up.

"It doesn't matter," she said. "I already have a comb."

Ali looked at his cousin, framed in the doorway of the kitchen, and he knew then that he had made the right decision. Fawziyah was not a delicate beauty, not the type to inspire poetry or a racing heart, but there was a certain charm in her smile, in the quiet confidence she brought to all her pursuits; and, in the past few months, she had grown into herself as a woman.

When Ali saw his bride the next day in her wedding garments—hands hennaed, hair dyed with saffron, eyes brushed with kohl, and cheeks glowing with the happiness of their future—he was stunned. He could not imagine a more beautiful woman. With a few words from the Imam, the bride and bridegroom placed their hands on the Koran and together recited its first surah. As he spoke them, Ali saw the words on the page spring into being. *In the name of God, the Beneficent, the Merciful . . . Master of the Day of Judgment . . . Show us the straight path.* And so they were married. After the ceremony, Ali and Fawziyah, her parents, and a few people from the neighborhood gathered in the courtyard of the mosque. They listened to a recitation from the Koran, and alms were distributed to the poor. No one from Ibn Ezra came to the wedding, which was understandable. Ali had not expected them. He had not even properly invited anyone.

After the reception, they loaded Fawziyah's trousseau onto a donkey cart and set off together for their new home. Riding along the road to Fustat, with his bride on his arm and the late-autumn sun warming his face, Ali thought about those first words of the first surah of the Holy Koran. *In the name of God, the Beneficent, the Merciful.* These divine attributes, he thought, these names of God, they were the qualities we should work to foster in ourselves. For in our generosity, love, and forgiveness we reflected the Generous, the Loving, the Forgiving, like a bit of iron warmed by the sun.

Ali was turning this thought over in his head, considering how it might be related to the story of the two brothers, when the cart pulled up to the gates of the synagogue. They were greeted there by a crowd of children.

"Hooray for Ali!" they shouted. "Hooray for al-Raqb!"

The bride and bridegroom were smiling down at the children when the gates of the synagogue opened and they saw the courtyard was set for a great feast. Everyone was there—the entire judicial council, all the men from outside Ephraim ibn Shemarya's fabric shop, and a number of people Ali did not recognize—all dressed in their finest clothing.

As Doctor Mevorakh's wife helped Fawziyah down from the donkey cart and led her over to the women's side, Ali understood that he and his new wife were the guests of honor. Before he could speak, he was carried off to the head of a table piled high with food, and the celebration began. It was a great feast, overflowing with wine and meat and pastries, and all of it to celebrate the marriage of a poor orphan, the watchman of the Ibn Ezra Synagogue.

Opening a jar of palm wine, al-Zikri laid a hand on Ali's shoulder.

"I knew I was right," he said and his eyes shone with a glint of happiness. "If this were the wedding of my own son, I couldn't be prouder."

"You are a good boy," Shemarya the Pious agreed, "and you will be an even better man."

Toward the end of the festivities, after he had eaten many times his fill of roast lamb and pistachio baklava, after a few too many glasses of mint tea, Ali thought for a moment that he saw the figure of his former beloved standing in the corner of the courtyard, in the very place where he had first noticed her. He felt a wave of desire break over him, spreading out from the pit of his stomach to the tips of his fingers. Even on his wedding night, he could not escape it. There was still that tiny part of him that wanted to be with her. For love never dies; it is only diverted. Ali knew this and yet, at the same time, he knew he had made the right decision. He loved Fawziyah and he was glad to be able to share his good fortune with her.

When the feast ended, when the music stopped, when everyone had gone home and the first blush of the next day played on the horizon, Ali led his bride into her new home. Following her gaze around the room, from the wall hangings and floor coverings to the tidy little kitchen, he felt the pride of a man who has provided for his wife more than she could ever have hoped to attain. When she noticed his kittens, sleeping in the corner of the room, Fawziyah clucked her tongue and crossed the room toward them. For a moment, Ali worried that she might ask for them to be put out of the house, but when he saw the tender way she bent down and scratched between their ears, he knew that she would love them as much as he did.

That next spring, Ali and Fawziyah were blessed with their first child. They named her Nafisa, after the great saint whose wisdom had brought them together. The following year, they were blessed with a son, Hassan, who was followed by Hussein and then Zaynab. Their house was full, their children healthy, and Ali found a joy in his family such as he could never have imagined.

Thus the generations passed from one to the next. Old men died and young men grew old. Shemarya the Pious passed away in the company of his beloved grandchildren; Ibn Kammuna's son joined his father on the judicial council. The Ezra Scroll stayed sheltered in its dark closet. The descendants of Ali's kittens filled the courtyard with gray. And Hasdi il-Sephardi passed his days in exile. Over time, Ali took on the name of his position, al-Raqb, the watcher, and he continued in the role until he was nearly fifty years old. At that point the leaders of Ibn Ezra decided to pass his responsibilities to Ali's son Hassan, who in turn passed the watch to his son, Ali. And so the al-Raqb line continued through the centuries, through famine and plague, fire and flood, civil war and occupation, demolition and deportation, through riot, assassination, and the violent suppression of dissent. The watch continued through all this, from father to son, father to son, a single chain stretched tight over a thousand springs and a thousand new years.

14

THE MAP Mr. Mosseri had drawn for me—sketched with his fountain pen on the back of our bill for lunch at the Nile Hilton—indicated my father's grave with a little square and two Hebrew letters. He had drawn a fence around the northeast corner of the cemetery to show the small section reserved for non-Jews, where my father was buried. A few dashes and a circle marked the main entrance, the undertaker's house, a large tree, and the mausoleum of Moïse Cattaui. But the map wouldn't be much use until I found the cemetery itself.

"The City of the Dead," I said as I slid into the passenger seat of a cab idling outside the hotel across the street from my apartment.

The Jewish cemetery—Bassatine—wasn't on any of the maps. But from what Mr. Mosseri had said, it didn't sound particularly difficult to find, tucked in along the base of the Muqattam Hills, between the Citadel and the Southern Cemetery, somewhere in that vast necropolis known as the City of the Dead.

"Where are you going?" the driver asked me in English.

"The City of the Dead," I repeated, "the Southern Cemetery."

I had spent most of the previous week trying to understand the significance of what my mother and Uncle Hassan had told me. I went back over my parents' letters, talked to Aisha, Aunt Basimah, and Mr. Mosseri, trying to piece it all together. The questions regarding my mother weren't particularly difficult to answer. But the ones involving my father—how he must have felt after the Ezra Scroll was taken from the synagogue, what it was like for him moving in with his younger brother, why he wrote that question mark on the newspaper clipping, where he thought the Ezra Scroll might have disappeared to, whether there might be some way to redeem him—those were questions I couldn't answer.

And so there I was, riding south along the Nile toward the City of the Dead, on my way, as Abdullah had put it, to ask him myself.

"Where are you going? Where are you from?" the cab-driver sang as he merged into the weave of traffic. "Where are you going? Where are you from?"

It wasn't a song, really, at least not in the strictest sense of the term, more like a melodic mantra, a poetic commentary on the ephemeral nature of life.

"You're a philosopher," I observed.

The driver smiled broadly at this and raised a finger toward the drooping ceiling of his cab, indicating that everything was in God's hands. If he had any philosophical inclinations, he owed all thanks to the divine.

"*In sha Allah,*" he said, annunciating each word of the saying. If God wills it.

Then he pointed at the shiny green-and-gold tissue-box holder affixed to his dashboard. I couldn't make out the calligraphy on the side of the box, but I assumed it said something about the will of God.

"*Inshaallah,*" I repeated and he smiled again.

"You know where you are going?" he asked a few minutes later, as we pulled up in front of the entrance to the Southern Cemetery.

I told him that I was going to Bassatine, the Jewish cemetery, and he shook his head.

"In the Southern Cemetery we have the Mosque of Qaitbay, Mosque of Barquq, and many very poor people living in the tombs. There is no Bassatine," he said; then he drove off.

The City of the Dead was a slum built on top of a cemetery. Or maybe it was a cemetery built on a slum. The *Lonely Planet* wasn't particularly clear on the question of which came first. Regardless, it was an arrangement that had persisted for hundreds of years. The wide dirt paths of the cemetery were lined with ornate stone tombs and mausoleums, each inhabited by a family or occupied by a little store selling cigarettes and candy bars. It was a fully functioning neighborhood, with produce vendors, taxis, and electricity jerry-rigged from a nearby substation.

I wouldn't want to romanticize the probably very difficult lives of those who made their homes there. Still, there was an inescapable poignancy to the neighborhood. And its residents all seemed to possess a certain tranquility, an uncomplicated coexistence with the deceased judges and merchants among whose graves they lived. The woman peeking through shutters the same mint-green color as the mausoleum next door, the man selling cell phone chargers under the ribbed dome of a saint's tomb, the young girl beating a carpet hung between two gravestones: they were all keepers of the past, guardians of that translucent border between life and death.

After wandering around the neighborhood for ten or fifteen minutes, I stopped to buy myself a bottle of water from a makeshift corner store. Across the way, a woman in a faded purple housedress was sweeping the ground in front of the mausoleum where she and her family appeared to live.

"Excuse me," I called out to her, "do you know where I might find the Jewish cemetery?"

"The Jewish cemetery," she repeated and, shaking her head at the preposterousness of the idea, went back to her sweeping. "There are no Jews here."

An older man sitting on an empty oilcan nearby overheard our exchange and motioned for me to sit down next to him.

"You are looking for the Jewish cemetery?" he asked. I told him that I was.

"Gone," he said. "Mubarak paved it over three years ago. It's a shopping mall now. Soon, all this will be a shopping mall."

I knew it wasn't true. It couldn't be. If the cemetery had been paved over three years ago, how could my father have been buried there? But in the City of the Dead, anything seemed possible, if only for a moment.

After an hour of searching with no success, I stopped to rest in the shade of a squat little building with a crested dome. According to the *Lonely Planet,* this was the Tomb of the Abbasid Caliphs, one of the more notable mausoleums in the Southern Cemetery. Peeking in, I saw that the interior was decorated with a cascade of stucco niches rising toward the peak of the dome. I was about to step inside when I felt someone standing next to me.

"Ten pounds to enter," he said.

The guard didn't look particularly official, in his old suit jacket and dingy gray galabiya. But it could be difficult sometimes to separate the legitimate authorities from the self-appointed ones, those micro-entrepreneurs who granted themselves dominion over various parking spots, street corners, and tourist attractions. To a certain extent, the distinction was immaterial. If you stood in front of something, you became its guardian.

"I'm just looking," I said.

Without batting an eye, the guard put out his hand.

"To look is five pounds."

I laughed and gave him the money. After spending most of the morning surrounded by abject poverty, searching for my father and a cemetery that might not exist, I was happy to engage in a simple transaction, an exchange of currency for labor. Handing over the five pounds, I took a step back, to really look at the building, and the guard followed alongside, determined to give me my money's worth. He rattled off the names of the Abbasid caliphs, then explained how their remnants had been transported from Baghdad to Cairo in the thirteenth century, after Baghdad was sacked by the Mongols.

"Everyone wants to be close to the tomb of Sayyida Nafisa," he added, shielding his eyes from the sun as he pointed up at the dome of the mosque above us, "even the great caliphs. She is the protector of Cairo. She is protecting the mother of the world."

It had always seemed strange to me, that saying—*Cairo is the mother of the world*—but looking up at the Sayyida Nafisa Mosque, its yellow stone dome presiding over the past and the present, the living, the dead, and those yet to come, I understood how this dusty metropolis might have given birth to the rest of the world.

"You are Egyptian?" the guard asked, pausing to examine my face as he led me to the next section of the tour.

"I was born in America," I explained. "But my parents are Egyptian."

"Yes," he said and he shook my hand, as if to congratulate me on the good fortune of my heritage. "I knew it. I always know an Egyptian."

"Actually," I told him, "I'm looking for my father's grave."

"You know where he is buried?"

"In Bassatine," I said, then paused, "the Jewish cemetery."

"Jewish cemetery?" the guard repeated, squinting a little as he inspected me more closely.

"He wasn't Jewish," I said, "my father. My mother is. But my father—"

I stopped myself and tried to start over, tried to explain why my father, who was Muslim, was buried in a Jewish cemetery, but before I could get the words out, the guard put his hand on my shoulder.

"This is your cemetery," he said and he threw his arms out to encompass all the tombs and mosques and gravestones around us. "When we die, there is no Jew or Muslim, no Christian. In the City of the Dead, there is only one God."

In a way, he was right. It was my cemetery, regardless of

who my father was or where he was buried. For the dead were always all around us, in their letters and their stories, in those plane trees and in that wispy white cloud cutting like a river through the sky. As I walked back through the cemetery and out along Khalifah Street, I thought about the lives of those interred around me, overlapping and intersecting with the millions of souls currently passing through the realm of the living. That woman selling sugarcane juice, the man guarding the Tomb of the Abbasid Caliphs, the Abbasid caliphs themselves, the Mongols, the al-Raqbs, the Shemaryas, and that mottled little tabby cat digging for scraps in a mound of trash, we were all living in the same city. For every city is a city of the dead, every one of us a dweller of this particular slum.

I had two voice messages when I woke up from my nap later that afternoon, one from Aisha, calling to see if I was free for dinner, and one from Mr. Mosseri, telling me that Simchat Torah was on Saturday and he would be honored if I could join him for a special celebration at the old synagogue, Ibn Ezra. There was going to be dancing and vodka, he said. If we were lucky, Rabbi Saada might join us as well. I called him back, hoping he might be able to give me better directions to the cemetery, but all he wanted to talk about was Simchat Torah.

"It is the end and it is the beginning," he said. "The Torah is a circle, always re-creating itself, always in the process of becoming. Simchat Torah is that point of inflection where the book folds in on itself and is born anew. We celebrate the end of the story and then we start over again at the beginning, with Genesis and 'Let there be light.'"

"But the cemetery," I began, trying to bring us back to my original question.

"Yes, yes," he said. "Of course. We can talk about that on Saturday."

Before we got off the phone, Mr. Mosseri said that the synagogue could be difficult to find at night. Even though I had been there just a few weeks earlier, he repeated his directions twice. Walk up the passageway that leads through the middle of the neighborhood; take a right at the Nunnery of St. George and a left at the Abu Serga Church. If I found myself at the entrance to the Greek Orthodox cemetery, I had gone too far.

A few days later, when my taxi dropped me off and drove into the darkness, I was glad Mr. Mosseri had insisted on repeating his directions. After passing through the main gates of Old Cairo, the moonlight settled into a dark purple gloom tinged with the buzz of the nearby Metro station. Aside from a banged-up ATM and a restaurant serving what smelled like lentil soup, the storefronts were all shuttered with rolling steel. The few people I saw along the passageway were either closing up, hurrying home, or huddled into some dark corner for the night. Following Mr. Mosseri's directions, I took a right at the Nunnery of St. George and a left at what I thought was Abu Serga. But I couldn't find the synagogue. No matter which way I turned, no matter how long I spent trying to decipher the inscriptions carved into the walls, I found myself again and again at the entrance to the Greek Orthodox cemetery.

I had gone too far a fourth time, and was beginning to think that I had misremembered the directions, when I heard the tinny beat of Egyptian pop music coming from behind a stone wall. A bit more investigation led me down a dark alley to a tall iron gate topped with a Star of David. Even then, I almost didn't recognize where I was. The courtyard was completely dark except for the moon and a bright yellow arc of light that swung out from the open door of the prayer hall. Mr. Mosseri and a man I assumed was Rabbi Saada were sitting at the tip of the arc, warming themselves around a coal brazier. There was a boom box on the ground and Rabbi Saada was holding a Torah scroll in his lap.

"Here he is!"

Jumping up from his chair, Mr. Mosseri introduced me to Rabbi Saada and to Khalid, a watchman from Abu Serga whom they paid to look in on the synagogue every so often.

"Am I early?" I asked, looking around the courtyard. Aside from a pair of silver cats slinking about the edges of the light, it was just the four of us.

"No, no," Rabbi Saada said. "You're right on time."

"There was a service earlier this evening, at the new synagogue downtown," Mr. Mosseri explained. "This is something we like to do for fun, a special celebration."

With a conspiratorial wink, he pulled a bottle of Smirnoff out from under his chair and poured a healthy shot for each of us. Handing the scroll to Mr. Mosseri for a moment, Rabbi Saada made a toast and we all drank. The first shot burned its way down my throat, but the second went down more smoothly, and the third I hardly felt. Half listening to Rabbi Saada expound upon the final chapter of Deuteronomy—how Moses saw the promised land from the top of a mountain but never reached it himself—I let my gaze wander to the open door leading into the prayer hall, from the pews to the ark to the white marble dais in the middle of the room.

"And so we pass," Rabbi Saada said, "each generation building on those who came before. We can climb the mountain. If we're lucky, we might catch a glimpse of the promised land. But we must rely on the next generation to continue our journey."

It was always just out of reach, the promised land, always over that next rise. Still, the wandering continued, generation after generation. The same stories were repeated, year after year, and always with the same hope, that the end of the journey was close at hand. After so many years of wandering, there had to be something at the end.

Unless, of course, the wandering was the story, an end unto itself. In which case, there was only the desert, an infinite scroll of sand fixed at the far distance with the hope of an oasis. And in two or three hundred years, the synagogues of San Francisco and New York would look no different from this one, dusty husks of grandeur one might stop in to visit on the way to the Golden Gate Bridge or the Statue of Liberty. It was a strangely comforting thought, that a few centuries from now, a group of Jews would be telling these same stories in Bangkok or Kolkata, believing once more that they had found their safe harbor, that their long journey had finally come to an end.

"And this is the blessing," Rabbi Saada concluded. He laid a hand on the place where the Torah's shoulder would be, if Torahs had shoulders. "Joseph buried his father with his own hands. Moses watched over the bones of Joseph. And the burial of Moses was presided over by none other than the blessed lord our God."

"Wonderful," Mr. Mosseri said, and he poured out another round of shots. "It's a shame we can't have you here all year."

I watched Rabbi Saada throw back his shot.

"I thought you were the rabbi here," I said, "in Cairo."

As the words stumbled out, I could hear the slur of vodka rounding out the edges of my harder consonants.

"Oh no." Rabbi Saada laughed. "I'm a rabbi for hire. I was born here, in Maadi. But I've lived most of my life in England, right down the road from the geniza."

"The geniza?"

I glanced reflexively at the attic of the synagogue and noticed an old wooden ladder leaning into the open mouth of its entrance.

"The geniza documents," Mr. Mosseri corrected, then turned toward me. "Most of the documents from the geniza are in Cambridge."

"Cambridge," I said, trying the shape of the word in my mouth. "How did they—"

The outline of an idea appeared, then vanished into fog.

"Now then," Rabbi Saada said and, rising with the help of my knee, pulled me up to standing, "we need some music."

Khalid turned up his boom box and, as the electricity of the beat worked through me, Mr. Mosseri joined hands with Khalid and Rabbi Saada. They all circled around me, dancing a kind of makeshift hora, slow enough for Rabbi Saada to keep up, but fast enough to give me the spins.

"You hold it like a baby," Mr. Mosseri said as he handed me the Torah scroll.

I had never held a baby before. But I understood the basic idea: cradle the head and support the body. Closing my eyes, I swayed with the beat, felt the steady pulse of the scroll and its warmth, like a stone that's been in the sun all day. There were only three in the circle, but beyond them I could sense the presence of those who came before us, all the Shemaryas and the al-Raqbs whose lives revolved around this place, those who prayed in the synagogue and those who watched over it.

After a few songs, we sat down again and Mr. Mosseri took the scroll inside. The pews were gleaming like a movie set, like a postcard from a dream. The light bent as I watched Mr. Mosseri climb the stairs to the women's section. He disappeared behind a copse of pillars. Then he was halfway up the ladder to the attic, still cradling the scroll like a baby. It was only then that I considered what it was I had been holding. Only in its absence could I really feel that tingling sensation, like a distant hum of electricity. Looking from Rabbi Saada to Khalid and back again, I tried to formulate a question, about the scroll, about my father, about the fragment, the documents in Cambridge.

"Was that—"

Before I could complete the thought, Mr. Mosseri emerged empty-handed and I swallowed back the final words of the sentence.

• • •

"Do you think it was the Ezra Scroll?" Abdullah asked, later that night, after I told him about Rabbi Saada and the scroll.

"I don't know," I said.

I was still swirling slightly from the Smirnoff, still felt the beat of the music. I didn't want to talk about all that. Stretching out on the couch, I tried to pull him down to me.

"Maybe your uncle was wrong," Abdullah persisted, sitting up straight. "Maybe the scroll wasn't stolen. Maybe they got it back from the police."

"Maybe," I said.

Maneuvering my head to the arm of the couch, I watched the reflections of the chandelier on the wall, trying to recall what Rabbi Saada had said about Moses on the mountaintop, about the bones of Joseph, the promise of the promised land. I thought about the geniza—all those documents, all those stories—an infinity of paper scattered to libraries around the world, and the attic itself as empty as a mine. I thought about my father, packing up his things, moving into his younger brother's apartment, and I imagined him sitting there on the orange armchair in the corner of his room, running his thumb along the edge of the fragment.

It was the only thing he had, that scrap of paper, his only connection to a world that no longer existed, before the Yom Kippur War, before Nasser and Golda Meir, before the creation of the State of Israel and the rise of Arab nationalism. It was the only proof that his stories were anything more than a fantasy. It was the only thing he had, the only physical reminder of what he had lost. And yet, I would like to think that, in the depths of his dejection, as he traced the letters of the fragment with his index finger, going over the details of his great shame, I would like to think that, in those moments, he thought of me. And maybe it made him happy, thinking that one day he would pass the fragment to his son, to the final link of a chain that stretched back over a thousand years.

"What do you think?" Abdullah asked again, bringing us back to the question at hand. "Do you think it was the scroll?"

"I don't know," I said, flopping onto my stomach.

It would be nice, to redeem my father and rewrite the ending of Uncle Hassan's story, to prove that it was all nothing more than a misunderstanding, a secret the Jewish community had kept even from their trusted watchman.

"It's just that—"

In a way, it didn't really matter, whether or not the scroll was still there, hidden in the attic of the synagogue. For it was the question that mattered, not the answer. Any meaning the Ezra Scroll might possess wasn't in the scroll itself. It wasn't in the parchment or the letters or even the hand that formed them. The magic of the Ezra Scroll, if there was any, resided in its possibility, in the constellation of stories circling around it. And the beating heart of any story was an unanswerable question.

15

"HAVE I SHOWN you my letter, for *The Times*?"

Dr. Schechter, Miss de Witt, and the twins were standing together on an open train platform a few hundred yards from the primary bustle of Cairo Station, watching a team of stevedores load their precious crates into the brassy blue train compartment Lord Cromer had arranged for them.

"No," Agnes said, muffling a cough, "but if you have a copy we would be very eager to see it."

Fortunately, he did. With a flourish, Dr. Schechter produced the folded typescript from his breast pocket and began reading aloud. After a few paragraphs of introduction, the letter launched into a lengthy description of the geniza.

"It is a battlefield of books, and the literary production of many centuries had their share in the battle; their *disjecta membra* are now strewn over its area. Some of the belligerents have perished outright, and are literally ground to dust in the terrible struggle for space, whilst others, as if overtaken by a general crush, are squeezed into big unshapely lumps."

The letter went on to describe in great detail the range of belligerents found on this battlefield of books—old Bibles, ancient leases, marriage contracts, rationalist works denying the existence of angels and demons, and amulets invoking the assistance of the latter in matters of the heart—but not

246 ♦ MICHAEL DAVID LUKAS

once did Dr. Schechter mention the assistance or participation of anyone else, not Miss de Witt and certainly not Mrs.
Gibson or Mrs. Lewis. The twins had come to expect such
omissions. Still, it stung. When he finished reading, Dr.
Schechter refolded the letter and looked up at his audience.

"I could not have done it without your assistance," he said,
as if pasting one final sentence at the end of the letter.

"Yes," Margaret smiled, "thank you so much for mention-
ing that."

Whether Dr. Schechter heard the sarcasm in her voice,
Margaret could not be sure. He had never been one for anything but the most literal of interpretations and, indeed, she
could not be certain he had heard her at all. Even as he folded
the letter, his attention swung to a pair of stevedores attempting to fit an ungainly crate through the door of the train
compartment.

"Slowly," he shouted in Arabic as he bustled over to in-
struct them in the proper manner of handling the crates.
"Slowly, please."

"He is very excited," Miss de Witt said once he was out of
earshot.

"It would seem so."

"And he really does value your help."

"Yes," Margaret reflected, "everything has its value. Doesn't
it?"

Dr. Schechter had good reason to be excited. He had secured the geniza. And this letter to *The Times*—which the
editors had agreed to hold until the documents arrived safely
in the bosom of the Cambridge University Library—would
trumpet his name throughout England. Could Agnes and

Margaret blame him for neglecting to mention them, two fusty widows who had helped facilitate his success?

Watching Dr. Schechter give orders to the stevedores, the twins noticed a new confidence bubbling beneath his familiar scholarly aspect. The future was bright for Dr. Schechter. He would be invited to deliver lectures to learned societies. He would be asked to dine with peers of the realm and, after a few drinks, he would be convinced to tell his story, the famous story of how Dr. Schechter had discovered the geniza. Being Jewish, of course, he could not be a full professor at Cambridge. Still, he would have an illustrious career. One day, the name Solomon Schechter would brush the lips of schoolchildren around the world.

"You are leaving tomorrow?" Miss de Witt asked.

"Four o'Clock Mail to Suez," Margaret confirmed. "There we meet our camels and set off into the desert."

Although they were looking forward to the desert, the twins were both somewhat saddened by the prospect of leaving Cairo—and the Ezra Scroll—behind.

"How marvelous," Miss de Witt said, clapping her hands together. "You have been to the desert so many times, though; it probably feels like a second home."

"You would be surprised how difficult it is to accustom oneself," Agnes said. "Even after so many visits, the cold nights and long camel rides are no less cold and long."

"The scope of the place is beyond the limit of human comprehension," Margaret added. "I believe even the Bedouins must wake each morning with a sense of surprise."

As she tried to explain the feeling—of waking alone in the middle of the desert—the Chief Rabbi and Mr. Bechor arrived in a carriage conveying six long wooden panels, the same ones Dr. Schechter had pointed out on their first visit to the synagogue.

"We are very glad that Dr. Schechter agreed to find them a proper home," Rabbi Ben Shimon said, joining the ladies as Mr. Bechor went off to help supervise the stevedores, "and of course we wanted some way to express our gratitude."

For hundreds of years, he explained, these panels had served as a border around the entrance of the synagogue. Each was engraved with a passage from scripture or a few words of dedication, wishing blessings on those who had contributed to the building's refurbishment. Watching a particularly long panel disappear into the train car, Agnes thought she recognized a phrase from one of her favorite psalms.

"'Enter into his gates with thanksgiving,'" she murmured, "'and into his courts with praise; thankful unto him, and bless his name.'"

"If there is any way we can thank you," Rabbi Ben Shimon said as if responding to the psalm, "for your generosity and for your expert navigation of the Customs Authority, I do hope you will let us know."

The twins seemed to let this offer pass. They were both silent for a moment, watching the panels as they were carried from carriage to train like sections of a broken crown. Then Margaret spoke.

"There might be something, actually."

"We are at your service."

"My sister and I have become enamored recently of the idea of the Ezra Scroll."

She did not elaborate any further. She did not actually make the request, but the Chief Rabbi's tiny cough made clear that he understood her perfectly.

"I think we might be able to arrange something," he said, glancing across the platform in the direction of Mr. Bechor. "Do you have any engagements tonight?"

"None at all."

"Then I will meet you at your hotel at nine o'clock."

"Nine o'clock tonight," Agnes confirmed.

"Mr. al-Raqb speaks very highly of you," Rabbi Ben Shimon added, implying that his invitation rested heavily on the watchman's recommendation.

"I trust he will be there tonight," Agnes said. "We have a small token of gratitude we would like to present to him."

"A token of gratitude?" Mr. Bechor asked, interjecting himself into their circle as he bounded across the platform. "It is you, my fine ladies, who deserve our gratitude. Not the other way around."

He bowed and took each of the fine ladies by her hand.

"And you, Mr. Bechor," Margaret said. "You must be very happy to know that the geniza is secure."

"Indeed," he said and, pausing, he adjusted a button on the cuff of his shirt. "There is one thing that—"

"Yes," Agnes said, though her tone was not particularly inviting.

"Have you had a chance to write the letter of introduction, for my son Marcel?"

Margaret opened her mouth, ready to deliver the tirade she had been preparing the past few days. But, feeling her sister's hand at her elbow, she paused to reconsider her approach.

"We haven't written yet," Agnes said, "but we will this afternoon, and I should think that you will be pleased with the results."

Margaret stared at her sister in disbelief as Mr. Bechor thanked them, kissed their hands again, and turned to leave.

"You really intend to write that letter?" she asked on their way back to the hotel.

"It's not the boy's fault," Agnes said. "If anything, he deserves our sympathy."

She then paused for a moment and cocked her head as if trying to speed the path of a memory.

"What was it Father said, after that trouble with his cousin?"

"'Mercy is more powerful than justice,'" Margaret recited, imitating their dear father's thick, gravelly voice. "'Forgiveness is greater than revenge.'"

"I was thinking that perhaps Lord Cromer would be willing to intercede on young Marcel's behalf," Agnes suggested.

"I should think he would," Margaret said, and she smiled inwardly at her sister's unexpected fount of compassion. "If we asked, I should think he would."

Huddled together in the Chief Rabbi's carriage, Agnes and Margaret were both very much aware of their own lamplight, the sound of horseshoes clacking against the pavement, and the smell of dinner being prepared in surrounding homes. How long had they waited for this moment? How many nights had they lain awake contemplating the possibility of the Ezra Scroll? And now there they were, on their way to see it. They had needed to ask, of course; one always needed to ask. But once they had put forth the request, it was answered as easily as that.

"Mr. Bechor will not be joining us?" Mr. al-Raqb asked as he opened the gates of the synagogue.

Rabbi Ben Shimon did not respond, but a flash of recognition passed between them, and the watchman nodded. Observing this exchange, Agnes and Margaret knew that there was no need to expose Mr. Bechor. Rabbi Ben Shimon and Mr. al-Raqb both already knew about the leak, the black-market document dealers, the cemetery, and much more, one would imagine. If Mr. Bechor hadn't yet been judged, he soon would be, and by the harshest of tribunals, the aggrieved members of his own community.

"This way," Mr. al-Raqb said, as if welcoming unexpected guests into his home.

Knowing what they now knew, the twins both felt rather silly for ever suspecting Mr. al-Raqb. But, of course, our mortifications are always sharper in hindsight.

"Thank you," Agnes said, with a small bow.

As they walked toward the golden flicker that illuminated the interior of the synagogue, Agnes glanced in the direction of Mr. al-Raqb's home. On his doorstep, a dozen or so light gray cats gathered around the feet of a young man, no older than sixteen, who appeared to be feeding them the remnants of his dinner. Teeming about the food, the cats looked like a single organism flashing silver in the lamplight.

"My younger son, Rashid," Mr. al-Raqb said and, as if embarrassed by the boy's charity, he added: "He is very attached to the cats."

Agnes and Margaret both looked at the boy. He was the son who had been caught in unnatural congress with Marcel Bechor, a rather slight child with green eyes and an unkempt gust of dark brown hair. When he saw the twins looking at him, he collected his things and went inside.

"He's a good boy," Mr. al-Raqb said, mostly to himself, "but he needs something to keep him busy."

"If you don't mind," Margaret put in, "I think we might have just the thing. When we saw him the other day, Lord Cromer mentioned that he was looking for household help. If you think your son would be willing—"

Agnes raised an eyebrow. Lord Cromer had said no such thing, but it was an awfully good idea. Whether he was looking for help or not, the Consul-General would certainly be able to find a suitable position for the boy, far from the disapproving gaze of Old Cairo.

"Yes," Mr. al-Raqb said, "thank you."

"Which reminds me," Agnes added, reaching into her bag. "My sister and I have a small token of appreciation for you."

They had spent a good portion of the afternoon procuring a glass covering and a red leather case suitable for the fragment they wished to present to the watchman.

"It was the least we could do," Margaret said, "after all your assistance."

Mr. al-Raqb thanked them again as he turned the presentation case over in his hands. He opened it, inspected the plaque, and ran his thumb along the black velvet interior. Whether or not he understood the significance of the fragment nestled inside, he seemed to appreciate the sentiment behind the gift. After staring at it for a long while, he shut the case and slipped it into the pocket of his galabiya. Then he led them into the warm yellow light of the synagogue.

"Here it is," Rabbi Ben Shimon said and, stepping aside, he extended his arm.

In the middle of the prayer hall, unfurled atop a hexagonal marble bima, was an ancient Torah scroll. Agnes held her breath while Margaret stepped up and leaned over to inspect the scroll, bringing her face nearly to the parchment. Cracked and brown at the edges, it was open to that passage in the middle of Exodus where Moses observes the burning bush, the bush that burned but was not consumed. Four hundred years before Christ, she thought, Ezra—the great scribe, the flower that appeared on earth—took it upon himself to compile an unimpeachable version of the Hebrew Scriptures, without error or innovation. And here it was, the original against which all others would be measured. The building had been named for him. Ibn Ezra, it was called: Son of Ezra. For all believers were, in one way or another, the children of Ezra. They all owed the basis of their faith to this text.

Margaret shivered as she lowered her nose to the ancient parchment and inhaled its slightly sour smell. One could not hear the word of God except in the perfect empty chambers of one's heart. She believed this to the very depths of her being. And yet, as she stood at the bima, she felt her face warmed by those letters, their soft slant and their tiny fiery embellishments. If she had a burning bush of her own, it was this very scroll.

"Wonderful," she said and, smiling with girlish delight, stepped down to give her sister a chance to look.

The first thing Agnes noticed about the scroll was the

color of the parchment, particularly that of the reverse. Over the centuries, it had taken on the distinctive brownish-gray color of denatured goatskin. What really struck her, though, was the parchment's exceedingly smooth texture, indicating that the animal's hair had been removed with lime. This was quite troubling indeed. As far as she knew, the process of dehairing with lime was first developed in Italy, nearly a thousand years after the birth of Christ. Agnes brought her face closer to the parchment. She could almost smell it, the lime, more than a millennium after it had been applied.

It was possible, of course, that this particular dehairing process had been developed earlier than previously known. It was possible that Ezra had chosen goatskin for his scroll, instead of the typically more highly prized calf- or sheepskin. Still, if she had to guess, knowing nothing of its true provenance, Agnes would date the scroll sometime between the tenth and fourteenth centuries, and she would have to presume that the parchment had been prepared in southern Europe.

"Amazing," Agnes said. Avoiding her sister's gaze, she turned to Rabbi Ben Shimon. "Thank you so much for this opportunity."

What else could she say? She couldn't very well announce her theory. To do so would strip the community of its most treasured possession or, even worse, accuse the Chief Rabbi of willful misrepresentation. So she kept her thoughts to herself until she and her sister were lying alone in the darkness of their hotel room.

"Meggie," she whispered.

"What is it?"

"The parchment," she said, "I'm fairly certain it was goat-skin, treated with lime."

Margaret knew far less than her sister about the identification of ancient documents, but she understood at once the implication of this conjecture. A long silence pressed down on them, during which Agnes reached out and took her sister's hand.

"How certain?" Margaret asked.

"We cannot be absolutely certain about such things."

"We cannot be absolutely certain about anything, can we?"

"No, I should think not."

Perhaps it would have been better if they had never seen the scroll, if they had been allowed to persist in the illusion of its perfection. At the same time, they both took some comfort in the absence of certainty, in the muddled space between the true word of God and its interpretation. Was it not the pursuit of the divine that gave us meaning? The chasm of faith between the Eucharist and the blood of Christ, Kierkegaard's battle of the living room, the chain of transmission between the Hadith and the true words of Muhammad, the black cloth separating the Kaaba from the pilgrims circling around it, the impossible longing of the Jewish people for their home in Jerusalem, for a temple always already destroyed, these leaps to faith were divine in their own right. The idea of the scroll was as real as the scroll itself.

And they could still hope, couldn't they? Might it not be possible that the scroll they had seen was nothing more than a feint? In which case, the Ezra Scroll really did exist, buried still in a closet somewhere, waiting patiently for a future scholar to uncover it. Or maybe the true scroll was not meant to be uncovered. Perhaps the Ezra Scroll was meant to remain forever in its dark closet, tucked away in the backstreets of Old Cairo, forgotten, untouched and undiscovered until the end of humanity.

16

A FEW DAYS BEFORE I left Cairo, I went over to Uncle Hassan and Aunt Basimah's for my final Sunday lunch. Aunt Basimah made my childhood favorite, lemon breaded chicken, and we talked about my plans for the following semester. I thanked them for all their kindness. And, as he hugged me goodbye, Uncle Hassan told me I was welcome back anytime.

"You are a good boy," he said, holding me out by the shoulders to get a better look. "Your father would be proud."

After lunch, Aisha offered to give me a ride home. We drove the first few blocks in silence, past the gilt-lettered entrance of the Maadi Sporting Club, over the Metro tracks, and through the center of Maadi, its streets crowded with fast-food restaurants and men selling electronics off the sidewalk. As she turned onto the main road leading north toward downtown, the outline of the Muqattam Hills rose up at the edge of the horizon.

"Do you know how to get to Bassatine?" I asked.

"The cemetery?" she said. "Sure. It's just off the road to Heliopolis."

"You wouldn't mind?" I said. "Stopping by on the way home?"

"Not at all."

A few minutes later we were on the road to Heliopolis, one side of the freeway speckled with apartment buildings and half-finished shopping malls, the other a vast expanse of factories, radio towers, and military installations. After a while, we turned off and continued on a dirt frontage road that led into an industrial area crowded with stonecutters and brick makers. The air was thick with pulverized building material and the only other vehicles in sight were forklifts and pickup trucks laden with red roof tiles, stone pillars, and tired dusty men.

Past the warehouses, backed up against a curve of the freeway, was the Jewish cemetery, Bassatine, its front gates secured with a thick chain and a padlock that looked as if it hadn't been opened in years. While Aisha waited in the car, I looked around for another entrance and shouted for someone to let me in. After a few minutes a stonecutter from one of the nearby workshops wandered over to see what I was going on about.

"No entry," he said, and pointed to the padlock.

"Do you know if there's another way in?" I asked him. "My father is buried here."

The stonecutter shook his head. Then, after considering the situation, he linked his hands together and positioned himself next to the front gates.

"Be careful," he warned as he boosted me up over the wall. "There are ghosts in there."

Once inside the cemetery, I was able to find my father's grave without much difficulty. Set off by a short brick wall, the non-Jewish section of the cemetery was located in a far corner between the main gate and the mausoleum of Moïse

Cattaui. My father's grave was near the back, a simple black headstone engraved with his name, his date of birth, his date of death, and a short verse from the Koran. *God is watchful over all things.* I stood next to the grave for a long while. Then I knelt down and rested my forehead against the warm black marble. I closed my eyes and when I opened them again I could see the condensation of my breath collected on the surface of the stone.

There was so much I wanted to tell him, about the fragment, Abdullah, and Mr. Mosseri; about the scroll I had held like a baby, which may or may not have been the scroll from the newspaper clipping, which may or may not have been the scroll that was taken from the synagogue. But in the end, instead of telling him, I asked the question I had been wanting to ask for years.

"Will you tell me a story?"

I waited a moment, looked up at the outline of the Muqattam Hills, listened to the sound of the stonecutters, the freeway, and the birds chattering in the branches of a nearby plane tree. Then I stood, brushed the dirt from my knees and placed a small stone on top of his grave. On my way out, I found the gravestones of my mother's grandparents. After paying my respects to them and to an entire row of Shemaryas, I climbed back over the fence and asked Aisha to take me home.

"Did you find him?" she asked when we were back on the main road.

"I did," I said. "He was right there all along."

My last days in Cairo were spent tying up loose ends, packing, and buying presents in Khan el-Khalili, but that final evening I reserved for Abdullah. He couldn't leave his post until later that night, so we ate dinner together on the front steps of the building. When we were finished, I balled up the paper wrappers and pushed an errant curl back behind his ear.

"You should come with me," I said, only half serious.

He shook his head.

"You'll be back," he said. And he was right.

Over the years, I've come back to Cairo more times than I can count: for research and for pleasure; for Aisha's wedding and the birth of her first daughter, Mariyam; for colloquia about the medieval Mediterranean world, the fall of Mubarak, and the poetics of Judeo-Arabic verse; to visit Mr. Mosseri and to pay my respects after the death of his mother; to tend the graves of Shemaryas and al-Raqbs, to watch over the memories of those whose descendants no longer remember. But that night the city was frozen in place. Abdullah put on *Astral Weeks* and we listened through the first side, sipping green apple Fayrouz and lightheaded with each other, watching the city pass by like stars across the desert sky.

In the years since, I've often wondered—for my father's sake and my own—whether it really was the Ezra Scroll, propped up on the chair between Mr. Mosseri and Rabbi Saada. Could that scroll really have been the same one my father tried to protect from the police, the soft-glowing magical object Ali al-Raqb used to woo his beloved, the perfect text Agnes and Margaret wanted so much to discover? The question pops up at odd hours of the day, while I'm in line at the cafeteria or hunched over an ancient marriage contract; it's sparked by the smell of parchment, the shudder of a fluorescent light coming to life, or a splatter of sunshine on the River Cam.

Whatever it was I held that night in the courtyard of the synagogue, it did its work. The morning after dancing with Mr. Mosseri, Rabbi Saada, and Khalid, I woke up with a pounding headache, a pasty mouth, and an intense, immutable desire to spend the following semester at Cambridge, in the company of the geniza documents. That afternoon I changed my plane ticket. I told my adviser that I was planning to extend my leave of absence and found a new subletter for my apartment in Berkeley. Rabbi Saada helped me to find a job at the Geniza Research Unit, and that is where I've been ever since.

It's not a particularly glamorous life. I wake up every morning at seven, have a quick breakfast, then cut across town to the back entrance of the Cambridge University Library. The Geniza Research Unit is on the second floor, between the stacks and a row of administrative offices. My desk is at the back of the conservation room, an old drafting table topped with an acid-free blotter and a blue tackle box containing the tools of my trade, the brushes and blades, magnifying glasses, wheat-starch paste, and archival plastic sheets. Aside from the occasional palimpsest or illuminated manuscript, the work is relatively simple. First I remove the fragment from its box and carefully brush away any ancient detritus. Then I cut a sheet of plastic down to the appropriate size and anchor the fragment to the plastic with a single stitch of acid-free thread. Finally, I cut a second piece of plastic and sew it up around the edges. When I'm finished, I tag the fragment for the catalogue and send it off to the photographers. Then I begin again.

There are hundreds of thousands of fragments, waiting in a climate-controlled vault on the third floor of this great brick library. We did the math the other day at lunch. With three of us working forty hours a week, fifty weeks a year, it would take somewhere in the realm of three hundred years to work through all the fragments. It can be humbling, chipping away at a project beyond the scale of a human life. But in my moments of doubt, I remind myself of what Rabbi Tarfon said, nearly two thousand years ago: *You are not obligated to complete the task, but neither are you free to desist from it.*

Over the years, my Hebrew and Arabic have gotten quite good. I can read some Syriac and I'm comfortable with the grammatical quirks of Judeo-Arabic. But to truly understand the fragments, you need to be fluent in another language, the idiom of paper and dust, the anxious slant of a scribe trying to finish a letter before sundown, the urgency of a peculiar crease. You have to be able to read the meaning in food stains and sun damage, misspellings and half-erased words. Each fragment contains dozens of stories, entangled in the weave of the paper, the cure of the parchment, the degradation of various inks. And it's my job to raise these stories from the dead, to release them, protect them, and preserve them for the scholars of the future.

At first, I told myself the job was only temporary, something to get out of my system before I went back to Berkeley and finished up my doctorate. Or perhaps, I thought, I could start over again at Cambridge, get a D.Phil. in Middle Eastern Studies. And maybe one day I will. But for the time being, I'm happy with the life I've chosen. I know my father would be proud. And my mother, eventually she came around to the idea too. When she and Bill visited a few years ago, I took them up to my little office and, as I was explaining the various tools of my trade, their technical names and functions, her eyes welled up. She took off her glasses, and when she hugged me I could feel her tears against my cheek.

"It's all a mother wants," she said, "to see her child happy."

And I am. After so many years in my head, it was a revelation to work with my hands, to feel the texture of a story beneath my fingers. I'm a reader above all else, bearing witness to the marriages, domestic squabbles, and business agreements of people who died centuries ago. But with so many stories swirling about, it's probably no surprise that, eventually, I felt compelled to set down my own. A few years ago, not long after the July 2011 revolution, I began writing, in the mornings before work, on weekends and holidays, attempting to arrange the shards of my family history into a coherent whole.

I went back to Cairo last year to sit down with Mr. Mosseri, Madame el-Tantawi, Uncle Hassan, and Aunt Basimah. I asked them all the questions I had been saving up over the years. Why did the Jews of Cairo give Solomon Schechter the geniza documents? Who told my father all the stories he told me? I spent a week digging through the archives of the Jewish community. I sought out distant cousins, took rubbings from gravestones at Bassatine. And slowly, the stories began to emerge. Mr. Mosseri told me family legends I had never before heard. Aunt Basimah described the first time she met my grandfather, how impressed she was by the elegant cut of his suit. And Madame el-Tantawi told me the story of my father's great-uncle Rashid—the youngest son of Muhammad al-Raqb—the one who, in his youth, was found in unnatural congress, as she put it, with a Jewish boy named Marcel Bechor.

According to Madame el-Tantawi, Great-Uncle Rashid had worked for many years in the kitchen of the British Consul-General's residence, then found a position at the Nile Hilton and eventually worked his way up to become the head chef. Uncle Hassan remembered him as a strict and somewhat reserved man, but neither he nor Mr. Mosseri knew anything more about his life, how he got the job at Lord Cromer's house, whether it might be connected somehow to the scandal with Marcel Bechor. It wasn't until I got back to Cambridge that I found the story—or part of it, at least—in Agnes and Margaret's papers.

Before leaving Cairo for the Sinai, the twins had written a letter to Lord Cromer, in which they recommended the services of a very capable young man called Rashid al-Raqb. When they returned home three weeks later, they found a note from the young man himself, thanking them for their kind assistance. *You cannot imagine how much this new environment has ameliorated my situation, of which I think you have been informed. I hope that one day I will be able to repay your generosity.*

At first I wanted to write a book that would contain all of these stories, a thousand pages encompassing a thousand years of Jewish life in Cairo. Over time, however, my project settled into a more modest frame, this fragmented account of fathers and sons, cousins and strangers, grief, forgiveness, and forbidden love. I'm well aware of the book's shortcomings. It's imperfect and incomplete. But what novel isn't? Language is a gesture—a finger pointing at the moon, not the moon itself—and eventually, all stories must come to an end.

Whatever comes of these pages, I have found satisfaction in writing them. In my research and in the shape of my days, in the wheat-starch paste and the acid-free thread, in the long hours hunched over ancient paper and my walks home along the River Cam, I have found myself, in more ways than one. I wouldn't call myself religious, not in the conventional sense—that would require me to actually choose one—but there's a spark there that wasn't before. And who am I to say what that is? Or isn't? Like my father and his father before him, I am but a watcher, a guardian, protecting the geniza documents, and content to persist in their mystery.

Author's Note

The story contained within these pages is, like all novels, a mix of fact and fiction. Some of the characters are based on historical personages, some are inspired by people I've known, some are entirely invented. The same can be said for the various plot lines. With a few small exceptions, the story of the Cairo Geniza and its "discovery" is based on historical record (particularly Janet Soskice's book *The Sisters of Sinai*, Amitav Ghosh's *In an Antique Land*, Adina Hoffman and Peter Cole's *Sacred Trash*, and S. D. Goitein's *A Mediterranean Society*). The story of the al-Raqb family was inspired by a conversation I had on an airplane with a Bengali Muslim woman whose family served for generations as watchmen of a synagogue in Kolkata. The story of Joseph and the descriptions of contemporary Cairo are based in part on my own experience living there in the fall of 2000. In general, I have tried to render the historical, cultural, and geographic context as accurately as possible. To that end, I have been assisted greatly by the work of scholars like Timothy Mitchell, Joel Beinin, David Sims, and André Raymond. Any inaccuracies, intentional or otherwise, are my own. As the poet Edmond Jabès wrote: "The writer, like the historian, lends a meaning to the past but, contrary to the latter, he destroys the past by giving it form."

Acknowledgments

Endless gratitude, first and foremost, to Nicole Aragi—literary agent, guardian angel, and dragon slayer, maker of baba ghanoush, provider of slippers, and so much more—for reading this book in its many different forms, for shaping it, for shepherding it into the world. And to my amazing editor, Emi Ikkanda, for believing in it and for seeing what it might become, for being the type of editor people say no longer exists, and for championing the book near and wide. Thank you also to the inimitable Duvall Osteen, and to the wonderful team at Spiegel & Grau and Random House, especially Cindy Spiegel, Julie Grau, and Denise Cronin.

For the time, space, and inspiration needed to write this book, enormous appreciation to: Montalvo Arts Center, Santa Maddalena Foundation, Bread Loaf Writers' Conference, Book Passage, Pizzaiolo, the Anne and Robert Cowan Writers Award, the Center for Middle East Studies at UC Berkeley, and the Geniza Research Unit at the University of Cambridge.

Thanks so much to everyone who read the book and supported me through the writing process: Anna Akullian, Rabih Alameddine, Rachel Brand, Maud Casey, Carolyn Cooke, John Engell, Mark Epstein, Danny Fingerman, Daniela Gerson, Rebecca Jefferson, Billy Karp, Reese Kwon, Ben Lavender, Krys Lee, Ben Outhwaite, Jeffrey Rotter, Melonie Schmeirer-Lee, Amy Smith, David Stein, Indira Stewart, Christina Toma, and Tristam

Wolff. And special thanks to those stalwart souls who read more than one draft: Adam Akullian, David Akullian, Lillie Brum, Jonah Charney-Sirott, Kevin Fingerman, Joy Johannesen, and Reif Larsen.

Most of all, I would like to give thanks to and for the members of my little family: to Rashi for his endless love and excitement; to Mona for expanding the borders of my heartland, far beyond anything I could have imagined; and to Haley for everything, always.

About the Author

MICHAEL DAVID LUKAS is the author of the international bestselling novel *The Oracle of Stamboul*, which was a finalist for the California Book Award, the NCIBA Book of the Year Award, and the Harold U. Ribalow Prize, and has been published in fifteen languages. He has been a Fulbright Scholar in Turkey, a student at the American University of Cairo, and a night-shift proofreader in Tel Aviv. A graduate of Brown University, he has received fellowships from the National Endowment for the Arts, Bread Loaf Writers' Conference, and the Santa Maddalena Foundation, and his writing has appeared in *The New York Times, The Wall Street Journal, Slate,* and *VQR*. He works in the Center for Middle Eastern Studies at UC Berkeley and lives in Oakland, California.

About the Type

This book was set in Figural, a typeface originally designed in 1940 by the Czech calligrapher and book designer Oldrich Menhart (1897–1962). It is an expressionistic face, echoing the forms of rough, pen-made letters.